The Names they Gave Us

Also by Emery Lord

When We Collided

The Names they Gave Us

EMERY LORD

BLOOMSBURY

LONDON OXFORD NEW YORK NEW DELHI SYDNEY

Bloomsbury Publishing, London, Oxford, New York, New Delhi and Sydney

First published in Great Britain in June 2017 by Bloomsbury Publishing Plc
50 Bedford Square, London WC1B 3DP

First published in the USA in May 2017 by Bloomsbury Children's Books
1385 Broadway, New York, New York 10018

www.bloomsbury.com
www.emerylord.com

A CIP catalogue record for this book is available from the British Library

ISBN 978 1 4088 7781 4

Typeset by Newgen Knowledge Works (P) Ltd., Chennai, India
Printed and bound in Great Britain by CPI Group (UK) Ltd, Croydon CR0 4YY

1 3 5 7 9 10 8 6 4 2

This one is for my mom

There is a crack in everything. That's how the light gets in.

—Leonard Cohen

APRIL

APRIL

THE FIRST PROM CRISIS IS MANAGEABLE. I'M REAPPLYING MY LIP color in the ladies' room when one of the swim team girls bursts in, sobbing. Our senior captain, Mallory, is right behind her.

"Brianna?" I spin, red mouth dropping open. Her cheeks are lashed with watery, gray mascara trails. "What's wrong?"

"He's been dancing with Chloe. For, like, half an hour!" The scent of spicy, floral perfume has flooded in with them. It takes a lot to cover up the chlorine smell that sticks to our hair and skin.

"Mark's a jerk who doesn't deserve you," Mallory says.

Brianna huffs. "But I *like* him!"

As newly appointed captain for next year, I feel a sense of responsibility here. Part of Coach's announcement speech was about my leadership abilities and dedication.

"Okay, first of all, deep breaths," I tell her. Like many

asthma sufferers, this is my go-to mantra. "Is he really worth ruining your makeup over?"

When she glances at her streaky face, Brianna lets out a horrified sob. Okay, I need to fix this.

I reach for my satin clutch, which took my mom and me hours of shopping to find. This purse was our holy grail: elegant, a deep red to add color to my ensemble, *and* actually big enough for all my essentials. "I can redo your makeup, if you'd like."

"You'd do my makeup?" Brianna asks.

"Of course!" I open my bag like it's a medical supply kit and I'm the first responder. It's going to take me at least four Q-tips to clean up the mascara stains. "Do you think you're all cried out? We can wait till you feel better."

"She's done," Mallory insists. "Because if someone asks you to be his date and then ditches you, he's not a good guy. So, no loss."

I have to agree—especially since Mark's a senior and Brianna's a sophomore. She knows the junior and senior girls on the swim team, but there aren't many people in her grade here.

"I'm done," Brianna says, concentrating on a slow inhale. I begin the careful work of desmudging without taking off all her foundation. Her skin has warm undertones, so my tinted moisturizer won't look right on her. "But it's, like . . . I got this dress and these shoes, and I was so excited. This is so humiliating."

"It is not, and you look *great*!" Mallory says, handing her a few squares of toilet paper. "Let's think of Mark as a free ticket. He bought yours, right?"

"Yeah." She sniffles into the makeshift tissue.

"And now you're here in your beautiful dress," I add. "Look up. No blinking. This makeup is salvageable, and so is your night."

"But what am I supposed to do?" she asks as I reline her eyes, smudging the edges with a careful fingertip. "Dance alone? That's so pathetic. Everyone else is with their dates!"

"You can dance with the girls," I suggest, meaning the swim team. I apply the first coat of high-drama mascara, as wet and black as ink.

"With other girls?" Brianna asks, confused.

"Ahem." This is from Mallory, who is here with her girlfriend. "Lucy means you should have the best time possible with everyone, even if it feels like you're faking it. Then you can remember this as the night you rubbed it in his face."

She smiles a little. "I do like that."

"Final touch," I say, dabbing a few dots of concealer on her now-pink nose. It's a bare-bones patch job, but it works. "You know what? Hold on."

I have to add a little more blush, and I blend her bronzer while I'm at it.

"Thank you," she says, examining her face in the mirror.

"Anytime. Now, freshen up your lipstick, take a few breaths, and go out with your head up. Yeah?"

"Yeah."

Mallory walks out beside me, nudging her shoulder against mine. "You're going to be great with them next year, Captain Hansson."

"Thanks. I wish you didn't have to graduate for me to be captain, though." Mallory is one of the girls who's on both the school team and the Hammerheads club team with me, so we've been teammates for years. She's a true shark in the pool, and she keeps me on my game.

"Well, you'll visit me at the U next year, yeah? Let me sell you on trying out for the team?"

"Sure," I say, although it's strange to think of visiting Mal. Would I stay with her? She's a friend, sure, and we have a lot of fun during our shared activities, but we don't really talk about personal stuff. "Have a great night! See you Monday."

It's not just one thing that makes me feel a little separate from the swim team girls; it's everything. I didn't start at White Hills High till freshman year. And I stay up at the lake all summer, helping my parents run our church camp, which means I miss all the bonding moments of summer club team. Then there's the fact that I have family movie night every Friday, and I won't ditch it, even for social events.

Kids my age usually have a *carpe diem* attitude about high school—hyperaware that these days don't last forever. And I know that too. But when your mom gets cancer on your third day as a freshman in a new school, you realize time with your parents is precious too.

I find Lukas where I left him, near the refreshment table. He ducks out of his conversation with the track team guys, frowning a little. "Everything okay? You were gone awhile."

"Yep. Swim team stuff."

He leans down to peck my cheek, an elegant motion that makes me feel like we're at a gala or a fund-raiser. Lukas wants to be a doctor, but tonight, I can see him as a young senator. He's thoughtful and engaged in every conversation, and, especially in his traditional black tux, he cuts a regal figure. Blond hair just long enough to comb, a healthy tan, and a strong nose.

"Is my tie okay?" he asks. "I've got to announce king and queen soon."

"Your first official act as Senior Class President Pratt!" I grin, teasing him a little as I straighten his bowtie. "Fancy!"

He smiles a bit sheepishly, though I know he's proud to have been reelected. It's a nice addition to his already impressive CV. Mine's not bad either, though I can't bear to think about it. Unlike Lukas, I have absolutely no idea where I want to go to college, or for what.

The lights dim lower around us as the DJ transitions to a slow song, and I nod toward the dance floor. "Shall we?"

"All right," Lukas says, taking my hand. He's much more comfortable chatting with people than dancing. He confessed this before our first homecoming together, to make sure I wouldn't have a disappointing evening. But at least he'll entertain a few slow dances. Even though we're only swaying, he wears his *working on calculus homework* expression.

"What?" he asks.

"Nothing." I smile, my pressed lips trapping the laughter.

This dress would be a little hard to truly dance in anyway. I thought I'd go for a pale pink or blue gown—something simple and floaty. But I surprised myself with this one: the color of milky tea, with crystals like a dusting of sugar. I tend to think of my coloring as plain: pale, freckled skin; unremarkably blue eyes; and ash-brown hair that falls nearly to my waist. But the neutral-tone dress works somehow, makes me look brighter by comparison. I think the mermaid silhouette and Hollywood glamour look surprised Lukas too. On the way here, he glanced at my neckline and tugged at his collar. "Are you sure it's not . . . a little . . . showy?"

I laughed and said that if my pastor dad was okay with the dress, it was fine. He still looked a little disquieted, which I hoped was a compliment. Lukas is fast to share his well-thought-out opinions in class, but he can be hard to read in other ways.

In fact, it took me all of freshman year to realize that he liked me. We were both the new kids—me transferring from Sotherby Christian so I could join the swim team, him from North Carolina. He brought his faint Southern drawl with him, along with a collection of brightly colored polo shirts and his impeccable manners.

We met in second-period freshman biology, two days before my mom's cancer diagnosis. Sometimes, when memories of that time come back like tremors, I think about what a good friend Lukas was to me. He handled the havoc with such grace—looking up statistics to comfort me, earnestly sharing scripture for whatever I was feeling. I'm a pastor's kid; I know Bible verses. But sometimes it's nice to have people present them to you. Like they thought so deeply about your situation that they sought outside help. He did all that without ever even holding my hand.

"What are you thinking about?" he asks.

"When we met."

He smiles, his gaze passing over my face. "It's so different to see you with all this makeup on."

"Good different?" My deep lipstick needed bold wings of eyeliner to balance it. Even though I have an online channel where I share makeup tutorials, I don't use many products day to day. My parents don't exactly love when I wear lots of makeup. And my parents don't exactly know about the video channel.

"Sure," Lukas decides. "Just different. You look like a slightly alternate-universe Lucy."

"Hollywood Luce," I suggest.

"Your parents didn't think anything of all the makeup?"

I lift one shoulder. He's unduly reverent toward my parents, so he considers my video channel a lie by omission. Whereas I think I'm keeping them from unnecessary worry.

But in this moment, with my best makeup artistry and my hair swept to one side, it feels like the culmination of what I hoped high school would be, all at once. I compose a quick prayer of gratitude—that I have both my parents still; that I have Lukas, who is steady and good; that I have swim team and a chance to be a good leader. Tonight, everything feels like it's supposed to.

The second crisis cracks my world into pieces.

Lukas and I stay after the lights go up, exposing a sticky dance floor. He and the rest of the student council take down the balloon arches, and I pick up a few corsage petals that have been trampled underfoot. Most of the chaperones are seeing students out, making sure no one is drunk or being particularly stupid as the limos take them to afterprom.

I'm waiting for Lukas outside the ballroom when Principal Cortez comes back up the stairs. "Lucy, sweetie, what are you still doing here?"

"Oh, Lukas is helping tear down, so I figured—"

"Well, he can go too." She touches my arm. "You've got enough going on."

"Okay . . . ," I reply. I guess I do have a lot going on, with swimming and my AP classes.

Her smile is an attempt to encourage me, I think, but she only looks sad. "Give your mom our love, okay? We're all thinking about her."

Because I don't know what else to say, I reply, "Will do."

She heads inside, flagging down a nearby hotel employee with a question I can't make out.

Give my mom their love? They're thinking about her? These are the sounds of freshman year, after everyone heard she had breast cancer. And *everyone* heard; when you're a school nurse and a pastor's wife, half the community knows you.

But she's fine now—has been for a long time. If she weren't, my parents would obviously have told me.

My dress itches at the neckline, and the straps bite into my shoulders. Moments ago, the ceiling outside the ballroom seemed lofty. Now, I feel trapped inside a too-small box with not enough air.

Maybe my parents have been a little preoccupied the past few days, but my dad is just struggling with this week's sermon. I can always tell by the sound of his pencil on the legal pad, the sharp scratch as he crosses out ideas. And I did notice my mom twisting the ends of her hair, as she does when she's worried. But the flu is getting passed around school, so work has been busy for her.

Still, a shudder slips down my spine, something deeply off in the world. My hands tremble as I pull my cell phone from my purse. I scroll to my dad's number, since he's the world's clumsiest liar. Even his reactions to unflattering haircuts are badly acted.

"Luce? What's wrong?" my dad demands. Of course he's alarmed—his only daughter is calling home on prom night.

"Nothing! I hope." Now I feel dramatic. Principal Cortez probably misheard some teachers' lounge gossip. "Is everything . . . I mean, Mom's okay, right?"

The silence. That's what gives him away. It stretches out, a chasm carved into the conversation, and blood rushes to the center of my body. Flashes of heat in my arms and thighs. The feeling that comes after you slam your brakes, hard, to avoid an accident. No. *No.* It can't be bad health news; she had a lumpectomy. *Please, Lord, I will do anything if it's not that.*

Finally, my dad manages to say, "You know what, honey? Everything's gonna be fine. The three of us will talk when you get home."

"*Dad.*" The hotel is a too-fast carousel, blurs of color and light around me. *Please, God. Let me be wrong.*

"Luce?" Lukas's voice is somewhere nearby, but the word floats over me, drifting past. I don't know where it came from or where it lands.

"I'll leave now," I tell my dad. "I'm leaving now. Just please tell me. I can't . . . I can't drive home wondering, okay?"

Wait, I didn't drive. Lukas did. He appears behind me, hand on my lower back and guiding me to the exit.

My mom's soft alto enters the background, calm as she confers with my dad.

"It's back, isn't it?" I whisper.

More silence. Space enough for a gulp or a pained sigh or a pang to ache through your chest. "That's what the doctors are saying. Yes."

I don't cry. But water springs to my eyes, the reaction to a slap.

I whisper, "I'm on my way," as my phone slips from my hand, dropping to the floor.

This is what I'll remember later: Lukas gathering up the pieces—of my cracked cell phone case, of me. Ushering me to the passenger seat. Getting my inhaler out of my purse and pressing it into my hand. It will occur to me later how unhesitating he was.

The first time, the diagnosis shook my world like an earthquake. I clutched the door frames; I fell to my knees. And when it was over, we straightened the photos on the walls. We swept broken vases into the dustbin. I let myself feel relieved, even if I never forgot the fear.

"This isn't possible," I whisper, somewhere between downtown and my house.

I can hear everything: the low blast of the air-conditioning, the hum of the engine. The cringing silence from Lukas.

"She had a lumpectomy." I say this as if it refutes a new diagnosis. I say this as if he hasn't been there with me through everything. "They said it worked. She didn't even need a mastectomy or chemo."

Lukas scratches the back of his neck. "We just don't have all the information yet. It could be really, really minor. I'm sure everything will be fine."

The first time, we repeated that refrain over and over. It was our credo, our hymn. I prayed while scrubbing dishes after dinner. I prayed with every stroke, back and forth, back and forth, down my swim lane. I prayed while walking between classes.

I didn't even beg God—I said I trusted that His will would be done.

I should have begged.

"But . . . you're *not* sure," I realize out loud, turning to Lukas. "No one can be sure."

"Well, it doesn't help to think like that. We have to trust God on this one."

He turns onto my street—how did we get here so quickly and so slowly? We've lived in the parsonage for ten years, and it's felt cozy and worn in since the first day. It's ancient—silver-sheened radiators, narrow hallways, and floral wallpaper in the bathroom that we never bothered to take down. Instead, my mom decided to embrace antiquity. She hung lace curtains, bought a beautiful brass bed for my room, and put out her collection of old quilts. Why am I thinking about this? My present reality has detached, and it is floating away like a child's lost balloon.

"Wait." I reach across the console to grip Lukas's arm. "Pull over."

Lukas obeys, drifting the car to the side of my tree-lined street. The church looms ahead of us. It's so close to our house that in the daylight, the steeple casts a shadow across our roof.

Leaning forward, I try to slow my breathing. "I just . . . I need to get it together before I walk in there."

He nods. Of anyone in the world, Lukas would understand my need for composure. It's like a tacit agreement in his family: straight-back shoulders, soft expressions, always in control. Their whole house is full of tall windows and cream linen upholstery. The possibility of smudges or stains will simply not be indulged.

"It's my mom, Lukas. My mom." These are only two words, but they glint with a hundred facets. She's my closest friend, my cheering section, my nurse, my teacher, my confidant. The least I can do is collect myself and *try* to handle this with grace.

"I know," Lukas says quietly.

When my mom was originally diagnosed, I tried to memorize her. Even in small moments—ducking her head into my room to say good night, singing along to the radio in the kitchen—I mentally freeze-framed every detail. Curly hair to her shoulders, always pulled back to reveal her trademark dangly earrings. The soft, pale skin that she rarely covers with makeup. The wide-set hips, so like mine, that she has never once complained about.

Deep breaths, air expanding my lungs until they ache.

"Hey. You've got this." Lukas reaches over to clasp my hand.

He says this when I'm nervous before a swim meet. But these types of inner strength pull from different reservoirs. Competition jitters call for adrenaline, for confidence. Your mother's mortality? I have no idea what that requires. Faith? Because I tried that before.

Lukas means well, though, with his clammy hand on mine.

I give myself one last slow exhale, then a puff of my inhaler.

"Good?" Lukas asks. He's seen a few stress-induced asthma attacks, and each time, he calmly talks me through it.

"You've got this," he repeats, with one last hand squeeze.

This is what I'll never, ever forget: My parents waiting for me on the couch. The stiffness of my beaded dress as I sink into the armchair. *It's in my breasts again.* My mom's soft hands holding mine. *Gonna fight it.* The teakettle shrilling. *Double mastectomy.* Sipping for the comfort of the heat, not even able to taste the mint. *Trusting in God like we always have.* How quickly I fastened a mask of bravery onto my face.

"We don't want you to worry," my mom says. "Surgery is scheduled for Monday morning. That's the first and hopefully only step."

"*This* Monday morning?" I gesture down at my ridiculous, jewel-encrusted dress. "You let me get all dressed up and go to prom when . . . when *this* is happening?"

"Oh, honey." She looks so genuinely sad, like telling me is the worst part of all this. Pressure builds behind my eyes, but I refuse to succumb to tears. "We wanted you to have your night. You deserved that much."

But don't they see? Prom night—my perfect prom night—doesn't matter at all compared to this. Why do they think I've stayed home every Friday of high school for our family movie night? Because I swore—to myself and to God—I'd never take this for granted, and I meant it.

"How long have you known?"

My parents exchange guilty glances, and for the first time in my life, I wonder if they've lied to me before. If protecting your child trumps the ninth commandment. It's my dad who speaks this time. "They found a lump at a checkup two weeks ago, and the biopsy came back pretty quickly."

Maybe it would be different if I had a sibling, but it's the three of us. I'm the only one who's been going on her merry way while the rest of this family worried, suffered, planned ahead without her.

"And when were you going to tell me?"

My dad answers more steadily this time. "Tomorrow morning. Before I tell the congregation. We didn't want you to worry for any longer than you had to."

I understand their good intentions—I do. But understanding doesn't make me feel any less lied to.

"Oh, Luce," my mom says. "I'm sorry it happened like this."

"I'm sorry it's happening at all." Yes, I feel burned by their secrecy. We're supposed to be a team, and I'm old enough to handle this. But mostly, I wish there was no awful diagnosis to keep secret in the first place.

"You should head up to bed," my mom suggests gently. "Change out of that pretty gown. It's been a long night. We can talk about it more tomorrow, okay?"

I acquiesce, but mostly so I can react in private. Clutching the stair rails with both hands, I feel the air thin; I feel my vision tunnel. And behind the bedroom door, my dress closes around me, squeezing like a fist. The crystals feel too hard, rock fragments trapping me in this too-tight casing. I contort my arms to reach the zipper, bending in a way that should hurt. But I feel nothing.

The dress drops from my body as I reach for my inhaler. The last time I glanced in the vanity mirror, I was zipped-up and sparkling—the very picture of prom night. Now, I am freckled skin squeezed into nude spandex, hands on my knees as I gasp for breath. My perfect hair coming loose, gown pooled on the floor. Behind me, a bookcase full of stories my mother read to me, full of swimming trophies and jewel-toned ribbons, full of certificates from childhood piano recitals. What is any of it worth? What is any of it without my mom?

Without her, who would call me Bird because of the way I squawked as a baby? Who would listen to every detail of my dates with Lukas? Who would have movie nights in and girls' nights out with me? Who would make faces at me from the choir loft when no one was looking?

Don't cry, I command as I peel the spandex off my body. *Do not.*

In the bathroom, I scrub the makeup from my face. I scrub until it hurts, until my skin is pink and clean. And when the warm water hits my hands, I think up at God: *We had a deal. How could you?*

How could *you?*

CHAPTER TWO

THE MORNING AFTER BAD NEWS IS THE CRUELEST OF THEM ALL. In the first, still-sleepy moments, I think of prom and smile dreamily. My mind lingers on the memory of Lukas's arm around me as we posed in the garden. As my mom beamed, teary-eyed.

And, like that, last night comes back over me like a collapsing roof—shards of slate and plaster dust crumbling down on my bed.

Taking a shower does nothing to wash the grime of dread away. As the water hits me, my brain starts reciting a gratitude prayer: *Dear God, thank you for Mom and Dad, Lukas and Aunt Rachel, for—*. It's automatic, and I stop myself. *No. Not today.* It's a childish and possibly blasphemous impulse, to give God the cold shoulder out of anger. But I'm just too mad—too betrayed—to pretend like nothing has changed between us.

I tense up, waiting for the lightning to hit me. There is nothing but the sound like falling rain.

Being a Christian kid and slightly neurotic besides, I used to worry I wasn't praying enough. Somewhere around second grade, I decided I'd thank God every time I washed my hands—that would be my reminder, the cold water on my hands. Then I found myself praying at the drinking fountain. When I got into the bath. It became habit, this ritual: water touches my skin and I send up a prayer of gratitude. But not today. Not now.

My mom is in the kitchen, pushing a spatula across the griddle. She's wrapped in her flannel robe, humming to herself. Could the doctors be wrong? It's a dangerous thought, and I know better. She just looks so healthy.

"Scrambled eggs sound good?" she asks, even though she's already piling them onto a plate for me.

"Perfect!" My enthusiasm is an overshot. I am an alien wearing Lucy skin, trying to mimic her usual behavior so her mom won't worry.

Eggs are one of the few things she can make with reliable success—plus some chicken recipes and casseroles. For church events, she always volunteers to bring the beverages. Sometimes my dad cooks, or—if he's at the church late—we order in, gleefully. If he's not home, we eat on the couch in front of the TV. My dad always walks in and pretends to disapprove. *Well, looky here*, he says. *The Takeout Twins ride again.*

As I sit there stabbing at my eggs, I start to wonder: Did I actually wash my hair in the shower? Or did I stand under the water, staring into nothing?

I dry my hair on autopilot, vacant eyes staring back at me. My mind hasn't done this—gone hypnotically empty—since my mom got sick. The first time, I mean. Since my mom got sick the first time. How long will it take me to internalize that it's happening again?

"Hey, kiddo," my dad says, ducking into my room as I finish my makeup. "I just got a call from Miss Rosa. She's under the weather. Would you mind heading over early to play some prelude music?"

"Oh. Sure. I'll head over there." In light of my unconvincing portrayal of someone who is fine, I'm relieved for an excuse to leave the house. Besides, it'll be nice to reconnect my hands to the piano. Until I was fourteen, I played competitively. Somewhere along the way, swimming nudged it out of place. But muscle memory is a funny thing, saving skills beneath your skin.

Alone in the church, I sit at the piano and press the keys gently, feeling out the resistance. Piano keys and pedals are like car brakes—they all do the same thing, but sometimes the necessary pressure differs from model to model. This piano is second nature to me. When my dad accepted the call to be White Hills United Methodist's pastor, my mom was still working at the hospital. Some nights, if my dad had to work late, I'd hang out here with him and practice. That was before my mom got her job as a school nurse so she could have summers off with me.

By the time Mrs. Edelman—our congregation's earliest early bird—is settled in her pew, I've decided on a lineup of hymns I know by heart: "A Mighty Fortress Is Our God," "Abide with Me," "How Firm a Foundation." The first is my hope, the second my prayer, the last a personal failing.

Lukas waves at me from the third pew, where I normally sit with him. He's early and by himself, which means he drove separately from his parents—probably in case I needed him. He's always thinking of things like that, always making himself available.

"*You okay?*" he mouths.

I nod, a quick jerk of my chin telling the lie for me.

Playing the prelude, it turns out, is a godsend. Since I'm up here, people won't approach me to say hi, so I don't have to pretend to be okay. Lukas gamely chats with them in my stead, doing a convincing *everything is great* routine, as usual.

As I move through my selections, the words scroll in my mind. What the heck is a bulwark anyway? And I wonder if every pastor's kid knows that Martin Luther himself wrote "A Mighty Fortress." It's something my dad likes to announce proudly, as if Martin Luther is his son instead of a forebear. The hymn always makes me think of Psalm 46: *God is our refuge and strength, a very present help in trouble.*

Really, God? Where? I mean, seriously. Give me a dove with white flapping wings. A rainbow stretched over our house. Give me literally anything—a feeling, a holy light, a burning bush. A barely flickering bush! One little match strike in the boxwoods outside our house.

In my attempt to avoid the congregation, my eyes settle on the altar.

And this is how I wind up initiating an epic stare-down: me versus Jesus Christ our Lord.

From my seat on the piano bench, I narrow my eyes against His alabaster ones, thinking: *Blink. Come on, blink.* He refuses.

This is because He's a sculpture—which, in a staring contest, really seems like cheating.

He stands on the altar, stone arms wide and ivory palms up—a pose that used to look welcoming. Now He looks halfway to a shrug. *Your mom has cancer again and there's nothing you can do about it.* He's right. I feel helpless, hapless, planless.

No member of White Hills United Methodist filing into the pews would believe the nasty voice in my head is mine. I substitute-teach elementary Sunday school, I play the "Hallelujah Chorus" on the pipe organ with gusto every Easter, and I've been able recite the books of the Bible in chronological order since I was six.

And I love this church—the stained glass, the carved wood, the familiar faces. I love my dad's little office and the kitchen downstairs and the rec room, even though it's old and musty. I know every closet and nook; I've watered every plant in the courtyard a hundred times. I love Christmas here, our tall evergreen and the candlelight, every drawn-out "gloria" that fills the rafters as we sing.

Cancer is like seeing all the magic of Christmas stuffed into clearance bins. The beautiful pine tree stripped to rust-colored needles in a garbage bag. White candles melted to stubs, blackened with scorch marks.

I can't unsee it. I have discovered the presents from Santa in my parents' closet. And I wish I could go back.

I'm on the last verse of my final selection when the choir files in. This hymn finishes: *I'll never, no, never, no, never forsake.* I almost laugh darkly at the irony.

When no one is looking, my mom turns, green robe swishing, to stick her tongue out at me. I can't quite laugh. How can she laugh?

Normally, I'd get up from the piano so the choir accompanist could sit, I'd walk down the side hallway, and I'd slide into the pew next to Lukas.

But the walls tilt inward, my eyes blurred. My lungs ache as if filled with hot smoke.

I cannot listen to my dad tell the congregation the news. I lived through it once, their dabbed tears and covered mouths. I can't do it again, with their gazes crawling over me and watching for a reaction, for reassurance, for something.

I can't be here. I cannot be here.

As calmly as I can, I smooth my skirt and exit through the side door where the choir has just filed in. But I don't duck into the end pew. I keep going, ballet flats tapping down the hallway as I hurry out. I can't stop; I'm in the sunshine now, propelled away from my church like we're opposing magnets.

The rational part of me is screeching: *What are you doing? You can't leave! Stop! Are you insane?* Maybe I *am* insane, but I can't stop. I grab my inhaler from my purse and take a deep pull.

I'm across the street, almost on my front lawn, before Lukas catches up with me. With all his varsity letters in track and cross-country, I'm not sure why I'm surprised.

"Luce. Hey. What's goin' on? You okay?"

"I'm fine. I just . . ." I gesture backward to the church, unable to look it in the face. "I can't be there right now."

He catches my hand. "Are you not feeling well?"

"Yeah, tell people that's what it is."

"But that's *not* what it is?"

I pull away to punch in the code on our front door. The electronic padlock was a Christmas gift from my dad, a joke for my mom, who loses keys even in her smallest purse. "My mom has cancer *again*, Lukas."

"I know," he says quietly.

"I can't be in there."

"Okay . . ." He's looking down at me—I can feel it—but I stare at the decorative bows on my shoes. "Can you help me understand? Is it that you need some space to cry?"

"No. I need . . . I need to scream."

He almost takes a half step back, surprised, but he stops himself. "You're angry?

"No, I'm *pissed*."

Lukas leans back now, put off. But "pissed" is a more sat-isfying word than "angry," which could be French: *ang-ree*. It's lovely, no hard sounds to press your lips against. "Pissed" is a hiss and a thud. Do you hear that, God? *Pissed*.

I thought saying it would be a release, that it would exor-cise some of my anger. But in fact, it only amps me up. "Like, honestly, *fuck* this. The entire situation."

"Lucy!" I'm as shocked by my language as he is. I've never said that word in my life. Thought it a few times, sure—but felt guilty about even that.

But no thunder shakes the ground beneath me; the clouds do not part to reveal a wrathful God. It is only me, almost incoherent as I yell, "I did everything right! I do! Everything! Right!"

Lukas stands utterly still in my yard, as proud and golden as our spring daffodils. "I know you do. But—"

"Do you remember freshman year?" I prayed without ceasing; I fasted like Moses and David and Esther. No one had more faith—more belief—than me.

"Of course I do, Luce . . ."

"And I still don't drink or smoke or skip class or even do anything *sinful* with you." I'd blush if my face weren't already enflamed. "I trusted that God would heal my mom, and He did. Except He *didn't*."

Before he can stick up for Our Heavenly Abandoner, I add, "My mom is the best person I know. Why her? It doesn't make any sense. She lost her parents when she was five, and then wound up in foster care. Hasn't she been through enough? Seriously."

Lukas's mouth twitches into a frown. "Well, sometimes God's plan doesn't make sense at the time it's happening. If we knew everything, it wouldn't be faith, right?"

Normally, I find Lukas so helpful. His calm insights—about everything from the excellent success rates of lumpectomies to the most relevant scriptures for serious illness—kept me sane freshman year. But this question clicks something in me, and my blood rises to a simmer.

It's just so *patronizing*. Like he's talking to a particularly stupid first grader, instead of his honor-roll, pastor's daughter girlfriend. I *know* how faith is supposed to work.

"Well, Lukas, it's easy to say that when nothing bad has ever happened to you."

He recoils from me as if dodging a punch. "That's not fair."

It actually is. All four of his grandparents are alive, even. "I can't do this right now."

"Can't do what, Luce?" He sounds pained, his empathy muscles stretching to reach me. But he can't quite get there.

"Church, this conversation." I laugh, gesturing widely at the world around us. "Anything."

I slam the door behind me, and the brass knocker handle slaps against its base—a bonus slam.

It takes less than one minute for the mortification to set in. When I peer outside, Lukas is gone. I yelled. I said the

F-word. But what can I do? Go back into the service? That will only draw more attention to my freak-out.

So I do the logical things: still in my church dress, I schedule a few videos for LucyEsMakeup, reorganize my entire vanity, and google "stage iii breast cancer." Two out of the three are emotionally healthy choices.

By the time my parents get home, I've removed the last of my winter clothes from my closet and drawers. While I'm at it, I figure I might as well pull some items for donation. Around me, K100 the Path blares a song's chorus: *"He is more, He is more."* More than what? More than fear? More than doubt?

I've never asked these questions of the radio before. I've just sung along.

My dad pops his head in, and I brace for the lecture of a lifetime. Instead, he asks if I'm okay (yes) and if I'm hungry (no). But later, when I step out into the hallway on my way to reorganize the bathroom, I hear my parents conferring. Deciding my punishment, I assume. I can't hear the words— just the low rumble of my dad's voice and the calm, higher octave of my mom's.

It's not until I smell dinner—the savory scent of roast chicken, herbed and with rice—that my mom knocks on my door. "Hey, Bird."

I glance up and then back to the lines I'm ironing into a pair of khakis. Another sensible choice—eliminating wrinkles from my closet can only improve things. "I'm really sorry about this morning. It won't happen again, I promise. I just had the worst stomachache."

Honestly, at this point, Saint Peter can just put that lie in my filing cabinet.

"Lukas said you were very upset."

That Judas. An excuse slithers out of my grasp, like so much else. I press down hard on the thick chino, steam huffing out of the iron.

"Luce," my mom says quietly. "Look at me. I know this is so hard."

"You know, I'm really fine," I lie. "I don't know what came over me."

"Can you put down the iron and talk to me?"

"Okay," I say, though my hands are twitchy—desperate to grasp on to something.

"Surgery tomorrow is going to be *fine*. We already got you excused from school, so you'll be there for everything. And remember, I've had surgery before. I'm pretty tough."

"Ha," I say, because it's an understatement. One of my clearest memories is the first time I saw her go into nurse mode in public. How instinctively she ran toward that hive-covered kid at Cracker Barrel. Toward his mom, who was too panicked to act. All at once, my mom's calm voice, the EpiPen, the soothing words as she popped the needle into the little boy's leg. Like it was an everyday thing. Because it is.

"Luce?" she says, nudging me back to her.

"Sorry. I'm really fine, Mom. It was just a lot to take in, finding out last night and processing. I didn't want the whole congregation looking at me."

"Believe it or not, I understand that very well." Her voice is quiet, almost penitent, but she doesn't apologize. "Well, dinner in ten."

I want to follow her out of the room, to put my head on her lap as we watch TV, to sit at her feet while she does the dishes. I want proof of her in my sight at all times. But if I want to be treated like an adult in this family, I can't act like a child.

So, instead, I reach for my Bible, a gift for my confirmation when I was twelve. My name glints across the cover, embossed in gold: *Lucy Esther Hansson*. In the back, there's an alphabetical table of contents by subject. I can search for verses about anger, forgiveness, peace, zeal.

Under "E," nothing is listed for Everything is falling apart.

MAY

CHAPTER THREE

ON THE FIRST DAY OF MAY, BOTH MY MOTHER'S BREASTS ARE removed in a surgery that takes 3 hours and 6 minutes. She spends 2 days in the hospital. The doctor is happy with how it went, though he had to remove some lymph node tissue as well. We'll have to wait for more detailed results as she recovers.

We watch 5 movies lying in her bed at home. She falls asleep during 4 of them, pain meds tugging her eyelids down.

I set a personal record as anchor for the Hammerheads' 400-meter relay. For the first time, neither of my parents is there to see it.

I take 5 exams, attend 11 graduation parties, hand out 158 programs at graduation.

My mom receives 8 bouquets of flowers and more casseroles than fit in our refrigerator.

We order takeout 7 times anyway.

She has 3 follow-up appointments. Zero are explained to me; all I'm told is, "That's how cancer goes. It's routine."

I take 8 sips of cranberry juice mixed with vodka at Mallory's graduation party, just to see what happens. What happens is that it tastes disgusting and I get really sleepy. Lukas drives me home in stony silence.

The world moves twice as fast. Or twice as slow. It's hard to tell when it feels like you're watching your own life instead of living it.

During the month of May, Lukas asks me 14 times if I'm okay. I lie 14 times.

I kiss him twice as often, at least. Maybe to prove I'm okay or maybe because it feels like the world might be ending or maybe because I'm just trying to feel not-alone.

He takes me on 5 dates, an attempt to take my mind off everything. After an afternoon at the aquarium, I slip out of my shirt on the couch in his parents' basement. Just to see what happens.

What happens is that Lukas goes along with it, but seems silly-embarrassed afterward.

Three times, he tries to mention trusting God's plan. The last time, I stare out the passenger's-side window and whisper, "Please don't."

My dad gives 8 sermons, 2 each Sunday. He cancels at least 10 evening events that I know of—everything but the Saturday weddings. He putters around, inventing chores to keep busy.

Every night, I play piano before bed. It's a place between waking and sleep, where I don't have to think in words. Most nights, my dad works on his laptop beside me in his favorite armchair. Keeping me company or trying to feel not-alone—I'm not sure.

My mom has 2 more follow-up appointments. She waves me off, saying they're tracking her blood cell counts—it's routine. My dad stares at his reheated casserole, pushing it around with his fork.

I start 0 college applications. I receive more than 30 brochures. The pile on the hallway table is stacked like bonfire kindling.

We have all 4 Friday movie nights, as if nothing is different.

I record only 2 videos for the makeup channel, both while my parents are at doctor appointments. One is a waterproof eye makeup tutorial for when you're going somewhere—a sad movie, say—where you might cry. Smiling into the camera, I refer to the look as "perfect for wedding criers." I can't bring myself to mention funerals.

I cry in only 3 places: in the locker room shower at the swim club, in my bathroom with the fan on, and in the car alone.

Every single night, I stare up at my bedroom's speckled ceiling, wondering if God sees me. Wondering if He feels even a little bit bad.

I try to pray more times than I can count. But it won't come. Something that has always been as easy as speaking now feels like reciting lines.

For the first time in my life, I consider that I am being looked down on by no one, by nothing.

The verdict comes in on the penultimate day of the month, a sunny Saturday. Or maybe that's just when my parents deign to tell me. They need to tell the congregation in the morning, before we leave for camp this week.

It's still in her lymph nodes. Six cycles of chemotherapy that we'll drive home from camp for once a week. My mom won't be able to help kids at camp or be school nurse next fall—too dangerous for her feeble immune system.

Between the two of them, they tell me 5 times that everything will be fine.

I know, I reply.

Everything will be fine.

Except I have seen behind the curtain now, and the wizard is only a man.

JUNE

CHAPTER FOUR

THE MORNING BEFORE WE LEAVE FOR CAMP, MY MOM FINDS me in my room, deep into one of my new coping mechanisms: organization! In this case, I'm sitting on the floor, surrounded by exact packing piles of clean laundry. To me, this is progress! A practical use of my fretful energy! Based on my mom's expression, however, this may look like very sad preschool circle time: me on the carpet, surrounded by obsessively ironed stacks of clothing.

She sits on the edge of my bed, studying me with a soft look on her face. "Hey, honey."

"Hey. Everything okay?" Her first chemo treatment isn't till next week, but you never know what other ugly news will snake its way into our lives.

"Fine! Just fine." She clasps her hands on her lap, settling in. "Listen, I got a phone call from Rhea Mills this morning."

"From Daybreak?" It's the camp closest to Holyoke, a mile away along the arc of the lake.

"Mm-hmm. Their camp just started, and they had a girls' counselor quit. Which is quite a coincidence."

I settle a pile of shorts into my suitcase. "You don't believe in coincidences."

"Exactly. This was a God thing, through and through. Because I've been thinking and praying—what can I do to help you through all this?"

"What? No. I'm going to help *you*."

"Well, I was thinking: What if you were a counselor at Daybreak this summer?"

"Ha. Okay." When she doesn't laugh too, I jerk my head up. "Wait, what? What if I went to the *hippie camp*?"

"Don't call it that, Luce," she says. "And yes. I want you to consider it."

"Are you serious? *Why?*"

"Well." She sits up a little straighter, as if prepping for her opening arguments. "A few reasons. I know you love Holyoke, but the visiting church groups come and go every week."

"Yeah?" I say, but the tone is more *So what?*

"I think a whole summer with the same kids would be a great way to make friends."

"I *have* friends." The words spring out too quickly—so obviously a sore spot. But I *do* have friends: the swim team and people at church who are my age and Lukas. I mean, maybe it's not like sisterhood-type friends, but it's not my fault that I transferred from private school to White Hills High freshman year. The friend groups were already formed.

And I wanted to spend time at home with her and up at camp instead of bonding at sleepovers or whatever. Does she want me to *not* like hanging out with her and Dad?

"I know you have friends." She says this so carefully that it's embarrassing.

"And I'll make new friends when I get to college. Just because you met Aunt Rachel at camp doesn't mean I have to find a best friend there."

"I agree." She squeezes her eyes shut for a moment. "But Daybreak is for kids who have experienced hard times in their lives—some trauma or difficulty like losing a parent or sibling. It's mostly fun camp stuff, but there are some aspects to help with coping too."

I didn't know that. I figured they did drugs and sang around the campfire. My heart is going full-on prestissimo. "Well, I wouldn't know how to help them."

"Honey." She says this word in the same tone that people say *C'mon.* Like she knows better and so do I. "What I mean is that I think the environment there would help *you* handle my experience with cancer."

She always phrases it that way. Not "my illness" or "this difficult time."

"I can't be at a non-Christian camp. I can't." I whisper this, mortified. But it's true: I *need* Camp Holyoke. I need to live with my parents in our little cabin and lead prayers and talk to kids about Jesus. I'm falling away so fast, and I can't find anything to grab onto.

46

"Oh, Luce." For a moment, I fear she's going to cry. Of all the things that can unhinge a person, seeing your mother cry has to be the quickest. "Faith isn't like getting a tan from the sun. You don't get it from being around Christians. It's already in you, and there's so much ministry and good you can offer Daybreak." She closes her eyes. "Do this for me. I'm asking."

"I can't! Mom!" My voice cracks, but I push back against the urge to cry. "I'm not leaving you. How can we even be talking about this?"

"Because there's one last reason. It's selfish." When she opens her eyes, they're filled with tears. "I need to know that you'd be okay."

We stare at each other, just a few feet of beige carpet away—her on the bed, me looking up from the floor. What is she saying? That she needs to push me away now, so she can see for herself that I could survive without her?

"Mom, I'm fine. I'd be fine." My voice cracks, betraying me. It's like she can see invisible sentences across my face, every thought I've had about losing her. This is what she'd read: *I think I might die if you die. I'll never get over it, not even when I'm forty and have kids of my own. And even if heaven is real, I can't wait all those years to see you again.* "You're going to be sick from the chemo, and I need to be there to help when—"

"I'll be right around the lake. You can come over every week on your day off. Give me this." Her voice is a whisper, pleading. "Please. Do this one thing for me."

How can I deny her? But how can I actually go? Didn't

I promise God I'd do anything? He can't want me to go to heathen camp.

"I'll pray about it," I say, and somewhere, Satan chuckles at how completely untrue this is.

"Good." She lets out a soft exhale. "Thank you."

In the quiet of my room, I kneel beside my bed—but not so I can pray as I promised I would. So I can cry into my quilt and still feel my legs on solid ground.

I'll do it. Of course I'll go to Daybreak. Because the darkest thought is the most convincing of all: What if this is the last thing she ever asks of me?

After a long, meditative swim, I text Lukas to meet me at our usual Starbucks. My hair is still damp, piled on top of my head. I didn't even put on mascara, because it seems like a truly ridiculous thing to care about these days.

When the bells on the door announce his entrance, I turn with a tentative smile. He raises one hand in greeting and walks straight to the counter for his black tea—no cream or sugar. Today's polo shirt is vibrantly tangerine, which makes him look more tan.

I pick at my scone, turning it into crumbs.

"Hi," I say weakly as he sits across from me.

"Good morning. Is everything okay?"

"Fine. I just wanted to talk to you about something."

"Okay. Yeah, me too."

"It's kind of a doozy," I say, leaning in. "My mom wants me to be a counselor at Daybreak."

It takes him a moment to comprehend, which I fully relate to. "The hippie camp?"

"Yeah." I explain her reasons, which actually seem sane as I repeat them.

Lukas shakes his head slowly. "Well, *that* doesn't seem like a good idea."

"I know," I reply automatically. "Wait, why?"

"Come on, Luce." His face is tender—almost apologetic. "Secular camp? After the past month?"

I wish I had to ask what he means. I guess I shouldn't be surprised that he noticed me pushing every boundary. But I could do without the condescending tone.

"Well, it's really important to her, so I'd appreciate if you could be supportive."

He stares down at his tea intently, as if it is the one speaking to him.

"Anyway, that's my news. What did you need to talk to me about?"

When he breathes out, I recognize the sound. I exhale like this on the starting block before I dive into my hardest heats. When I'm nervous and trying to calm myself.

"My parents and I have been scheduling college visits for this summer," he begins. "And with senior year on the horizon, I've been thinking a lot about the future."

"Okay . . ." I mean, this is not news. He's been planning for his future since the day I met him. Literally. He was taking meticulous notes on the first day of freshman bio, already preparing for his someday-career as a doctor.

He sets both hands on the table between us, wringing them. I don't understand why his expression is so pained. "Luce, I've been trying here. I've been trying so hard."

I cock my head, too confused to form a question.

"It feels like every day, you're slipping farther away. And I don't know how to help you."

"Well," I say, absorbing that blow. "My mom has cancer, Lukas. Again. It's not a super fun time for me."

"I know," he says, with total earnestness. "And I'm not insensitive to that. But I don't know what this means for us."

"For *us*?"

"Well, I know we've both alluded to eventually getting married, but is that still where you are on this?"

Okay, now he's lost me: college visits, me not handling cancer well, marriage?? I stare at him. "I was kind of thinking I'd go to college first."

He closes his eyes for a moment, almost a flinch. "Please don't be sarcastic about this."

"Well, I'm sorry, but how am I supposed to react? We're seventeen! This is a ridiculous line of thinking!"

"Is it? We're going into senior year. This is when huge, life-altering decisions start getting made. Do we want to intentionally go to the same college?"

"I have no idea. Yes?" I mean, I've always pictured that, I guess. But at the moment, I'm picturing Lukas as the deranged ringleader of the circus that my life is becoming. I don't even know what I want to major in!

"I'm a planner, Lucy, you know that. So, with all this

happening, our relationship and its . . . long-term viability have been on my mind."

Long-term viability?! Like we're a virus strain? "Well, this is the first I've heard of it."

He winces at my sharp tone. "I've thought and prayed about it a lot, and talked with my parents, and I even spoke with my old pastor from North Carolina."

"So what did you land on?" Pray tell! What conclusions did you—along with other people who are not me—reach about our relationship?

"Well, I have been thinking that this summer might be a good opportunity for us to take some time apart. To . . . recalibrate. A pause, if you will."

I open my mouth to say: *We* will *be apart—I'll be at camp.* But his real intent hits me, and I start to laugh softly. Great. Perfect. My mom's about to start aggressive chemo, I'm heading to a strange new camp—what could make this summer better? Definitely a breakup. Three for three on improvements to my life!

How's *that* for sarcasm?

His eyes widen at my less-than-analogous response, at my shoulders shaking with quiet laughter instead of tears. "Luce. I'm sorry if it sounds like—"

"You're right," I say simply. "We should consider it."

"Wait," he says. "Really?"

Maybe I'm prideful—I admit it. Maybe I like my makeup being perfect, maybe I like the compliments about my hair, maybe I like people knowing I'm a together person—a good kid. Maybe I can't stomach the thought of Lukas only staying with me because my mom got sick. "Really."

I gesture toward his side of the table, giving him the floor.

"Well, I'd like us to think of it as a pause. We'll already be in different locations, so I think it's the ideal time for us to reflect on what we each want before things get serious with senior year. We can reassess when I'm up at the lake with our congregation in July."

"*Reassess?* Can you be a human for a second? It sounds like you're my boss at some boring office job."

At this, his expression softens. Even his shoulders drop, so he looks less like a Collected Young Man and more like my sweet boyfriend. "I'm sorry. I should have practiced what I was going to say so it'd be . . . better than this."

He's *pausing* me, and yet I feel a flood of affection for Lukas Pratt. He cares so much about doing the right thing. I mean, he installs updates the moment his laptop tells him to. At every stop sign, he brakes for three full Mississippis. Of course he'd want to make sure our relationship is Right. Of course he'd table that thought when he heard the word "cancer."

"Lucy? Can you say something?"

"Do you want to go out with someone else?"

He looks startled by the thought of dating other people, so at least that's a relief. "I . . . hadn't considered that at all."

The shock of this conversation has worn off, and so has my mindless, nitrous-oxide laughter. I feel it, like a rock hitting the windshield. The on-contact snap stuns you, but then comes the slow-motion horror a moment later as the glass splinters.

I am broken up with. The initial impact happened, and now it carves a line, splitting right through me.

"Lucy?" Lukas asks gently. "Do *you* want to? See other people while we're apart?"

"No!" But then I add, because I want to hurt him, "Maybe? I don't *know*, Lukas."

He rubs his hand across his forehead. "You know I love you, right? That I want to do this *because* I love you, and I want to make sure we're doing the right thing for us."

The weird thing is that I *do* know he loves me. I don't doubt it, even now, as he is breaking up with me.

"I think that if you do find yourself wanting to go out with someone else, you should." He swallows. "That's hard for me to say. But that's the point of being apart. I want to know that we're sure about this before we factor each other into college decisions. Right now, I just don't know that I'm very confident about it."

"How long have you been thinking about this?" I mean, honestly, does everyone in my life just keep awful things from me, all the time?

When Lukas blushes, it's not a full-face pink. It's two pink splotches right on his cheeks. "Um, well. Obviously,

I've been concerned since your outburst, leaving church. But that concern rose further after the incident following our date to the aquarium."

I can feel the blush creeping up my forehead, down my neck. The incident? You have got to be kidding me, dude. So we made out sans shirts. We've been going out for two years! "Seriously?"

"Well, it was excruciating to sit in church the next day, wasn't it?" he asks. Actually, I didn't feel like we'd done anything that wrong. I felt guilty for not feeling guilty, maybe. "And I started to think about what a temptation it would be if we were at the same college. Since we're both committed to not having premarital sex . . . I don't know."

That's all it takes—the flame-burn of feeling judged—for a fire to be stoked inside me. So, I fooled around with my boyfriend of two years *once*. So, I'm hurt and confused by a God that has never hurt or confused me before. And because I'm human, Lukas needs to reconsider if I'll be his college girlfriend and future wife? What decade is this?

In the past two years, I've all but searched Lukas for a gift tag—*To: Lucy, From: God*. He showed up as the new kid right when I transferred to public school freshman year, right when I needed him. He opens the car door for me; he chats about marathon training with my dad. He sits at swim meets next to my mom. So why does he feel so much like Shruggy Jesus to me right now? Why am I tempted to place my hands on his shoulders and push?

"What would you do, Lukas? If *your* mom got cancer? Twice?" His mother wears a lot of candy-pink sundresses with paisley or even starfish prints. She has a Southern accent and a sleek, blond bob. I hope he's imagining clumps of it falling out. Because that will be my *reality*.

When Lukas opens his mouth to reply, I cut him off. "Because I know what *I'd* do for you if that happened. I'd pray and fast and cry with you. But I'd also be angry with you. I would crawl to wherever you were, emotionally, so that you wouldn't feel alone."

He already looks ashamed, staring down at the table between us, but I'm not done. "I would *not* climb up on my high horse and gallop around the Piedmont Square Starbucks, judging you for how you felt about a situation I could not possibly understand."

At this point, I'm loud enough that other coffee drinkers give us wary glances.

"This has not gone as well as I'd hoped, I admit," Lukas says miserably.

Lord. He wanted this—pausing our relationship—to go well. It would be absurd if it wasn't so earnest. He talked to his parents and a pastor to ensure this was the right decision. He doesn't want either of us to make a wrong choice about college or our futures. In a backward way, this dedication is part of why I admire him.

So.

I take one last sip of now-tepid tea. "Well, I better go."

"Lucy . . ." He reaches for my hand. "I don't want us to leave angry."

"I'm not angry," I lie.

He studies my face for a moment, then nods. Because this is what Lukas does: believes without question. The way I used to. I nearly resent him for it.

When he leans down to kiss my cheek, I almost jerk away. This kiss is a stamp pressed to a letter—the final touch before you send it off. But his cologne wraps around me, oaky and familiar and traitorously pleasant.

"I'll be praying for you, Luce," he says quietly.

"I'll be praying for you too." *That your chicken pox vaccine didn't work and you spend the whole summer with itchy spots spreading down your back and private parts, into crevices you can't even scratch.*

I may actually be the devil.

On the drive home, I do not cry. I do not hear the radio. I do not feel the AC blasting on my skin. I drive straight ahead, jaw set, intent on my path.

At home, I plunk the car keys on the kitchen table instead of in their designated bowl. It gets my parents' attention, and I lift my chin. "I wanted to let you both know that I'll be going to Daybreak this summer."

My parents' faces are the theater-symbol masks, comedy and tragedy. My mom beams while my dad's jaw drops in horror.

"So . . . ," he manages, "Lukas was supportive."

I dodge this. I don't want to talk about Lukas. The last thing my mom needs is confirmation of my turmoil. "I need to do something for myself. And I feel like I'm being called to this camp."

"Well, okay, then!" My mom clasps her hands together. "I'll call Rhea! She'll be delighted, just delighted! Oh, honey. Thank you."

That settles it: even if my entire summer is a nightmare, the joy on her face was worth it.

So I march upstairs to visit the Daybreak website again and reassess my packing needs. I pack the tin hidden in my desk drawer—the one with all my top-shelf makeup in it. If I'm not going to see my parents every day this summer, maybe I can wear some of it. It doesn't make sense at camp, necessarily, but you never know.

When I'm done, I sit at the piano downstairs and let my hands fly. I've remembered, these past weeks, why this was such a big part of my life. In fact, I don't even realize my dad's in the room until I've finished a fifteen-minute-long Mozart piece. "Oh. Hey."

"Hey. Sounded good." He's sitting in the Queen Anne chair, looking relaxed. "Bitten by the piano bug again?"

"I guess."

"About this camp thing. You sure about this, kiddo?"

"I'm sure. It's what Mom wants."

"Well, I know. But . . ." As he considers, his dark brows lower in consternation. My dad has a full head of hair, and it's white—has been since I was little. But it actually makes his face look younger by contrast. Skin smoother, blue eyes sharper. "She would understand, Bird."

"I know." But too much has changed now. "I can do it, though."

"Well, that I don't doubt. You'll be a wonderful counselor. We've always said how great you are with kids—even when you *were* a kid." He gets up, kissing the top of my head. "I'll just miss seeing you at Holyoke every day, that's all."

As he turns to go, he straightens the portrait of Jesus beside the piano.

I walk past the painting every day, but I haven't looked at it in ages. I picked it out with my mom when I was eight. So many renderings of Jesus make him look stern or so pious that He's not even human. But the one on this wall? He looks like someone who'd help a mom get a stroller up the stairs—like someone you'd ask for directions, knowing he'd find a way to help you even if he wasn't sure. "He has laughter in His eyes," my mom noted approvingly as she purchased it for me. And He does.

As I set my hands on the keys again, I can feel Him looking back at me, His eyes glinting with mirth.

"This isn't funny at *all*," I whisper. "Don't even look at me."

He keeps grinning like He knows something I don't.

CHAPTER FIVE

FROM MY VIEW INSIDE THE CAR, DAYBREAK LOOKS A LOT LIKE Holyoke—cabins set among the trees, a fire pit in the distance, and canoes racked up by the lake, in the same aged forest green and battered camp red. The pier is thin, splitting out into a T-shape. Down a little way, I can see campers in silhouette near the shoreline.

The lodge spans my entire view out our car's front window. It's wider than Holyoke's, with golden-wood siding and a porch. The sign above features a painted sun—half-risen and egg-yolk yellow—with "Daybreak" spelled in cornflower blue.

"Here we are!" my mom announces cheerfully. "Stay here for a minute, okay?"

In the backseat, I hug my knees to my chest, breath fogging up the window. *God, what am I doing here? Is this right? Am I really doing this?* No answer fills my soul. But as the doubt moves through me like a shudder, I think of Lukas, who didn't even text me to say *Have a good summer!* or *Good luck at camp!* But why would he? We're paused. In fact, I'm consumed with the urge to find some cute counselor here—maybe one with long hair or those big plugs in his ears, what do I care?—and lay one on him, just out of spite.

At least the camp is quiet right now, and, without strangers' faces nearby, it almost feels familiar. The lake glinting beyond us is mine, after all. I imagine dipping my head underwater, losing hours to the still water and the scent of the pines.

"Ready?" my dad asks, opening his door. My mom's exiting the lodge with a woman about her height, in shorts and a flannel shirt. It's been years, but I do remember Rhea—dark skin and gray hair in tight twists. She's old enough to be my grandmother, but she's not wrinkled like a tablecloth, like a fussy, too-precious thing. She's weathered, like thinly ridged tree bark.

When I emerge from the car, my mom looks at me the way she did when I won a breaststroke heat for the first time. I don't know what I did today besides agree to come here. "Rhea, you remember my daughter, Lucy."

"It's been a long, long while." She has one of those inward-glow smiles, calm but undeniably warm. The type that makes you feel like you're in safe hands. "Since you were a little thing. You probably don't remember."

"I do." I return a hesitant smile of my own. "And my mom has always told me about how you convinced the landowner to let us buy Holyoke."

"Ah, well. I can always recognize good caretakers. It's my spiritual gift. Holyoke was meant to be in your parents' hands."

I drop my polite smile, surprised at that word choice—"spiritual gift." Maybe Rhea's a Christian too. I didn't even consider that.

My mom puts an arm around my waist. "Rhea's fine with you coming over Sunday mornings. You'll have to get up early for sunrise chapel, of course, but you'd be doing that every week at Holyoke anyway."

"And we do have a piano in our rec room," Rhea says. "Do you still play?"

"A little. Just not competitively anymore."

"Well, you're welcome to it after lights-out for your campers, between eight and nine. One counselor always stays in the cabin, but one of your co-counselors is an early-to-bed type. So you'll have most evenings free."

"Great!" My voice is too bright, a false sheen.

I wait for my mom to look tortured, hearing the deceit in my voice, but she looks so . . . happy. "Well. You're going to have so much fun. I can't wait to hear about it."

I've never been away from her for more than a weekend trip to my aunt Rachel's house. That's all I get? I search her eyes for some other clue. "That's it? Not even a 'make good choices'?"

"That's it." She places her rose-petal palms on my cheeks. "Because I trust you. I trust the way we raised you, and I trust the young woman you've become."

This is because she doesn't know about me picking a fight with Shruggy Jesus or rolling around topless with Lukas. My soul has already put on a blinker for the Hell exit, and now I live at hippie camp. That's like sending me into the express lane.

"I'll see you in a few days!" My mom hugs me, gripping and fierce.

My dad kisses my cheek and whispers, "I'm proud of you, Bird. See you Sunday. We're a mile away if you need anything."

I bob my head, but it's not exactly a nod of agreement— more a reflex, self-soothing as I start to feel like I'm not fully inhabiting my body. Part of me believed my dad would back out last minute. But they're really leaving me here for the whole summer.

My mom turns to me again. "Don't forget your vitamins. And keep your inhaler in your shorts pocket, just in case, okay? And drink plenty of water, Luce, okay? I mean it."

There it is. Nurse Mom. "I will. Promise."

Rhea walks with her in those few steps toward the car. They hug when they reach the passenger's-side door. I don't hear Rhea say anything, but she must have because my mom is nodding against her shoulder.

My dad climbs into the driver's seat as Rhea returns to my side. And as our Subaru pulls away, my mom blows me a kiss. I pretend to catch it, a holdover from my kindergarten days. As I do, my mom covers her mouth like she's about to cry. I feel wickedly vindicated. Good. Be sad.

"Well, welcome, Lucy. I'm so happy to have you. First things first: your color-team band and your binder. It has the basic info," Rhea says. She hands me a blue rubber wristband and a navy binder with a "Hello, My Name Is" sticker slapped across the front. "Hansson" is written in all-capital letters. "The counselors go by last names here. We find it adds a little to your authority with the younger campers. Hope that's okay."

"No problem. I'm used to it from swim team." I crane my neck back as we start walking, but the car is out of sight. They really left me here.

"Oh, that's right! Your mom mentioned you're a swimmer."

"Yep. She was too, in high school and college."

Rhea rolls my suitcase down the path, and I pick up my duffel. With just a tote on my other shoulder, I can still examine the binder. The front has a schedule: *7:30 a.m.: sunrise yoga (optional).*

My cheeks puff out with my restrained laugh.

"There are six of you who are almost seniors, and you're all with the third and fourth graders. Each cabin has one college counselor, but most of them are responsible for the older kids." She gestures toward the path to the right, and I follow it beside her. "As you know, we've been in full swing for a week. I thought I'd give you some time to get settled, and then a fellow junior counselor will stop by to give you a tour. Does that sound okay?"

"Sure."

"Great. And here we are!"

"Here" is Cabin 3A, squat and standard with a screechy screen door. Inside already smells like the camp bunks that I help my parents clean before each new church arrives—damp towels, sunscreen, and bug spray. It looks, comfortingly, like elementary school: blue and green tie-dyed pillows, cartoon character T-shirts balled up on the shelves, glassy-eyed stuffed animals poised in waiting for their owners to return. It's hard to be intimidated by little girls who tuck into pink-speckled sheets, cradling plush dogs as the lights go out.

Nine bunks for campers, three for counselors. I try to imagine falling asleep in a room full of people, their tossing and turning or fitful sighs. I've never shared a room. At Holyoke, the church counselors who accompany the kids stay in the cabins with them, and I stay in the cabin with my parents, a tiny home away from home.

"You'll be right here. One of your co-counselors, Simmons, is on the top bunk." Rhea wheels my suitcase to a stop and taps the lower bunk to the immediate right of the door—the only one with a bare, waiting mattress. "Anything I can do for you now? Anna will stop by to give you a tour in about an hour, and she can also help you with any questions you come up with."

"That sounds good."

"Oh, and I put a waiver in the binder pocket. Your mom signed, but it's something we have all campers and counselors cosign. If you want to read over the materials and get that back to me this evening or tomorrow, I'd appreciate it."

"No problem." Fortunately, my mouth seems to be working. But I can't wrangle the other parts of me—my tear ducts, my nervous stomach, my racing mind. Faced with the details of my new life, they've gone wobbly on me.

"Welcome to the fray, Lucy," Rhea says. Her lips form a crescent moon, the slightest of smiles. "It's not an easy summer job—and some days, it's tremendously hard. The pay is next to nothing. But I wouldn't trade it. I hope it's the same for you."

"I hope so too." I make my voice peppy, so she'll leave.

Instead, she shakes her head—barely more than a twitch. Not in disapproval but in . . . marvel, I think. "My. You really do look just like your mother. It's arresting."

"Oh. Yeah." I push back a few curls. "Thank you."

When the sound of her hiking boots fades away, I examine my space. The top bunk is already someone's home, and I don't just mean the bed is taken. I mean someone fully lives there.

The bed is covered by rosebud sheets, a thin quilt, and a purple silk pillowcase. Pictures sprawl across the wall space behind the pillow like a headboard. The centerpiece picture was clearly drawn by one of her campers. It's a single name— Keely—drawn in purple pencil, with flower vines growing up each letter. The rest of the pictures form a collage: A span of stars with the words "Not All Who Wander Are Lost." Ripped-out magazine pages of tall redwoods, an Airstream trailer glinting like a silver bullet.

There are a few photographs, one of a little girl with plastic barrettes in her black hair. Another with two guys and two girls crammed together on a retro couch. I'm not sure which person my bunkmate is: the blonde with her mouth open in laughter or the dark-eyed girl with a lips-pressed smile, so content that she looks like she might close her eyes. The four of them sprawl and overlap like puppies. Like a pack, raised together from birth.

Whoever she is—Keely Simmons—she belongs here.

That's how my tiny room at our Holyoke cabin is. There's a picture of the three of us, art projects I've made at camp, a driftwood cross on the wall, a framed photo of Lukas and me on my bedside table. Here, I have one duffel bag, one suitcase, and one massive binder.

But I know cabins like these. I know the ebb and flow of camp life, these same trees and this swishing water, and I'm still Lucy Hansson. Even if this isn't my camp, and I'm a sort-of-single girl whose mother is possibly dying on the other side of the lake. It's like a dream where all the details are present but rearranged—it's your classroom, but the Target cashier is your teacher. It's your bedroom, but monsters from that movie you watched are attacking, smacking against your windows.

I unpack, convinced I can wrestle the details back into

order. My hands stretch the fitted sheet around my new mattress, smooth the flat sheet and duvet down, cram the pillow into its case. I stack T-shirts and shorts on my designated shelf, organize my makeup and shower products in the soft-sided basket I brought. I leave my Bible out on the bed next to my oldest Holyoke T-shirt—too small now, forest green with cracked white letters.

When I survey my completed bunk, it looks transient and spare. Heck, half these girls have their possessions strewn around like it's their own bedroom at home. Only one other bunk is neatly organized, bed made and a little pink suitcase still on the shelf.

It's all so daunting that I almost reach for my inhaler. I have mental pictures of all the worst times I've hyperventilated from stress: In middle school gym, where the teacher thought running laps was useful physical education. Before my seventh-grade piano recital, convinced everyone would somehow know I was wearing a tampon for the first time when I walked up to the piano bench. In the science-hallway bathroom, failing to control my breath on the first day of freshman year and public school. I am sincerely uninterested in adding to that little photo album.

When I settle in with the binder, I can't even get past the table of contents: Overview, Basic Rules, Self-Expression, Health/Medical, Talking about Death/Loss, and more.

I would like to say the word "shit" very loudly, savoring the "shhh" and the tap of the "t." Because, really, what the shit am I doing here?

And what, exactly, would Jesus do? Well, for starters, He wouldn't be as self-absorbed as I am. He'd be too busy helping others. What would Lukas do? Take charge like this was a leadership challenge. Pretend a college admissions board was watching his every move. What would my mom do? Be warm and loving, willing to ask questions without a trace of self-consciousness.

All these ideas have merit, so why am I still frozen, pretzel-legged on my bed that isn't mine, and thinking: *Is it too late to get out of this? What are the actual consequences? The third-grade girls would have only two cabin counselors? I think I can live with that. My mom is hugely disappointed?*

I don't think I could live with that.

There comes a time when you just have to put on some mascara and pull yourself together. And I know that, but I have very little experience with the *fake it till you make it* philosophy. It simply doesn't work for things I care about. Feigned confidence won't help you perfect a backstroke or a smoky eye or a concerto. It takes practice, skill, careful hands. And you can't fake faith. I mean, maybe you can to others—but that won't make faith manifest within you.

But I'll try to act like a capable and qualified and emotionally stable counselor until maybe it becomes true. I'll try. That's what echoes through me like a mantra, like a prayer, alone here on a sagging mattress. *I'm trying; I'm trying.* It's the friendliest I've been to God in a month. *Please see me trying. I'm trying to hold it together for my family, I'm trying to be a good person, and I'm trying to adapt in a biome that won't stop shifting—goodness,*

I'm trying so hard that I ache. Outside, the sun is trying to meet the horizon, the tall trees are trying to reach the clouds, and the campers are trying to perfect cannonballs off the pier. And I am really, really trying not to cry.

CHAPTER SIX

THE CABIN DOOR CLATTERS OPEN, STARTLING ME. "HEY! YOU
must be Hansson!"

The voice comes from a girl around my age with blond
hair, stylishly dark at the roots. The girl from the picture above
my bunkmate's bed. "Anna. Tour guide, at your service."

She bends into a goofy bow, hand wafting snootily like
a page in a royal court. When she looks up, I'm struck that
she's almost exactly my height, though waifish. And her
makeup is *good*—subtle mascara and expertly smudged
brown eyeliner. She either has naturally great eyebrows or
excellent pencil technique. So I guess some people do wear
makeup at this camp. It's a cheering thought, as much as
anything could be right now.

"Hi!" I bumble, remembering myself. "Yes. Lucy. Hansson."

"You okay?" Anna studies my face just as intently.
"I'm not being nosy! Well, I am. But you look a little . . .
overwhelmed."

"No! Well. I was just"—I heft the binder off my bunk—"looking at this."

"Oh, Christ. No wonder!" she says, and I tense at her choice of words. "I mean, don't get me wrong, that monstrosity is helpful. But it's stuffed full of exceptions. Most days around here are rules."

"Thank goodness. I was thinking I'd be helping with a seizure while explaining death and also running an art class."

"Nah. We try to juggle only *two* crises at any given time." She smiles, trying to cue me that she's joking. With makeup defining her high cheekbones and symmetrical nose, she could be as sharp and lovely as the runway models who strut down glossy magazine pages. But smiling, showcasing the full apples of her cheeks, she could never look anything but fun.

"Ha," I say, realizing how long I've been staring. "Great."

"Here are the main things, really." She ticks them off on one hand. "Some of the little campers might want to sit on your lap or hold your hand, get a piggyback, et cetera. That kind of touch is fine if they initiate it and you're comfortable with it. Um, you'll get to know any health issues, which is no biggie—we have a nurse. Try not to swear in front of the kids. If the older kids do, pull them aside and ask them to be a good example. Always try to de-escalate. If you have a concern about something a camper says or draws or whatever, give Rhea or Bryan the heads-up."

"Says or draws?" I repeat.

"Yeah. Like, in art class, they might draw . . . I don't know, needles or a coffin. Some of them have seen some messed-up shit."

Sure. Needles or a coffin. Great.

Anna notices my blank horror before I can shield it. "Hey, let's stop at the kitchen for a snack as part of the tour. You'll feel much better."

"Oh. I'm actually fine; I—"

"No, you need this snack. Trust me."

And . . . I do trust her. Her energy livens up the cabin, and all I can think is how much I want her to like me. As we head outside, I glance over hopefully. "So, are you in this cabin too?"

"No, you're with Simmons, who's our age—just finished junior year, right?" I nod, dully recalling that school ended barely a week ago. The last month is like a gray smear across the calendar, every day blurred together and dim. "Your third cabin counselor is Garcia. Camp is college internship credit for her and some of the other older counselors."

"So, I have nine third-graders, but also an all-age color group."

"Exactly. You're Blue Team. Color activities are usually in the evenings—sometimes for points against one another. Tug-of-war, cheer-offs. It's called Color Wars." She smiles grimly. "You're lucky you missed the naming of the color captains on Saturday. Lots of tears from those who didn't get it."

I'm about to ask more about competitions, when a group of campers walks by. They look fourteen or fifteen—the oldest camper age. It's funny, once you're going into senior year of high school, how young freshmen look—coltish legs, baby cheeks, adult noses taking shape. As they pass us, one of the girls calls hello to Anna, whose response becomes static to my ears. Because the girl's stomach protrudes out in a perfect sphere that leaves no space for doubt. I almost stop walking midstride. She's so young.

Somehow, my legs keep walking down the path, though the rest of me has stalled out. Finally, I stutter: "Was she . . . ? Is she—"

"Pregnant? Yeah. That's Tara." I can feel Anna looking at me. "You're not from a camp like Daybreak, huh?"

"Not exactly. Not grief camp."

"Well, we're not *all* grief campers, necessarily. It's more like, in the scheme of baggage we carry, all of us here have at least one big suitcase. My checked bag is my anxiety disorder, for example."

"Oh," I say. Am I supposed to drop that my mom has cancer? I can't seem to push the words out of my mouth. "Okay. That makes sense."

Anna takes me down to the water's edge, and I crane my head to see if Holyoke is visible. It's a silly thing to do—I'd need X-ray vision for the mile through the trees. But maybe I could make it out in the evening. My dad keeps the chapel lights on all night, in case any of the campers want to seek prayer time or solace there.

"There's another camp that way," Anna says. "But don't get excited. It's some crazy church camp, so not exactly boyfriend potential. Or girlfriend. Whatever!"

It lands like a smack. *Crazy church camp?* We're not crazy! Not even a little. In fact, we're pretty modern by Christian standards! But I like Anna already, and I don't want her to write me off.

She's moved on to explaining evening activities, but I'm tuning out. Was it cowardly to not mention that Holyoke is my camp? It's just that . . . telling people you're religious can make them assume a whole list of things about you. Like you've rolled out a scroll of all the ways you see the world. My dad always says: try to let it go if people judge you that way.

I know he does that himself. The truth is, there's theological disagreement within the church—between Methodist ministers, even. My dad comes home from state conferences looking wind-battered, even though he's been inside all week. His hair is mussed, shirt collar askew, skin dry. I imagine him in conference room sessions, frustrated and fidgety. I imagine him up late in his hotel room, jotting down notes as I hear my mom say on her end of the phone line, *I know, babe. But just keep speaking your heart—that's all you can do.*

We wind up at the lodge, and the porch beams creak in welcome. Inside smells like camp dinner, a not-unpleasant mix of starch and seasoning, with vegetables somewhere beneath it—green beans, maybe. With almond slivers, I bet.

"Behold," Anna says. "The mess hall. Standard."

It *is* standard—long tables in rows, a tall ceiling. But at Holyoke, we call this space the fellowship hall.

Ha. We have fellowship. They have a mess.

Anna has a bouncy walk, long arms swaying. It makes her look young. And happy. I think my walk must look like shuffled feet in funeral procession. "Our chef gets in the zone during dinner prep, so now is not the time to introduce you. I'll be right back. Wait, are you allergic to anything?"

I shake my head, and she leaves me at the end of a hallway, which is lined all the way down in framed photographs. The end picture, nearest me, is from last year—all the campers and counselors, with the year printed at the bottom. In it, I spot Anna beside the same threesome in the photo above my bunkmate's bed. My bunkmate, Keely Simmons, is sandwiched between the two boys—one with glasses and a wide grin, the other slim and smirking—with her arms slung over their shoulders. They look like they belong to one another.

I follow the pictures down the hall, watching the present-day recede and the hairstyles lift. Still, all the campers are alike in their comfortable smiles, in the easy way they pool together on the lodge's porch. At the end of the hall, I find the first few years of camp. In them, Rhea's hair is jet black, her skin smooth. Thirty years ago. There are three blank spaces on the wall nearby, like missing teeth in a big grin of frames.

"Sorry!" Anna reappears with heavy footsteps. "Whelan had to yell at me for interrupting his *process*, but I got the goods."

"The goods" appear to be two massive cookies. They're crammed full of chocolate chunks, oatmeal, some kind of nut—and that's only the ingredients I can decipher.

I nearly unhinge my jaw taking the first bite, and it's everything at once: sweet, salty, nutty, crunchy. My mouth waters in demand for more.

"What *is* that?" I stuff another bite in. "That crunch . . . Is it . . . ?"

"Crumbled-up potato chips. Secret ingredient. Whelan calls them First-Week Cookies. He keeps them in a secret jar. Big ones for counselors and staff, smaller ones for the kids."

"He only makes them the first week?" That's not acceptable. I will be needing more of these in the immediate future.

"Nah. But we need them especially now. You know—first-week blues. Homesick kids or exhausted counselors, all the summer breakups. That kind of thing."

The walnuts scratch against my throat as I cough. Could she just *tell* I got dumped? Are the hippies clairvoyant?

"You okay?"

I manage to swallow, my eyes watering. "Yeah. Just . . . apparently trying to eat this thing whole."

Anna's laugh is a quick, happy bark. "Totally understandable."

"So," she says, back to her tour-guide voice. "Rhea's office is at the other end of the hall, on the right. Bryan's is on the left. Have you met Bryan? That's her son. He's a therapist too. He lives in town with his wife and kid over the summer, but he's here a ton of the time."

Anna walks me down another hall to a big reading-and-rec room. Beaten-up leather couches square off, facing one another. There's a deer head mounted over the fireplace, sun-faded maps tacked up on the walls, and a few time-thinned Persian rugs. Old board game boxes are stacked on the shelves beside books—slim early readers on the lowest levels, thicker novels up higher. The piano my mom mentioned stands upright on the far side. On top of it, a globe, a brass trophy, a framed Michigan state flag.

"This is *nice*," I say, noticing floor cushions near the worn-in couches. The room looks like Ralph Lauren designed it twenty-five years ago, using East Coast antique stores and a tight budget.

"Yeah, Rhea knows how to make resources go the distance. She spends all her free time on grants and stuff. Sometimes for the whole place, like specific projects or objectives. Sometimes for individual kids. She's basically who I want to be when I grow up."

As we walk out, I run my hand across the knit blanket on the back of the couch. It's every color of green—near-black forest fading into palest honeydew.

"I made that," Anna comments.

"Seriously?" I turn to look at her in a slightly new light. "It's beautiful."

"Thanks. Rhea taught me my first summer. Knitting can be good for anxiety." She mimes moving two needles. "These days, I do whole sweaters."

And here I thought the hippies were around the lake growing marijuana or something. But no. They eat really great cookies and knit?

Near the rec room, Anna opens a door labeled "Maintenance."

"This," she says, "is the counselor meeting room. AKA the Bunker."

The room is small and wallpapered with notices, pictures, Post-its, neon flyers. A frayed plaid couch lines the back wall, and several tall bookshelves hold binders and bags of snack food. In the corner, a table and chairs have manifested straight from the 1970s: pale orange seats with metal legs.

"We do quick updates here or just hang after lights-out. One counselor stays in each cabin after nine o'clock, but the other two get free time after that. If we're not too tired, which sometimes we are."

Next, we visit the nurse's office, which is a small building right off the lodge. We're greeted by a nurse named Miss Suzette, the howls of a middle-school camper, and a TV blaring political commentary. Anna introduces me over the clamor.

"Nice to meet you, Lucy Hansson." Miss Suzette swivels toward the kid, who is whimpering with dramatic flair.

"You'll have to excuse Chase here. He is dealing with his discomfort vocally."

"Hey! That stuff you put on *burns*."

"I know, baby."

He holds out a hand, open-palmed. Miss Suzette smacks it like a high-five, and he scowls. "Just give me the Band-Aid."

She complies, and turns back to me. "Rhea tells me your mom is a camp nurse!"

Was. I don't say: *She's taking the summer off because doctors have to put poison in her body to kill the cancer.*

"Yeah! And a school nurse. Elementary." I don't say: *She can't return this fall because her weakened immune system won't be safe around sick kids.*

"Ah. So you understand my *triumphs* and *struggles*." Miss Suzette pats Chase's head as he applies his own Band-Aid, looking sour about it.

"All right. We should get back so you can meet your campers before dinner." Anna throws a conspiratorial glance at Miss Suzette. "Chicken casserole with mozzarella and tomato. I snooped."

"Yes, Lord," Miss Suzette says.

Outside, campers swarm toward the lodge. My view narrows into tunnel vision. All these kids I don't know. All these kids I'm now responsible for. At home and even seeing their bunks, it was only the idea of them. But they're entirely real—fast feet, waving arms, small bodies. With hair wet from the lake. Two little ones holding hands. Middle-school boys crowing with laughter over something whispered.

And I am an interloper. A guest at someone else's family dinner.

At Holyoke, I greet the campers with my parents, welcome them, and field any questions.

At Holyoke, I know the answers.

The Daybreak campers buzz with energy around the nearest counselor, chattering and a few half-climbing on him. He's one of the guys beside Keely and Anna in the hallway picture, easy to recognize by his thick, old-school glasses— dark frames on top, clear on bottom. He has deep brown skin and close-cropped hair and a short-sleeved oxford shirt. Linen, the kind my grandpa wore after he moved to Florida. Not that this guy looks like a grandpa.

He . . . really does not look like a grandpa.

The counselor claps a few times to get their attention, and I can already tell what's coming. A camp song is the easiest way to harness all the nebulous energy. As quickly as I think it, the campers start clapping too, forming two groups. They face one another, leaving a walkway between them.

To the sound of sharp claps, the first kid walks—no, *struts*—down the center aisle they've created, moving his arms in a dance I could never replicate. Next, a girl and her friend do a semi-synchronized dance that involves lots of hips and shoulders. Some of the kids are intent and solemn, others gleefully showing off.

"Hansson?" Anna says, nodding toward the group. It takes me a second to realize she is suggesting that I . . . what? Dance?

"No, no." I shake my head with the vehemence of some-one whose skills are limited to learning swing dancing in sixth grade. At school. With boys who really needed to discover deodorant.

She shrugs, still clapping, as the counselor who started the whole thing stands at the ready. The crowd cheers, "Jones! Jones! Jones!"

He strides purposefully down the center, then vogues—arms sharp and moving, framing his face. I've seen my mom do this move when my aunt Rachel visits. There's usually a part of the night, before I go up to bed, when they're amped up on ice cream and listening to Madonna, reminiscing. I always pretend to be mortified by their dorkiness. But really, I just wish I had a friendship like that, equal parts silly and devoted.

When Jones reaches the end the line, he snaps back into counselor mode.

"All right! Good work!" he says. "In you go."

He motions the campers inside like a marathon volunteer, with enthusiastic direction toward the correct way. As they head in, one little girl scrambles up Jones's back. He tucks her legs under his arms and turns toward the lodge.

"Anna!" the girl yells, spotting us. "There you are!"

"Nev. One of my fourth graders," Anna mutters to me, unable to suppress her smile. She waves at the girl.

The counselor spots us and heads our way. His grin changes his whole face, lights it up like the flash of a camera. Something about that smile—the lack of inhibition or the

way it makes his eyes squint—makes him look like a little kid.
It's the way you smile before you learn how to pose, how to
fake it and say cheese.

"You must be the relief pitcher." He reaches out one
hand, the other arm holding the girl in place. She studies me
with narrowed eyes, framed in a fan of lashes, as my hand
disappears in his. "I'm Jones. This is Neveah."

"Hansson," I say.

"And that's Tambe." He points to where his co-counselor
is hustling another group inside. I recognize him from the
photo in the lodge hallway—the wiry guy with bronze skin
and thick black hair that I can't explain other than to say it
swoops up. He's wearing a shirt that reads, in drippy, spray-
paint-like text: EVERYBODY'S WERKIN FOR THE
WEEKEND. "We've got the third-grade boys' cabin."

"And Yellow Team!" the girl on his back adds. "The best
team!"

"We're Yellow," Jones tells me, smiling. "Tambe's Blue, so
you'll be together for color activities."

Anna sticks her tongue out at Neveah, teasing. "Green
pride! C'mon, Hansson, I'll show you to your cabin table."

"Nice to meet you," I tell Jones. I give Neveah a special
little smile, but she's back to studying me, suspicious.

"Oh, there's your bunkmate. Simmons!" Anna calls.

She's crouched down, talking to a middle school–age
camper wearing purple hair clips. When they turn toward
us, it's striking how alike they look—wide brown eyes and
arched eyebrows.

"Lucy Hansson, this is Keely Simmons, your bunk-mate."

I'm taller than she is, but her presence somehow fills more space. Her stance is wide, feet in line with her hips. Next to her compact curves and dark skin, I feel lumbering, pear shaped, and chalk pale.

"Hey," she says. Her expression is inscrutable: neutral but not unfriendly. "Guess you heard we scared the last counselor off?"

I can't tell if I'm supposed to laugh at that, so I settle on a smile and a one-shoulder shrug. Super cool, Luce.

"Hm," she says. It sounds like a pronouncement about me. "The girls are inside already."

"I'll take you," Anna says. When we reach the table, Anna smiles brightly and introduces me to our third counselor, Garcia, who has a nose piercing and a bored, polite tone of voice that suggests I am totally beside the point. Something we agree on.

"All right, 3As!" Garcia says. "This is Hansson. She's your new counselor! Tell her your names."

They're studying me, top to bottom, taking me in, and I shift my weight, hoping I measure up and can remember all nine names. One of the girls hugs me; a few others look skeptical. Keely Simmons appears, examining her nails as a girl named Maya leans back against her.

"I'm Payton," one girl says. "Are you the new Ellis?"

"Ellis?" I ask.

"She was the counselor who quit," another girl says.

"She's not the new Ellis; she's Hansson," Simmons says. "And I know you'll all be welcoming to her. Right?"

They chorus their agreement, though they're all sizing me up. I picked out my outfit carefully—a white eyelet shirt with coral shorts—but it seems prissy now. A little too try-hard.

"We get to go second for dessert tonight," one girl says. I think her name is Nadia. "It's angel food cake, and we get whipped cream."

"That's awesome," I say, pushing away the image of my mom spraying whipped cream all over our ice cream, then directly into her mouth. Our impromptu girls' nights any-time my dad is called away for pastor duties. "I love whipped cream."

"Cabin 3A!" a loud voice yells from near the kitchen. "Line up!"

"That's us," Simmons says, appearing behind me. The girls are already prancing toward the counter, talking over one another and to Simmons.

"Well, thanks so much for showing me around," I tell Anna.

"My pleasure!" She says it like she totally means it. I like her even more than that cookie from earlier. Or it's a tie, anyway.

She's saying something about a talent show when, in my right ear, voices rise up. I see motion in my peripheral vision, but the rest happens fast. A warm body slams into my back, a sharp bone—elbow or shoulder—digging in.

"Oof!" I lose my balance, falling into Anna, who braces me.

Behind us, two boys are locked in a howling brawl, but my joints seize up, immobile. I'm wide-eyed, mouth open but soundless, stomach clenched so tightly I almost heave. They're no older than sixth grade, but they're a tornado of pale limbs, flying slaps, and fists.

"Hey!" Anna yells, moving in front of me. She backs up, arms out, forcing my legs to step away. "Cool it!"

Jones and Tambe are nearest—at the third-grade boys' table—and they step in. I wait to hear the snap of Jones's glasses, but it only takes him a moment to have one of the kids by the waist, lifting him back. His voice remains gentle even in commands. "Hey. Stop. Stop. Breathe."

Only then do I notice a yellow band around the kid's wrist. He's one of Jones's.

Tambe has the second boy loosely by both arms. Even though the kids have been detangled, they're still glaring at each other, breathing heavily and ready to pounce. All I can think is that they're so little—so wiry, their skin so close to their skeletons—to contain so much rage. Jones points at the kid that Tambe's holding. He has a bleeding scratch mark down his face. "Turn it off, dude. I mean it."

He directs his own detainee toward the door, hands gently laid on the kid's shoulders. I hear him say, with no trace of frustration, "C'mon, ya joker. Let's have a little heart-to-heart."

The tension hangs, suspended in the air, even after the two brawlers have been escorted out. When the campers begin to talk again, it's hushed.

"It's all right, guys," Simmons says. "Back to dinner."

My chest tightens in a telltale way, lungs unable to get enough air.

"Excuse me," I manage to say before hurrying toward the bathroom we passed on our tour. I just don't want the campers to see me struggling.

But Anna's right behind me, walking fast to catch up. "Oh no! Are you hurt?"

"No, no. Fine," I gasp out. Behind the restroom door, I press my inhaler to my lips.

Anna's mouth is slack as she watches my freak-out. "Jesus, I'm *so* sorry. Can I get you anything? Should I get Miss Suzette?"

I shake my head, taking the most even inhale that I can. "I'm really fine. Happens sometimes. It's a random thing."

More like a panic thing, but whatever. I'm in so far over my head. I don't know anyone, and I miss my parents and being the one who gives the tour. I don't have Lukas or any coping mechanism that feels within reach. The tears drip out before it occurs to me to stop them.

"I'm sorry! It's ridiculous that I'm crying! I'm fine!" I cover my face with my free hand. "I just don't know what I'm doing here! I've never been at a camp like this before, but my mom's sick, and she wanted me to come."

Once I get that out, I take another drag of my inhaler.

"Oh, Lucy." Anna's hand is warm on my arm. "It's okay. I've been coming to Daybreak since I was a kid, and my first year as a counselor—last year—was *still* hard. You learn quickly, as you go. I promise."

My throat warps from an attempted gasp into some kind of gross, sobbing hiccup. "I swear I'm not insane. Everything is just such a *mess*. I got dumped yesterday. Or . . . well, I got paused."

"You got what?"

"He paused us. Put our relationship on pause."

"Oh, God."

"I know."

Her hand drops from my arm, and I uncover my face to observe her expression. Probably horrified by this tragic puddle of emotions in front of her. Or judging me for having no perspective. I mean, there's a pregnant fourteen-year-old at this camp and I'm losing it over a breakup?

"Who *pauses* someone?" she asks, disgusted. "What an asshole!"

Casual swearwords don't exactly offend me; they just take me a moment to process—conversational speed bumps. But this one doesn't even make me feel defensive of Lukas. In fact, I let out a dark laugh.

"What an actual asshole," I repeat. How strange, the sound of my voice saying that word. It's like hearing yourself on a recording—*is that really me?* I wait for the pang of guilt that accompanies any bad language I use, but it doesn't come. I glance up at the water-stained ceiling, waiting for cracks to form, for God to rain down His holy wrath. There is only the buzz of fluorescent lights.

Anna seems to be on the edge of saying something, but

we're both distracted by the swinging bathroom door. It opens to Simmons's solid stance and cloud of dark curls.

She takes us in, then focuses on me—my heaving shoulders and wet eyelashes. "You can't cry in here."

Her tone doesn't have a trace of meanness. It's just a statement of fact.

Anna swivels to gasp at her. "Keely!"

"What? Brooklyn had to pee but heard crying, and it scared her. She came back to the table to tell me."

"She's having an asthma attack!"

I shake the inhaler in my hand and curve my mouth upward. It is not a smile.

"Well, go to Miss Suzette or the break room." Her face softens as she sighs. "I'm sorry; I'm really not trying to be harsh. But if we seem scared or off balance to the kids, then the world seems scary and off balance to them."

"I—Okay." Agreement feels easier. Always de-escalate, right? "Fine."

"And if you're going to quit, please just do it now." She says it gently, as if breaking bad news. "I'm sorry. I don't want the girls getting attached."

The door closes before I get a retort out of my fallen-open mouth. "Well, *this* is going great."

"Sorry about her," Anna says, turning back. "The girl she was talking to when I introduced you? That's her little sister. So to Keely, every camper is Kiana. She's protective."

"It's fine," I lie. "She's right. I should go to the nurse."

"You know, tonight's activity is just practice for our talent show. So I'm sure you could lie low in the bunk." Anna presses her forehead into her palm. "I'm so sorry. We're making a terrible first impression. It's not normally a shitshow like this, I swear."

"No—it's fine." But here's the thing about *It's fine*: The more it's said, the less it's true. "*I* made a terrible first impression. Geez."

"Not even close. Look, I'll tell Rhea you're going to Miss Suzette's. Can I do anything else for you?"

"No, I'm really fine." Sure I am. With my pinkened eyes, I'm the picture of stability and grace. "Actually . . . any chance you could forget all that stuff I babbled about?"

Anna smiles kindly. "Maybe not forget it. But I can promise I won't tell anyone. We Daybreakers may not make a great first impression, but we're excellent secret-keepers."

I hope she gets my gratitude through a simple nod.

Before I push out the door, I hear her voice. "Hey, Lucy?"

"Yeah?"

"I'm really sorry your mom's sick."

Those are the words she says, but I hear the ones that sit behind them: *You can talk to me about it if you want.* Even though we only met an hour ago. "Thank you."

The mess hall is full of discordant voices and forks scraping on plates, but I train my eyes downward as I walk out. My hair falls forward like tendrils of vines, hiding me until I emerge into the humid dusk.

I follow the curve of the lake, trying to find a vantage point where I can see the chapel light at Holyoke. I just want to know it's there—a harbor still waiting for me.

Instead, in the fading golden daylight, I spot Jones sitting on a log by the waterline. Near him, the boy from the fight runs a few paces and hurls a long stick into the lake. It smacks against the water, splashes cutting up. Next, he flings a rock, then what looks like a strip of tree bark—his skinny body pitching forward in a heave of rage.

When the last of his debris pile has dropped beneath the water's surface, he turns, stumbling back toward his counselor. Only then do I notice those little shoulders, shaking. Jones gets up to catch him beneath the arms, and the boy leans in, sobbing. I can't look away as Jones stands there, holding him but otherwise gazing out across the placid lake. Like this happens often, angry kids clutching at his shirt as they cry until they're emptied out.

And that's why I don't get to cry, I guess. Because they do. Because we're older but we're not the grown-ups who seem too far away to really understand. I tuck that thought inside me, warm and small like balled hands inside hoodie pockets. Beneath the beech trees and sugar maples, feet crunching against dead leaves, I hope for strength. Because as much as I want to be the one crying, I want to be the kind of person someone can hold on to.

CHAPTER SEVEN

6:45 a.m.

I startle awake, disoriented, and nearly smack my forehead against the bunk above me. Camp. Daybreak. A back that aches where it was elbowed. I remember now. After leaving the mess hall last night, I crashed into a dreamless, weighted-down sleep, barely even stirring when the cabin girls came in for lights-out. My co-counselors must think I'm an absolute moron.

If you're going to quit, please just do it now. Something about that comment makes me resolved to try again. I tiptoe out of bed and change in the communal bathroom, dim lightbulbs flickering overhead.

At the lake's edge, I pull my swim cap over my head and position my goggles. The sun is stretching its arms up slowly on the horizon line, and I stretch mine out as I dive. *Dear God,* my brain begins, *thank you for*—no. No thank-you. I reach my arm out, a sleek stroke against the water. *Make her better.* I kick my legs evenly, with extra force to propel me. *You owe me that. Don't you?*

I swim out and back, until I hear . . . a bugle? From somewhere. How retro. It blasts out the cheerful tune used in place of alarm clocks for the military. I wrap my towel around me and hurry back, hoping my absence hasn't been noticed. The girls are just getting out of bed, and I tug my swim cap off to untie my hair.

"You were swimming, Hansson?" asks the girl named Payton. "It's early!"

"Well, I'm on a swim team, so I have to practice."

"You wear a swim cap?" Nadia asks.

"Yep."

"I do too! To keep my hair nice."

"Hey," Simmons says, as she dismounts from the top bunk. Her eyes flick across my face, hunting for clues about my apparent insanity. "You're still here."

Well, I *was* going to apologize. But I truly don't appreciate the surprise in her voice. "I'm here."

She studies me for a second, then smiles. I hope this means she heard the determination in my voice. "Well, then. We have optional yoga on the Great Lawn, breakfast, then showers for those who want them. We also have rest time after lunch if you want to shower then."

"Okay." I straighten up. "And look, I—"

"It's fine. Maya! Out of bed. I mean it."

"Ugh," Maya says, face pressed into her pillow.

I really relate to Maya.

8:00–9:00 a.m. Breakfast

Simmons sits toward the end of the table, already surrounded by our cabin girls. I sit next to a girl with two shiny black braids, and a few others fill in around me.

"You eat a lot," a girl comments, staring at my pile of food. Her name is Clara, I think.

"Swimming makes me really hungry."

"Me too."

The girls sitting nearest me are just kind of watching me. And I have no idea what to talk to them about. At Holyoke, I'd ask about their churches: *What are you learning in Sunday school? Do you sing in choir? Are you doing Vacation Bible School this year?* Without that shared language, I don't know what to talk to third graders about. It's summer, so they don't want to talk about what they're learning in school, right?

One girl stares at me as she shovels oatmeal into her mouth. "You're pretty."

"Thank you. So are you."

"Yeah." She keeps studying me. "You have a lot of freck-les. Like, a *lot*. Have you ever tried to count them?"

"No, but how many do you think?"

She squints. "Probably a bamillion."

I only barely stifle my laugh. "How many is that?"

"It's like a bajillion but less."

"So. What's your favorite activity that you've done so far at camp?"

"We got to do beads," Clara says. "Everyone else made bracelets and stuff, but I made a key chain for my mom."

That's what I would have done with beads at her age. And now. "What colors did you use?"

I keep asking questions and listening, and I'm relieved when they start taking their plates to the dish drop-off. I made it through.

"G'morning, Hansson," a voice says. Jones settles onto the bench across from mine, next to Nadia, who beams at him. I might have reacted the same, except the two boys standing behind him distract me. I recognize them from the fight last night—one with a scabbed-over line across his cheek now. They're staring at the ground.

"Hi," I say, setting down my juice cup.

"How'd you sleep?"

He plucks a grape from Nadia's plate. She giggles and says, "Hey!"

"Um, pretty well, thanks."

Jones gestures at my plate. "That berry topping is so great on waffles, right? I miss it the entire school year."

"Yeah, it's good." I can't really focus on what he's saying because of the two solemn boys behind him, waiting.

"Well, anyway, Nolan and JJ have something they want to say to you."

The redhead I saw crying into Jones's shirt looks down at me, miserable. JJ, I think. "We feel real bad that we ran into you yesterday."

"It was an accident. I swear," Nolan says.

"I know it was. And I'm okay." I smile in a way that I hope looks reassuring.

"And?" Jones says, his tone hard. He pops another grape into his mouth, expression perfectly relaxed. But the boys can't see his face.

"We're sorry," Nolan says.

"We are," JJ says. "For real."

The boys glance inward, not quite making eye contact with each other. When Nolan speaks up, it's quiet and hurried. "Willyouforgiveus."

"What was that?" Jones asks.

"Will you forgive us?"

"Yes," I say quickly, putting them out of their misery. "You're forgiven. Thank you for apologizing."

Both boys stay put, clearly waiting for a cue from Jones. He gives them a dismissive wave, and they trudge off together. I can tell they wanted more affirmation—longed for Jones's respect. It's clear they'll have to earn it back.

"They got in trouble," Nadia says to Jones. "You were mad at them."

"Not mad. Disappointed." He gets up, leaning across the table toward me. "Thanks for being a good sport, Hansson."

On his way back to his table, he leans down to whisper something to Keely. He reaches one arm around her other shoulder, sneakily lifting a piece of bacon from her plate. She shoves at him, grinning, while the girls around her laugh. Jones grins back, crunching on the bacon. *Oh.* Missing Lukas aches like a splinter, small but piercing.

9:00–9:30 a.m. Pitch-In

Our cabin has cleanup duty. The kitchen isn't huge, but it's well organized, every surface portioned for use.

The chef is tall and broad, with ginger stubble like glitter on his jawline. He looks almost as old as my parents, but it's harder to tell with a bandanna covering his hair. "Okay, I need a leftover scooper and a saran wrapper."

All nine girls look at Simmons, who says, "Maya and Payton, you're up."

I'm tagged to supervise dish patrol—four girls on stepstools in a little line across the industrial sink. Brooklyn and Clara scrape food into a trash can, Emily washes dishes with the sprayer, and Sofia loads them into the massive dishwasher.

Sofia announces, "I like loading dishes because it's like a puzzle."

"You're good at it," I tell her.

Clara frowns at the piles of dirty plates. "I don't want to touch this stuff. It's gross. Can I spray instead?"

Simmons glances at me, a "no" already in her mouth.

But I have to prove that an eight-year-old can't steamroll me. "Nope. You'll be on a different chore next time."

"But I don't like scraping food."

"Well, I don't really like cleaning my bathroom at home, but I do it anyway."

"You do? Why?"

"Well, because it's my bathroom. It's my job to clean it up. I don't want to be a taker."

"A taker?"

"A person who takes and takes and doesn't give."

"I dunno." She winces as she picks up a plate. "Taking sounds pretty good to me."

When they have a steady little assembly line, I whisper to Simmons, "What do we normally do during this time? If we don't have cleanup duty?"

"Other chores around camp. A lot of what we do here is trying to teach life skills." Her eagle eye catches on something across the kitchen. "Nice mopping, Nadia and Nina! Love that teamwork."

9:30–10:00 a.m. Cabin time

My body is begging me to crawl back into bed; my eyelids sag as I clean up my bunk. But the girls are fully energized, nearly bouncing as they brush their teeth. There are three shower stalls, but all of them are taken. I settle for washing my face and redoing my ponytail, pausing to praise Thuy for how neatly she's made her bed.

"Where'd Simmons go?" I ask Garcia.

"She ducks out to teach astronomy class to the older campers."

"Oh. Cool." I drop my voice to add, "Um, is there tea in the kitchen? Like, caffeinated?"

Garcia laughs a little, like she truly understands. "Yeah. But I'd go straight for the coffee."

10:00–11:00 a.m. Learning

Our class is in the rec room, and nine girls pile onto the brown leather couches. We're about to get started—or so I think—when the third-grade boys clamber in. Of course it would be a combined class by age group. Jones gives me a wave and a friendly smile, which I manage to return before glancing down at my feet. I seem to have caught shyness from Nadia this morning. As the boys settle in, I sit down on the piano bench, which is nearby for extra seating.

"Owen," Tambe says to a kid who's still talking. "Snap it shut or else."

"Or else what?" he replies.

Tambe lowers his brows and tilts his head down just a little.

Owen snaps it shut.

Satisfied, Tambe plops down beside me and twists so he can whisper in my ear. "They driving you nuts yet?"

"Nah. They're sweet."

His smile is smug as he crosses his arms. "Good. Remember that during the first hissy fit. It will sustain you."

After everyone is settled, a college counselor named Flores guides the third graders through a hands-on activity. They do a multiplication worksheet using stacks of Legos. 3 x 1 = a stack of 1 green, 1 blue, and 1 yellow Lego. 3 x 2 = a stack of 2 greens, 2 blues, and 2 yellows.

"It's two, three times," Brooklyn whispers to herself as she presses the plastic blocks together.

Next, Flores talks to them about telling time, why it's important, and what about it seems hard. For the rest of the session, they practice with a big replica clock; each kid gets to spin the hour and minute hands.

When the clock truly does hit 10:55, we round up the girls for their next activity. I'm about to walk out the door, when a warm hand touches my arm and I'm looking up at Jones. I can see my own surprised expression reflected in his glasses.

"Hey," he says. "Just wanted to let you know that D'Souza called a quick junior counselor meeting before lunch."

"D'Souza," I repeat stupidly.

"The head counselor. She's a senior in college." He must notice my confusion because he adds, "It'll just be checking in and schedule stuff. Five minutes, tops. In the Bunker. The door that says 'Maintenance'—Anna told you that, right?"

"Right. Though she didn't mention why it's labeled 'Maintenance.'"

"Helps keep nosy campers out." His smile is rueful. Even when he's not breaking into that huge grin, something about his eyes—or cheeks? What *is* it?—makes him seem deeply, genuinely happy. "And honestly, the junk food and relative quiet in the Bunker help us *maintain* our sanity."

My laugh comes out as a snort. You just don't expect a dorky dad joke from someone so handsome. Not that I care that he's handsome. I don't.

But I do wish I hadn't snorted in front of him.

11:00 a.m.–noon

Our short outdoor activity is a nature walk. As we trek through the woods, Simmons points out types of trees and plants and asks questions: Who knows what poison ivy looks like? Which animals hibernate and why? The girls gather fallen leaves and tiny buds of wildflowers like they're treasure. I haven't done this since I was little—roamed around nature, letting my imagination fill in every gap. I used to notice unusual trees that might hold magic; I used to half-believe animals would talk to you if you were gentle and quiet enough.

Toward the end of our walk, we sit in a clearing and we talk about our favorite thing about being outdoors. The girls say "deer" and "creeks," "flowers" and "the moon." My shirt sticks to my lower back as the sun beats down on my bare legs.

"I like squirrels," Sofia says. "A group of squirrels is called a scurry."

We all agree that this is awesome.

When it's my turn, I answer, simply, "Clouds."

"Any reason?" Simmons asks.

Because they're always shifting, sometimes as pink as cotton candy, sometimes pearlescent with gold edges, sometimes like smoke across the moon. Because when you're little, it seems like clouds are solid, like you could sit on one. But then you grow up and cut through them in an airplane, and when you're high enough, they blanket the world with soft cotton.

Because when I learned the song "He's Got the Whole World in His Hands," I imagined God's hands made of clouds. For longer than I should have, I felt like clouds wrapped around the world, evidence that we are cradled—cherished, protected.

But the sky is unbrokenly blue today.

"It's fun to look for shapes in them," I say.

"Yeah!" one of the girls says. "I wish there were some to look at now!"

Me too.

"You didn't go yet, Simmons," Nadia says.

"My favorite thing about being outside is looking up at planets and stars," she says, and the girls murmur agreement. "Did you know that some of the parts of our bodies—the teeny, tiny parts that you need a fancy microscope to see—came from stars?"

"Nuh-uh," Payton says. "For real?"

"For real," Simmons says. "Elements called hydrogen and carbon were, millions of years ago, formed by stars called supernovas. So you, little girls, are made of stardust."

They all look around the circle, marveling at one another in a new light.

Noon

I report to the counselors' room with a cup of tea in my hand. The space looks even smaller with a few people already in there, the walls even more covered in notepaper. I study a few flyers for jazz shows in town and a picture of counselors I don't recognize sitting on each other's shoulders, playing chicken in the pool (strictly forbidden, per the binder). Nearest me, a scrap of neon yellow paper says: *TAMBE OWES SIMMONS 1 BASKET OF ONION RINGS AT TOM'S. NOT JUNIOR SIZE EITHER. THE WHOLE BASKET.*

"Hansson! Hey!" Anna's in the corner of the couch, sipping a soda.

"Hey." Before I can sit beside her, Tambe breezes in. He plops onto Anna's lap, squashing her.

"What a day!" he proclaims, then turns his head toward Anna. "Am I hurting you?"

"Nope. Like holding a puppy."

He gasps. "How dare you. I've been working out."

"A pit bull puppy," Anna amends.

"*Thank* you."

Simmons strolls into the room, eyes fixed on the shelves.

She digs around, then glares at Tambe. "Did you eat the last of the good pretzels?"

"I resent that you accuse *me* right away," he snaps. "But yes."

She jerks a chair back from the table and slumps down, breaking open a container of what I can only assume are the bad pretzels. "Where do you even store all the food that you eat?"

Beside me, Tambe splays out on Anna dramatically. "Why is everyone *persecuting* me today?"

A girl breezes in, wearing a floral top and striped canvas shoes. She's Asian and pretty—glossy hair to her shoulders, and a peachy blush on her cheeks. When she sits on the couch beside me, I press myself into the armrest, hoping I'm not sitting in someone's usual spot.

"Hi! You must be Hansson." When I nod dumbly, she says, "Min. Rose Min. I'm fourth-grade girls' cabin and Purple Team. Sorry I didn't get a chance to say hi yesterday. How's your first day so far?"

"Good! The food's great, and the girls seem really sweet." It's pathetic how happy I am that someone's acknowledging me. Tambe's not the puppy—I am. Yay, yay! Attention. Next I'll flop on my back and offer up my belly for rubs.

"Enjoy this moment with Rose." Tambe leans around so he can make eye contact with me. "She's in lurve with Davis, so she spends all her time with the college counselors. Too good for us now."

"Aw, Tambay-bee," she coos, glancing back at him. "I was too good for you before too."

Tambe gives me a look as if his point is made. "See? So sassy. This is why we miss her. Relish the little moments she graces us with."

"Oh, stop. I see you all the time."

"So sue for me for missing you, Min-y Muffin."

Lord help me if I don't want my own stupid nickname. Instead, I sit there on mute, wishing I could find an entrance to this conversation.

Jones jogs in last, easing himself onto the floor in front of Anna and Tambe. He's wearing another short-sleeved oxford today, this one rust red with tiny white diamonds on it. The print looks like it belongs on a vintage tie.

D'Souza turns out to be a very short girl with the kind of squared-shoulder posture that makes it clear she's in charge. After giving a few updates—seriously, Leo Leery can't have gluten no matter what he tells you, and whoever is finishing the coffee without making more, honestly, stop it—D'Souza puts her hands on her hips.

"Okay! I think that's it. Oh! Did you all meet Hansson?"

When everyone swivels to look at me, I eke out, "Uhh . . . hey."

"Let one of us know if you need anything. And they told you that you get Friday nights off, yes?" Before I can reply, she continues, "Junior counselors get Friday nights off; college counselors get Saturdays. No curfew, but you still have to be up at seven a.m., so make good choices. We have a zero-tolerance policy for anyone who is hungover or late."

"Oh, I wouldn't—"

"Zero. Tolerance," she repeats before I can explain that I would *never*. "Last weekend was good. Everyone was smart about it. Let's keep it that way. Okay. Any other quick questions or concerns?"

"Where'd we land on the Fourth of July?" Min asks.

"Oh, right." D'Souza crosses her arms like a drill sergeant with troops under review. "Rhea says you guys get the day off. College counselors will get the next evening off."

"GLORY!" Tambe cries, as Anna and Simmons whoop.

"Well, thank Jones for that one," D'Souza says curtly. "Since he's playing the festival, he's already off."

Jones raises his arms, bent at the elbow and palms up. It's a Saint Francis of Assisi pose, missing only a baroque halo and a flock of delicate birds. Half humility, half acknowledgment.

Playing the festival? The meeting is adjourned before I can ask what that means.

July Fourth feels like five years away.

Noon–1:30 p.m.

Lunch, then another half-hour set of chores: cleaning windows in the gym, although "gym" is a flattering word for this space. It's a small room off the lodge, used only on desperate rainy days, according to Simmons. The floor is made of indoor track material, rubbery and pilled, and the back wall has crates full of jump ropes, dodge balls, and even badminton rackets. They look like they were donated to Daybreak after a school finally replaced their gym class supplies. There's even a punching bag in the back corner, which I make a note of. I don't generally think of myself as a person who wants to hit things for catharsis, but . . . well. Things change.

The whining is *epic*. These girls make window cleaning into one of the labors of Hercules. Even though we counselors are right beside them, scrubbing the higher windows.

"It smells in here," Brooklyn moans.

"So bad," Maya agrees. "Like boys. Like boys' *armpits*."

"The mural's cool," I say, trying to be positive.

"I guess," Nadia says. "I like the rainbow."

Me too. There are elements of childhood fables—birds holding a banner, a tree made of stars.

"I helped paint that, you know," Simmons says. "My first summer here."

"Were you in third grade?" Maya asks hopefully.

"Fifth."

"Really? What part did you paint?"

Simmons points to the flowers growing around the tree.

"Well, it still smells like actual butts in here." This is from Brooklyn.

"One more complaint," Garcia says, "and I'll take away swim hour."

For a few minutes we scrub in silence, except for the squirts of spray bottles and the squeak of clean glass.

"Have you ever seen *Annie*?" Sofia asks, and Simmons shoots her a look. "Just saying."

1:30–2:30 p.m.

Arts class, which can apparently be everything from painting to crafts to dance.

Today, a college counselor teaches the girls about percussion instruments. There are little bongos and maracas, ribbed wooden sticks that they rub together. It's cacophony.

They're *delighted*.

"Jesus. Christ," Simmons mutters, rubbing her temple.

Garcia snorts. "Amen."

And even I know what they mean.

2:30–4:00 p.m.

By the time we get to the daily swim session with the fourth- and fifth-grade girls, I'm amazed these kids are still on their feet. But finally: something I know I'm good at.

"Anna!" I call, waving. She's in the water near Min, who also waves at me.

"You cool with shore duty?" Simmons asks. "I promised my sister we could play Marco Polo."

"Oh. Yeah. Fine." I already got my swim in this morning, I guess. And besides, after my emotional breakdown last night, I have zero room for negotiation.

Most of the Cabin 3A girls splash around, though a few are digging a massive hole in the sandbank. Garcia's off with the college counselors, who seem to flock together.

I sit down on a nearby towel, feeling like an afterthought. Maybe this is a preview of college, where everyone will know what they're supposed to be doing and I'll just . . . be there. The idea of living in a dorm, where I know absolutely no one, makes me feel preemptively homesick for my mom.

"Hey," a little voice says. I shield my eyes from the sun, looking up at Nadia.

"Hey." She sits beside me on the towel without asking, which is a surprisingly little kid move. Already, Nadia strikes me as a bit older, emotionally, than the other cabin girls. Her mind always seems to be chewing on something. "You okay?"

"Yeah," she says. "I just miss my mom."

I weigh the options automatically: reassure her or commiserate. "Hey, you know what? I was just sitting here thinking about missing my mom too."

"Really?"

"Really."

"Did she die? Your mom?"

"No," I say, surprised. "But she's pretty sick right now. Did your mom die?"

I should use the same language she did, right? She said it bluntly, so that's how she thinks of it.

"Yes. When I was seven." Like it was a lifetime ago, instead of a year.

Nadia's so tiny—just a baby. And yet, she's three years older than my mom was when she lost her parents to a car accident. At fourteen, after living with extended family for years, she was placed in foster care, with a couple who ultimately adopted her. I have never fully comprehended how young my mom was until this very moment.

"I'm so sorry that happened. Did you swim together? Is that what made you think of her?"

"Yeah. In the pool. She got in with me and played."

"I used to swim with my mom too." Here in this lake, feet kicking hard as she coached me in an encouraging voice. And now, swallowing a lump in my throat, I have to ask myself how I'd want people to treat me if she was gone. "Tell you what: Anytime you miss your mom, you come sit by me and we can miss our moms together, okay? And if you want to tell me any good memories about her, I'd like to hear them. Sound good?"

"Sounds good," she agrees.

"Hansson!" a voice yells from nearby. "Clara took my shovel! She needs a consequence!"

And here we go again.

4:30–5:30 p.m.
Finally, we get a full hour of cabin rest time.

"You know the drill, ladies! Nap or quiet reading."

I take the most grateful shower of my life. I don't even care that I have to wear flip-flops or get dressed in the stall after, not feeling quite dry enough.

For the half hour that remains post-shower, I ball up on my bed. Payton plops down next to me, touching the tips of her dark hair.

"Your hair is curly on its own?"

I push back the damp strands of my hair, which has fully spiraled. "Yep."

"Mine too. And Simmons's." She smiles contentedly. "We all have it! My mom's hair is smooth, but my dad's is curly. I think curly is good."

I prefer mine straightened, but I doubt I'll have time for it this summer. "I like it too."

As we walk to dinner, she's glued to my side, pushing her hair behind her ears when I do.

6:30–8:00 p.m.

After dinner, the evening activity is talent show prep again. In the rec room, Simmons has hauled a sewing machine from who knows where, and she's puttering over a length of black fabric. Kids practice dance moves in every corner, and the two ninth graders elected MCs write notes in the corner as if hosting the Oscars. On the floor, a group works on a long, painted-paper banner that reads: Daybreak Talent Show.

I help the decoration committee by cutting out yellow

construction paper stars. I'm half a decent constellation in when a shadow is cast over me.

"Lucy! Hi." Rhea is looking down. "I'm sorry I've been so busy since your arrival. You doing okay?"

"Fine, yeah."

"Great. Listen, I was wondering if you could stop by the meeting hall. We put together a choir for all the kids who didn't want to sing solos for the show, and . . . they could use some backup. Of the piano variety."

"Oh. Like accompaniment?"

"If you don't mind."

I don't, but I worry that she's imagining me as the middle-school virtuoso that I was. "Well, I'm a little rusty, but—"

"Believe me, your help will be most welcome."

"Okay. Should I head over there now or—"

"Yes. Please, if you would. Most appreciated."

I abandon my stars and head outside, where the real stars have yet to appear. The sky is a deep, watercolor blue swiped with thin clouds, and for a moment, I feel peace like a blanket laid across my shoulders.

It's short-lived, because I run smack into a very tall, very solid form. Rhea's son, who is easy to recognize—the only middle-aged guy around camp, lanky with a neatly trimmed beard.

"Sorry!" I exclaim. "I wasn't looking."

He takes a moment to reply, stunned by the surprise of our collision.

"No, no. My fault." His expression goes almost foggy, as if accessing the deepest part of his memory. Trying to place me. ". . . Lucy."

"Yeah!" The fact that he'd remember that is testament to Daybreak's level of actually caring.

"I'm Bryan Mills. Sorry I haven't had a chance to properly introduce myself. It's very nice to officially meet you."

"You too. I think my cabin girls have class with you next week. Group games?"

"Oh, yeah." He scrubs a hand through his short hair. "That's the phrase we use for trust exercises, word associations, drawing as expression . . . basically, psychologist tools for kids."

"I could use some of that," I admit, surprising myself. "So I'm looking forward to it."

"Of course. Yes. Good." His body language has this quality of bewilderment. It's something I associate with my pediatrician—very smart and a little awkward. "See you then, then."

I find the meeting hall, which is a small building off the lodge that, inside, looks like it was once a chapel. Tall, thin windows run down the sides, clear instead of stained glass. Plastic chairs instead of pews. But still, there's a piano at the front and a section that looks meant for a choir.

There, Jones has organized the campers into four sections. He's behind the piano, thumping on the middle C to give the altos their starting note. "That's where you are, okay? Try it on an *ah*."

I hoped I could be stealthy—ease my way in—but every head turns to look at me, and Jones follows their line of sight.

"Hey, Hansson. Come for a sneak preview?"

"Actually . . . Rhea mentioned you might like a piano player?"

He inclines his head toward me. "You play piano?"

"Yep."

"Hallelujah!" he says, raising his arms dramatically. "Come on down. Put me outta my misery. I barely know a basic scale."

His pleased smile flusters me as I take my place at the piano bench. Only there do I feel it—the ache in my knuckles, the longing for them to be set free.

"From the top!" Jones calls to his choir. "That means the beginning. Hansson, could you give me the first chord?"

The page in front of me is an online print of beginners' sheet music—"With a Little Help from My Friends." Whew. Easy—and a song I recognize.

I plink out notes for each section, then chords as they try to harmonize.

Jones conducts with his whole body, twisting at his waist, feeling it. His voice calls out encouragement even as they sing. "Yeah, tenors!"

An eighth-grade boy raises his hand. "Is this about drugs? Getting *high*?"

Jones opens his mouth, but not before Nadia scoffs at him. "No! It's like swings. Like having a friend push you helps you go higher."

The kid looks back at Jones for confirmation. "You heard her! It's a metaphor. Let's turn to the next page."

He twists so only I can see his face, making an "eep" expression as he pretends to wipe his brow in relief. I'm glad for my long hair, which falls forward to hide my laugh.

By eight o' clock, the song is . . . well, not great. But it's much better than when we started. They've been taking it section by section, and Jones says, "Who wants to try it all the way through before we break for the night?"

There's a cheer from the younger kids, but the older ones look disheartened. They want it to sound good. The little ones just want to belt it out.

"Hansson, beginning notes, if you would." I give them all four parts, but I add chords—no more a cappella. It's rudimentary accompaniment, but Jones's gaze jerks over to me, stunned.

"What? Yes!" he cries, delighted. "Keep goin', guys!"

With background notes beneath them, they stay more in tune. The added noise seems to make them feel less exposed, giving them confidence to put more breath behind their voices. Sure, it's still a little off-key with flubbed lyrics, but at least it's loud and proud.

"Wow," Jones says, after the last note rings out. "This is gonna be good, guys. Okay, folders away and meet up with your cabin counselors in the lodge."

"You," he says, leaning against the piano, "are a godsend."

"I'm just glad to contribute." A day of experience has proved that I can't reliably sustain his eye contact without blushing, so I glance down. "Do you want to do more of a Beatles sound or a Joe Cocker vibe?"

I demonstrate both quickly—Beatles with peppy quarter notes, and Joe Cocker with power chords, simpler but emotional.

His eyes widen, as if he can't believe his good luck. "What if the first chorus was Beatles, then we switched to Joe. That'd be fun, right? We can try it tomorrow."

"Jones!" a little voice calls from near the door. "You said you'd walk with us!"

"Duty calls." He walks backward a few steps. "Thanks again."

As I walk out with Nadia a few minutes later, I notice a line of symbols, hung in a neat line across the back wall. There's a cross—dark metal, but the same size and shape as the driftwood cross in my Holyoke bedroom. A Star of David, a crescent moon with a dangling star that I think is for Islam, and a star inside a circle. Then a spoked wheel like you'd see on a ship, and what looks like a number 3 with an added curve. That one I've seen before, but I can't place where. Each rests on a single nail. Pendants of faith.

I touch the bottom of the cross. *I hope you're seeing this,* I think at God. *I hope you see how hard I'm trying here. I hope you see that I'm trying to haul myself back up.*

I know it doesn't work this way, trading goodness for godly favors—for healing. I know that God's grace is just that: grace, undeserved. Unearned. Still, my mind sends whispers heavenward: *Please fix her. Make her better. Please. Please.*

Please.

CHAPTER EIGHT

THREE DAYS PASS IN A TORNADO OF MORNING LAPS, NAME LEARNING, cabin cleaning, watercolor painting, planet facts. Everything is a camper question: *What is this? Why are we doing this? What do you think about forest fairies? Can you do a handstand in the lake?* I go to bed when the girls do every night, eyes half-closed before my head finds the pillow. Somehow, I manage to get up early and swim, but I'm tired down to the core of myself—to the marrow, to my *skeleton*.

By the time we make it to Friday, I surprise myself by dreading my night off. The fullness of each day—the chatter, the activity, the flurry of on-to-the-next-thing—quiets my mind. When despair about my mom or confusion about Lukas drifts in, an earnest third grader pops up with her next question. Their little voices chase away the fog.

I wonder if my mom knew that this would happen—that constant, heavy-lidded busyness would give me peace.

The homemade banner announces the talent show in an

arch above the meeting hall's doorway. Yellow cut-out stars adorn the walls, already shedding gold glitter. I pity the cabin that has meeting hall cleanup for Pitch-In tomorrow.

"Hansson!" Anna calls out, waving to me. She's saved me a seat, and I can't even hide my relief.

"Welcome, Daybreak campers!" yells a boy who looks thirteen or fourteen. He's wearing a white T-shirt with a tie drawn on it in Sharpie. "I'm Jeremiah, and this is Lydia, and we're your hosts for the evening!"

As the night goes on, we watch fumbled magic tricks, belted-out solos, and self-choreographed dances. A spoken-word poem that gives me chills; a sincere, out-of-tune guitar performance that puts a lump in my throat; a sketch that is goofy and surprisingly well acted. Anna grips my hand as one of her Green Team campers showcases fancy soccer footwork, and whispers "yes" under her breath when it goes well. And between, the MCs introduce each act with index cards and charisma.

"Next up," Lydia says, "we have a special treat for you. Our biggest ensemble of the night! Give it up for Daybreak's choir: the Silver Linings!"

One of the older kids came up with the name yesterday, after "the Daybreakers" was deemed violent and "the Sunbeams" was vetoed for corniness. And so we—we nonviolent, noncorny choristers—amass before the entire camp.

Jones nods at me, signaling the start. I play cheerful, Beatles-style chords, and the kids stay on beat admirably. Their eyes are alert in concentration as they sing out each note. It's not perfect, but it's totally perfect. I just wish the audience could see Jones's face, his open-mouthed grin as he cues each section.

Before the last chorus, I cut out completely, like we practiced. Unaccompanied, the choir still sounds robust, full of life. In the front row, Rhea swipes a knuckle across her lower lid, blinking with glassy eyes as the kids insist, again and again: *With a little help from my friends.* And when everyone claps, our ragtag choristers look delighted with themselves, bowing. Jones holds a hand out to acknowledge the pianist, but I wave it off, embarrassed even as people cheer.

Thank you, Jones mouths to me. It's the first time this week that I've felt fully a part of something, this thing we made—even if it's just one song and a few rows of proud-to-the-brim kids.

When I sit back down, Anna clutches my arm. "Hansson, that was so good. I didn't know you could play the piano like that!"

Next up, five ninth-grade girls appear in matching clothes—white tanks and black shorts. Jones is still standing at the front, now holding a trumpet. *Playing the festival,* D'Souza had said about the Fourth of July day off. Apparently he'll be playing trumpet. He settles into a stance, loose hipped, the mouthpiece at his lips. He blasts the first notes, and the girls provide percussion, stomping and clapping in perfect unison. They speak the lyrics, which I vaguely recognize—a girl group song from a few years back.

The synchronicity is exact and graceful, somewhere

between a military company and a ballet company. Long hair flies as they stamp out choreography. Intensity, arms out in sharp lines.

The younger campers sit slack-jawed and mesmerized. Some sway their arms and rock their shoulders, getting into it. As the girls' last powerful step vibrates across the floor, the whole camp rises up in cheers and shouts of the girls' names.

Someone screams, "*Yeah, Jones!*" and he lifts one hand before turning it to display the girls like they're the Showcase Showdown prize on *The Price Is Right*.

"I didn't know he could play the trumpet," I whisper to Anna, echoing her words.

"Oh yeah. It's, like . . . what he *does*. Plays, teaches lessons."

Earlier this week, I questioned why Rhea would have a talent show the second week of camp. Why not wait till the end? It would give them more time to prepare, for the camp culture to gel. But I get it—I entirely get it. She's giving everyone the opportunity to say, *This is part of who I am. This is what I'm good at. This is what I want you to see in me.*

The show runs later than 8:00 p.m., and we herd the campers back for bedtime. Our girls are still singing and dancing as they change into pajamas, seemingly nowhere near sleep.

"Sorry they're all riled up for you," Simmons whispers to Garcia.

Garcia shrugs. "They're really into *Matilda*, so it's fine. Are you sure you want your night off? I don't know if I can live up to your narration."

"Ha," Simmons says, but she looks pleased. "You'll be great."

Every night, Simmons has been reading them a chapter of *Matilda* before bed. She reads with conviction—her voice sweet for Miss Honey and gruff for Miss Trunchbull. I listen with my eyes closed, smiling at how much Simmons sounds like a mom. Not *my* mom, just . . . *a* mom, that kind of loving effort, the comfort of a familiar voice as you drift off.

I use the bathroom and tame my flyaways in the mirror. I'm not sure what'll be going on in the Bunker tonight, but I figure a swipe of mascara can't hurt. I shimmy into my bathing suit, just in case they go swimming at night. It's good to be prepared.

When I duck out of the bathroom, the girls don't even look away from Garcia, who is making Matilda's parents sound thoroughly horrible. Simmons has a backpack on her shoulder, ready to head out the door.

"You going into town?" she asks.

"Oh," I say. I mean, if that's what people are doing, I'm totally in. "Yeah! I guess so."

"Cool. Have a good night." With that, she's gone. The screen door snaps behind her.

Wait. Does that mean she's *not* going into town? Is that not what people are doing? I'm frozen in place as I consider what just happened.

I step outside, hoping to find more information, and I do. I can barely make out, in the distance, four people disappearing down the path toward the woods—Anna's blond hair bright against the trees, a red tartan blanket thrown over Tambe's shoulder, the stark difference in height between Jones and Simmons.

Part of me expects Anna to turn around, to realize she'd forgotten me. But why would she? I told Simmons I was going into town. Besides, they've probably had this four-person routine for years. And so I'm alone, black-lashed, feeling a type of excluded that I thought I had left behind on the middle school playground.

I could go to bed—I do need the sleep—but it just seems too pathetic. So I head to the piano in the rec room. After a quick warm-up, I dance my fingers across my last-ever recital piece. It comes right back, like it was stored in my fingers this whole time. I play the full thing, with emotion, with passion, and when I hit the last chord, it resounds, echoing off the wooden floors and into the vast room.

I used to practice alone all the time, no audience but the portrait of Jesus above our piano.

But here, in this empty room, the keys' lingering hum sounds mournful. And I'm not sure why I feel lonely instead of just alone.

CHAPTER NINE

SUNDAY MORNING, I WALK A BIT OVER A MILE AROUND THE LAKE, finally straight toward Holyoke. The sun lifts over the horizon, and it feels metaphorical.

My family's little cabin is set away from the rest of camp, farther up the hill and nestled into trees. It looks like a kid's drawing of a house—a square with a triangle roof. Inside isn't much more than that, actually: a sink, oven, and refrigerator all crammed in a row; a pantry; and a three-person table against the wall. Then a cozy living room, one bathroom, and two bedrooms. If you call mine a bedroom. It might have originally been a closet. But it's mine.

I burst in the front door, expecting the teakettle to be squealing on the stovetop to my left and my mom reading devotions at the tiny table to my right. But it's quiet. They must already be setting up for the service.

"There she is!" my dad says when he spots me just inside the chapel doors. It feels too dramatic to run toward his wide-open arms, so I just hurry. My mom turns the corner behind him, happy but hesitant. As I wrap my arms around her, it takes all I have not to weep pitifully in relief, in the comfort of seeing her looking the same.

"Hi, sweetheart," she whispers into my hair.

"How are you feeling?" As I hear my words, they strike me as oddly formal—a doctor's query instead of a daughter's. "Was the first treatment okay?"

"It was fine." Her hand runs over my curls. "I'm just fine."

My dad gives us a few moments of hanging on before he clears his throat. "Luce, I wanted to ask you. Would you play something to start the service?"

"Sure. Which hymn?"

"Oh, anything you feel like. Just something to wake people up."

My mind leafs through the pages of the red Methodist hymnal I know so well. "Come, Thou Fount."

He nods.

I breathe the chapel in like it's a candle scent. Wood polish and dust, altar candles, and crisp leaves outside. My camp. The campers from Bethel Methodist in Ohio start to file in, and I wave at a few familiar faces from years past. They're sleepy-eyed in rumpled T-shirts and swishy athletic shorts. It's always felt so scandalous, to attend camp chapel in casual clothes.

My mom squeezes my arm before I take my spot at the piano. It's old, a little more *pang* to the keys than I'd prefer, but I love that it gives each song a specific, Holyoke tenor.

"Good morning, Bethel campers and counselors!" my dad says from the platform. "Please turn to number 265 in the red hymnal in front of you."

I play an intro and the first chords, nodding to cue the congregation. The chords are straightforward, but they sound too plodding to me. Too stale for such beautiful words. *Tune my heart to sing thy grace; streams of mercy, never ceasing.* The bass clef chords should be triads, but I break them on the second verse, pulling my fingers long across the keys. I coax my right hand into sixteenth notes like trotting footfalls—into a staccato, and then, next verse, fluid as violin bow strings. Every pounding chord is a plea, since I can't seem to find the words or will to pray the way I should.

When I finally slam my hands into full chords, I press it all into the piano. The notes widen through the chapel. There's a drama to it, a weight that resounds. I'm moving my shoulders, my head swaying, forcing out my sadness and frustration through my fingers. *Prone to wander, Lord, I feel it.* This is a fugue state; I'm not even fully here.

And when I sit back, music still ringing off the strings, my cheeks burn. I only play like that when I'm alone. Not when there are rows full of random Ohioans.

Someone in the pews sneezes. No one says, "Bless you."

"Thank you, Lucy," my dad says, looking back at me from the pulpit, "for that passionate rendition of an old favorite. That was . . . something."

He's smiling, but his eyes are unblinking, searching

for why I almost went full-on Holy Ghost this early in the morning. I don't know, Dad. I'm losing it. But, God help me—God literally help me—that's the closest I've felt to faith in weeks.

I sit beside my mom in a back pew, too embarrassed to look at her. I don't want to know what she'll see.

"That was beautiful, Luce," she whispers. She takes a sip from the big water bottle she has by her side. This is a new addition, and I file it away in my mind. I already hate being out of the loop on her treatment and side effects.

My dad preaches about the prophet Jonah, about miracles in the Bible, about where we see God today. Some of the younger kids fidget and whisper, and are scolded by camp counselors. But the older kids—my age and even a bit younger—scribble notes in their journals. I watch the back of their heads, bobbing at the finer points of my dad's sermon.

And I'm jealous—disgustingly, hotly jealous. My heart aches like the sore muscle it is. I covet their innocence, their easy belief. They trust the world; they trust God. They see Him everywhere. Like I did, my whole life, and I didn't even know to appreciate how good I had it.

After the service, my mom leans in. "Let's have breakfast at the cabin, yeah?"

I say good-bye to my dad, who will drive an hour home to our church for the ten-thirty service. My mom and I walk back, just the two of us, as she tells me about the hospital visit. The way she describes it, she might as well have been at bridge club, chatting with the other women hooked up to IVs. I assume the positivity is for my benefit. She gathers up some fruit in a big bowl, and we take our tea out to the porch.

She settles into her Adirondack chair, plucking a prune out of the bowl. It is beyond me why she thought that belonged with green grapes and strawberries. "So. Tell me about your week."

"Well," I say. "I'm exhausted, for starters."

"Are you drinking enough water? Getting enough sleep?"

"Yes, Mom."

"Are you sure? Are you regular? Here, eat a few prunes. They'll—"

"*Mom.* I'm fine. Although sharing a bathroom is the worst."

"Ha," she says.

It's not rational, but I wanted her genuine pity—even for something so stupid. Because I can't tell her about the ache I felt, watching the counselors go off on Friday night without me. I huff out a breath, annoyed. "I don't fit in there, Mom."

"In the bathroom?" She smiles.

"Don't joke."

The expression drops. "I'm sorry. Why do you say that?"

"I just . . . don't belong. I'm too different from them."

"Different how?" She's genuinely perplexed.

"I don't know. But I am." It seems too dorky to admit

that I cringe when my fellow counselors mutter "Jesus" like a swearword. That my face flushed when Tambe made a sex joke in the Bunker yesterday. Everyone else laughed and clearly got the punch line, which I'm not totally sure I did.

"Hm." My mom scans the woods around us, eyes following a pair of birds flapping upward. "Remember that field-of-lavender puzzle we did a few Christmases ago?"

Of course I do. We do a puzzle every winter break—a difficult one, with one thousand pieces. But the lavender one, oh man. We drove ourselves mad trying to finish it. But I have no idea how it comes into play here. "Yeah . . ."

"It's easy to sort by pieces that look alike. But it's two differently shaped pieces that connect."

"You sound like Dad," I mutter. Straight out of the sermon. "It's just hard because they have, like . . . years of memories and inside jokes. I can't compete with that!"

"Ah. Well, maybe you don't compete. You add to it. That's how it was when you started public school, right? And how Lukas felt when he was new to town. But he found friends and you."

I jerk my head over, wondering why she'd bring up something so cruel. It takes me a moment to remember: she doesn't know. It's the first time the omission has felt like a lie, but I still don't want to tell her. Because how do I explain why Lukas broke up with me? It's a humiliating reminder of all the ways I'm failing.

"Oh, Luce," she says, taking my silence as despair. Which maybe it is. "It's only been a week. It's going to get so much easier."

Only then do I notice the worn edges around her eyes and mouth. Maybe it's something only a daughter could notice: the very earliest fraying. I'm sitting here complaining about Daybreak while cancer warps my mom's healthy cells. While she stares down more chemotherapy.

"I'm sorry." My voice comes out softer than I meant it to. "It's just been a hard week, and I hate not being here with you."

The last phrase cracks in my throat. *Here with you.* I want to be here with her. I want her to be here with me. Forever, indefinitely. That's the heart of the problem—the entire, breaking heart of the problem.

"I miss you too, Bird." I expected my emotion would choke her up too, but she says this happily. She scans the lake, as if letting the beauty hit her skin. "But I feel so peaceful here. I take naps. I brought a lot of books, and I'm knitting. And I'm reading the book of Psalms, which is so illuminating! King David was so deeply flawed. Sometimes brave and trusting, but sometimes cowardly and sinful. But his relationship with the Lord was rich, so passionate."

I almost ask why, at Stage III, she'd find herself in songs of praise and gratitude. But I memorized Psalm 23 at Vacation Bible School years ago, and it sticks in my mind still.

Even though I walk through the darkest valley, I will fear no evil, for you are with me.

"Are you scared of chemo getting worse?" The question leaps from my mouth, bounces awkwardly across the porch's wooden planks, and lands at my mother's feet.

But she reacts only with a quick tug of her eyebrows. Her eyes move to my face—watching closely for, I suppose, a trembling lower lip. "I'm scared of how terribly sick I'll feel, yes. But I'm trying to focus on how grateful I am that this treatment is available to me. I'd be more scared to not have chemo. Does that make sense?"

"Yes." I've never felt more fear-frozen than when she was wheeled away for her surgery. Once she was out of sight, I wanted to wail like a little kid lost at the mall. But I know I would have been more scared if her cancer was totally inoperable.

"Mom," I say. "I need to be here with you. You're going to need someone at the cabin when Dad is busy, and I gave Daybreak a shot, but—"

"Out of the question." Her tone is still pleasant, and her hand flutters as if she can bat away this gnat of an idea. She's not *hearing* me. She doesn't understand how much better off we'd all be if I was here.

It hits me like divine inspiration—how I can change her mind. "There's a girl at Daybreak who's pregnant, Mom. A camper. *Pregnant.*"

Her face darkens like I knew it would. Ha! I'll be packing

for Holyoke by this afternoon. "Well, I hope you're making her feel loved and supported."

Wait, what? Our church is all about the *true love waits* message, and I can't believe my mom would condone anything else. This is a woman who tried to convince me to talk to the swim team girls before prom about being safe! Her exact words included *Birth control pills don't protect against STDs. Make sure they realize that.* As if I'd ever talk about that kind of thing! "Mom. She's *fourteen*."

"Then I hope so even more." Her cheeks flush pink, her voice hushed with severity. "She's a child. Imagine what she's going through."

If I did *it* and got pregnant, my parents would disown me. Well, that's not fair to say. They wouldn't kick me out to the streets. But they'd never look at me the same way, never love me the same way. This is what I've always believed. And yet my mom seems disappointed in *me* for being shocked?

Nothing makes sense anymore.

"Well, I should probably get back."

"Already?" My mom sits up. "We haven't even had real breakfast yet."

"Yeah. I, uh . . . have Blue Team stuff."

"Lucy . . ." She grabs my hand as I get up. "You're going to walk out on your cancer-ridden mother just because this is difficult?"

I blink at her, breaking my trance of anger. What am

I *doing*? She's battling a serious illness and I can't keep my temper in check? "I'm sorry. I'm so sorry, Mom. You're right."

As I settle back into my chair, she marvels at herself. "Wow, the cancer guilt packs a punch. Huh! Hadn't used it yet. Nasty weapon, that."

I meet her eyes with a grim smile. "I deserved it."

She sips her tea, pleased and calm as the Queen of England. "Okay, tell me something you actually do like about Daybreak. There's got to be something."

"Well, it's different than here at Holyoke, where I'm just leading activities. Being with the girls all the time, I get to see how they take everything in. They're fiery and honest, sometimes such quiet little thinkers. They're . . ."

"Totally exhausting?"

"*Yes.*" I laugh a little, but stop short: Was *I* totally exhausting as a third grader? I wish I could remember my entire relationship with my mom—every day together, instead of just the biggest moments of childhood. "Um. What else . . . Oh, we got to do a self-defense class."

"Really!"

"Yeah. We learned maneuvers for disabling an aggressor." I throw an elbow back, demonstrating what Tambe taught us. The entire class, he led us with total solemnity. Not necessarily what you expect from a teen guy wearing a Beyoncé T-shirt. "The older kids get to do boxing, I guess. There's a punching bag and everything. But the little ones just learn how to protect themselves if they get attacked. I thought it was a bit extreme; they're third graders, you know? But . . . but I think some of them have pretty hard lives."

"Yes," she says quietly, and I have to figure she and Rhea have discussed this. "They sure do."

My mom would be a good resource for Rhea, though she doesn't talk about her childhood with me. I have asked only once why she left her family for foster care—a fact I don't think she ever meant me to know. She said, simply, "They were not nice to me."

When she told me that, I must have been in middle school. I don't know what I thought "not nice" might mean. I think I imagined the Dursleys from Harry Potter—shut off and unkind. Now, I wonder sometimes: Did they leave her alone? Not feed her as punishment? Something worse? The earliest picture she has of herself is at age fourteen, and I can't quite imagine her as a little girl. If what everyone says is true, I look just like her.

She's the one who breaks the silence, reaching over to take my hand. "This is nice, huh?"

The words batter at my chest like pounding fists: *Mom, please tell me everything about you while we still have time. Mom, let's just be totally honest. Mom, Lukas broke up with me.* It goes against every instinct not to blurt everything out to her. But the lake's surface is liquid gold beneath the rising sun, and my mom's hand is cool in mine, and all I can do is try to see my dad's message from the pulpit. That there are traces of heaven in everything—in shifts of summer sun, in your palm curled around a cup of strong tea, in the clasp of your mother's hand. So I close my eyes, and I try to memorize the way the world feels all around us.

CHAPTER TEN

TOP FIVE MOST EMBARRASSING MOMENTS OF CAMP, WEEK TWO
1. After my Monday morning swim, I'm toweling off on my way back to the cabin. I'm not sure of the exact time, but I haven't heard the bugle yet.

And then I nearly run into the bugle. Or rather, the bugler. Jones. So it's been him these past mornings, waking everyone up for the day. I didn't put it together.

"Morning!" he says with a friendly wave. His trumpet is in one hand, glinting in the earliest sunlight. He is wearing a T-shirt and shorts like a normal human being. I am wearing a still-sopping swimsuit. And I know from experience that my goggles have pressed red ovals around my eyes.

"Heh," I reply. *Heh.* Not "hi," not "hey." Very distinctly: *heh.*

And instead of trying to recover from that, I scamper away like a third grader.

2. During our Tuesday night activity—watching *The Sandlot* after playing all-camp softball—Brooklyn tugs on my sleeve and asks if I have a boyfriend or a girlfriend. We're sitting on blankets outside, a projector playing the pool kiss scene.

"A boyfriend," I whisper automatically, before I remember. "I mean, neither."

"So you *don't* have a boyfriend?"

"Well, I kind of do. It's . . . I mean, sometimes relationships are complicated when you're older."

"What's your kind-of boyfriend's name? Have you kissed him? Are you in love with him?"

Lukas. Yes. And . . . I thought I was. Can you be truly in love with someone who would put you in storage for summer, like a nice enough but unnecessary winter coat?

"Watch the movie," I whisper.

"That means yes," Brooklyn says to herself, smug, as Anna pats my hand.

3. On Thursday morning, Anna and I are sitting together at breakfast. She's flanked by her fourth graders, and I have a row of 3As at my side. We're taking our trays up, when I see Jones and Simmons in the hallway to Rhea's office. They're nearly toe-to-toe, conferring about something, arms crossed as they whisper.

When Anna catches me staring at them, I mutter sheepishly, "They're cute."

"'They' as in Simmons and Jones? No, no. That's a brother-sister thing."

My first reaction is surprise; I never would have guessed. They have different last names, for starters. So maybe they have different dads or something. Simmons is short, with arched eyebrows, higher cheekbones. I guess they do both have heart-shaped faces?

Regardless, I don't think anything of it when, while trying to make small talk during morning Pitch-In, I say to Simmons, "It's so nice that you get to be at camp with your brother and sister."

She gives me the most epic *Excuse me?* look the world has ever seen. "I don't have a brother."

"Jones," I say, not understanding.

As I stand there, heart pounding with confusion, she levels me with a side eye that could split the horizon line from the earth. "Do I really have to tell you that not all black people are related?"

My face lights itself on fire. "No! What? I mean— Anna . . . she told me you guys are a brother-sister thing!"

Her tight expression relaxes. "Oh, Jesus. Ha! She meant he's like a brother to me. We grew up together. Same high school, too. Our moms are close. He dated my best friend for over a year. That kind of thing."

"Oh. Cool." And my stupid, stupid mouth adds, "Dat*ed*? Like, they broke up?"

"Yeah. In the spring."

4. Simmons's stare homes in on me, her brows lowered. "Why? You interested?"

"Oh gosh, no! I just asked because I thought how hard that would be for you, two of your best friends breaking up. I mean, I have a boyfriend. Well, I had a boyfriend. We're taking a little time off. You know what? It doesn't matter."

Shut up, *Lucy.* My words sound like the thumps of a football when it has been fumbled.

5. I play touch football with the Blue Team on Thursday evening. I actually fumble.

CHAPTER ELEVEN

Friday evening after dinner, we're outside for our color-team activity—a friendly game of kickball against the Yellow Team—when a little voice shrieks, "Help! She's allergic!"

I turn to see one girl sprawled on the grass. My prayers fly as fast as my feet: *Help me, guide me, let her be okay.* Oh, Lord, it's Neveah, Anna's fourth grader who I met on the first day. D'Souza is holding her hand, wide-eyed but trying to soothe her. I drop to my knees, taking in the hives across her neck, her puffy eyes. She's lucid, groping around her pocket. She has an EpiPen there—*oh, thank God, thank you*—and I close my fingers around it.

"Hi, Nev." I look into her dark eyes, wide with panic. Tears slide down her cheeks. "I've got you, okay? Promise."

"Okay," she manages.

"Something she ate? Wasps? What?" I demand of her friend, the one who screamed. I'm pulling the pen out of its case.

"Bees."

I glance back at D'Souza. "I got it. Go."

She sprints off toward Miss Suzette's. Somewhere in the noise around me, I register fellow Blue Team counselors getting our campers to back away, giving us space.

"I didn't," Neveah gasps, "feel a sting."

"It's okay. We're gonna fix you right up. Ready?" I swing my arm and pop the needle into her outer thigh, feeling it release. She groans but doesn't cry out as I hold it for ten seconds. "Good girl. That's gonna help so soon. Just relax. You're fine now. All fine."

I scan her legs, up and down, up and down, but I see no entry wound. Still searching, I run my hands over her arms. Ah, there. Right above her elbow, where skin is less sensitive. I scrape my thumbnail across the raised mark, removing the stinger.

Glancing around desperately, I find Jones's eyes. "Can you get her up?"

Before he can get to us, Neveah grasps my hand. Her brown eyes are wide now, lashes wet. "Hansson. I don't want to die."

"Hey. Look at me. Do I look like I think that's even remotely a possibility?"

She stares into my eyes, and I do not blink, holding my breath until my chest aches. I hope it hides my panic, how fast my heart is beating. I'll need my inhaler from my own pocket soon enough.

"No," she decides.

"No," I agree, and Jones scoops his arms beneath her neck and knees, lifting her.

"Okay, lady, Jones Towing at your service. Here we go."

I trot beside them, trying to monitor her symptoms. We meet Miss Suzette on the path to her cabin, D'Souza by her side. My relief whooshes out in loud exhales, heavy breathing unhidden now. It's out of my hands. I did what I could.

"Hey, baby girl," Miss Suzette tells Neveah. Her gaze moves to me. "You got the Epi in?"

I nod.

"You sure? It can feel like—"

"I'm positive."

Inside the cabin, Jones lays Neveah down on Miss Suzette's own bed. I didn't realize she slept here, but of course she would. Camp nurses are needed day and night. She coos at Neveah, supplies already laid out. "Hey, tough stuff. Look at you, riding this thing out."

"It only happened one time. When I was little," Nev says. *Oh boy*, I think. *You're still little!* "I just remember it was so, so bad."

"I know, baby," Suzette says.

"Sting entry is right arm," I tell her. "Above her elbow."

Nev reaches for my hand as Miss Suzette gives her a liquid antihistamine and sets to work cleaning out the sting. Suzette hums a little—calming herself and her patient or filling the tense silence, I don't know.

When she's done, she turns back to us counselors. We've remained in reverent silence, afraid to disturb such a precarious situation. "All right. I've got it from here. Go reassure everyone that she's gonna be fine."

"Can Hansson stay?" Nev asks. "Please."

Miss Suzette doesn't glance at me. "Of course she can."

Rhea comes in as Jones and D'Souza head out. She runs a hand over Neveah's forehead—like a mother checking for a fever—and says, "I heard we had some excitement."

"Do I have to go to the hospital?" Nev whines. "I don't want to."

"Well, we're going to monitor your symptoms. We'll call the squad if we have to."

More tears from Neveah. "Okay. But I'm not leaving camp. No matter what my mom says."

"You were so brave," I tell Neveah as we help her settle onto the couch. She'll get to eat Popsicles and watch TV with Rhea and Miss Suzette.

"Hansson?" she whispers. Her eyes and skin already look much better.

"Yeah?"

"That was scary."

"It was. But you're tough."

She unwraps the Popsicle that Rhea hands to her, giving me a sneaky smile. In a whispered voice, she adds, "I liked the part where Jones carried me."

I step away for a minute, to use my inhaler in Miss

Suzette's bathroom, which has pink tile and leafy wallpaper and a jar of potpourri. A quick glance in the mirror shows my sunburn and the slightly crazed expression of some-one staving off asthma. I look like a madwoman in some Victorian-era crime novel, losing her mind among soft colors and florals. *Why would Lukas break up with such a lovely girl?* I laugh darkly.

"Let me get you a glass of water," Miss Suzette says when I emerge.

"Oh, I'm okay."

Suzette turns with an appraising look. "Did you hear me ask a question?"

Well, then.

I sit at the table in front of a cold glass of water, unaware of how thirsty I was until it hits my lips.

"You did well out there, baby. Kept a cool head. Your mama will be proud."

"Thank you." My voice cracks, and just like that, I'm cry-ing. Ugh, how mortifying. I don't want Rhea or Neveah to hear.

"There it is," Suzette says quietly.

"I don't know why I'm crying," I whisper. "I'm honestly fine!"

"It's the adrenaline letting up. It's relief. That was scary."

"I really thought she might die."

"I know. But you never showed that to her. You're tough stuff too, baby. Real tough stuff."

Somehow, I'm sniffing pitifully inside her arms. And I think—as I worry I will even when I am old and gray—*I want my mom.* When does it stop—the longing to be mothered?

It's almost dark when I leave Miss Suzette's cabin, and the camp has gone quiet. Another Friday night off, but I guess I'll go to bed early.

"Hey, Hansson!" Anna's voice calls. "Where ya going?"

When I turn, they're pooled at the mouth of the woods. Waiting. Anna, Simmons, Tambe, Jones. In plaid button-downs to protect from mosquitoes. Backpacks slung over their shoulders, just like last week. Anna's holding a thermos and a bag of marshmallows. Jones is carrying a gallon jug of water and a few long metal skewers. The other two have unlit camping lanterns, glossy green and burnt red.

Taking my confusion as hesitancy, Anna hollers, "*Don't* tell us you're practicing piano. You can take a night off."

When I approach, Jones steps forward a few paces, asking quietly, "Are you okay? We'll stay back with you, if you want."

"I did *not* agree to that," Tambe grumbles.

"We heard you could use a s'more," Anna says. "And by 's'more,' I mean a s'more and a stiff drink."

"Well, tell her the rules," Simmons says flatly. "She might not want to come."

Anna hip-bumps her. "Oh, Keels. You're the only one who hates feelings."

Okay, now I'm confused: alcohol, s'mores, and feelings?

Tambe takes pity on me and explains. "What happens on Friday nights stays on Friday nights. Can you handle that?"

I want to say, scornfully: *Who am I going to tell?* But instead I say, "Sure."

"Then let's *go*," Tambe says, his back already to me. The lantern swings at his side, the rusty handle creaking. Anna and Simmons troop after him, chattering about funny things the campers have said this week.

"Can I carry something?" I ask Jones. The leaves crunch under our shoes as I walk alongside him.

"Oh, sure." He reaches over to hand me the skewers. Just having something to hold makes me feel included. The metal is warm from his palm. "You're sure you're okay? I've seen a lot of stuff, but . . . that was intense."

"I'm okay now. But yeah, I was terrified."

"Were you?" He glances over. "Fooled me. You looked so sure that she would be fine."

"I was just trying to keep her calm. My mom's a nurse, and that's always what she does."

"I was gonna say . . ." He smiles, rubbing at the back of his neck. "You must have experience. I was just frozen."

"My mom has a, like, very mild peanut allergy. Her throat gets a little itchy. But she basically uses it to get an epinephrine prescription in case I'm ever discovered to have a bad allergy."

Jones laughs, a surprised *ha!* "That's, like, questionable ethics as a nurse . . . but excellent mom skills."

"Exactly," I say, rolling my eyes. "And she made me use the practice pen to learn and everything. She's going to be *thrilled* it came to good use, which I swore it never would."

As we hike, Anna and Tambe are practically bouncing, talking over each other and occasionally breaking into song. Simmons collects fallen branches in a stack across her arms.

It's not long before I'm following them off the trail, dodging between trees. I notice that a few small plants beneath our feet are squashed, clearly trod on last week. The path opens to a little clearing surrounded by trees—as near a circle as you'd find in nature. There's a metal fire pit in the center and logs arranged around it. We're closer to the lake than even on the standard trail, but a little higher up. It feels farther removed than a five-minute hike from camp.

The routine unfolds quickly, and I have no place in it. Simmons arranges the kindling in the fire pit, and Tambe leans over it, focusing. Anna airs out a cherry-red tartan blanket while Jones unloads the rest of his backpack. As the fire sparks and snaps, filling the small space with the scent of summer and burning, I wish I had something to set up.

"That's an impressive fire," I tell Tambe.

Jones surveys the flames. "I think that's a record, even for you."

Tambe raises his arms and shrugs his shoulders in some kind of dance. "Scouting, bitches!"

I wait for Simmons to sit down before I pick a log spot. Once I do, she reaches over to me, holding out a clear glass bottle. It has a green cap and a label that I can't read, but I'm almost positive it's alcohol.

"Oh, no thanks." I've only tried alcohol twice. The first time was at a party freshman year, the weekend before Lukas moved to town. That alcohol was also clear. It felt fizzy on my tongue and tasted like raspberries that had been in the fridge about a year too long.

She shrugs and takes an extra drink. I have the distinct feeling that she only offered it to make me feel childish for passing.

"So, Lucy," Anna says. She's settled on the blanket, peeling open a chocolate bar. I realize it's jarring to hear my first name. "How was your week?"

"Oh, good." The lie dissipates over the fire, a single syllable that seems to create silence. "Yeah."

"Mohan," Simmons says. "Tell her."

Tambe shoots me a look. Apparently, they use first names when alone, and his is Mohan. "Friday nights, we speak the truth. Even if it's ugly. Even if we have to bitch about campers to get it out. It's necessary, yeah? To vent, to have a place where we turn off the counselor for a bit."

"Okay . . . ," I say, hesitant. I'm wondering if I just agreed to high-stakes Truth or Dare.

"Okay." Anna's smile is pointed. "So how was your second week at Daybreak, *really*?"

Now I wish I'd taken a swig of alcohol. "I'm . . . really tired. Like, bone-deep tired. I feel like I could curl up anywhere—on the ground here—and just pass out."

Anna snorts. "Me too. I do not have my camp legs yet."

"So," Jones says. "You're from White Hills. You play the piano like a boss. What else? Family?"

They're trying to get to know you, I remind myself. This is a good thing. "Mom and dad. No siblings."

"What do your parents do?" This question is from Anna, who is now breaking the chocolate bar into squares.

"My mom's a school nurse." Do I say it? I mean, what am I going to do, lie? "My dad's a pastor."

That gets their attention. Anna snaps her head up. "You're a Preacher's Kid?"

"Ah. A PK. So that explains the no drinking," Tambe says.

But Simmons, I notice, retracts her head a little, studying me. It's a protective expression, though I'm not sure what I'm threatening. Or maybe she's just adding this new information to what she knows of me. I don't get the sense that it's in the Pro column.

"Nah," I say—my attempt at nonchalance. "I'm just nervous I'd throw up or act stupid in front of you guys."

How's that for honest? Jones tilts his head down to hide his grin. Then he bails me out. "Got any other fun facts up your sleeve?"

"Um, I'm swim team captain?" For something that takes up so much of my time, it doesn't land as very interesting.

My heart pounds out a pathetic rhythm. *Please still like me; please still like me.* "And I have an online makeup channel. That's about it."

"Whoa, whoa, wait." Anna sits up. "Oh my God. Oh my actual Lord in heaven."

"What?"

She's clapping her hands, shocked by her own delight or delighted by her own shock—I have no idea. "Shit! I thought you just had one of those *faces*, you know? That looks familiar? You taught me how to do winged eyeliner."

"I did *not*." No way. I mean, my videos get quite a lot of hits, but I'm not an Internet celebrity or anything. Yeah, companies offer to send me products sometimes, but I almost always decline. It makes me feel too sneaky, intercepting packages from my parents.

Anna's shaking her head. "Yeah! Totally. I mean, I watched a lot of winged eyeliner videos, but oh my God. Yours was definitely one. I can't believe it."

"You're famous!" Tambe tells me. "Have you ever been recognized before now?"

"Once. By a girl coming into Sephora as I was leaving." She gasped, "*LucyEsMakeup?*" And I awkwardly said hello, thanking God that my mom and I had agreed to meet back up at the Starbucks on the first floor of the mall.

"You're doing my makeup," Anna announces. "I don't know when, but you are. Okay? Like, you can go full on, no holds barred."

"You're on," I say, smiling.

"All right," Simmons says. "Ready to get on with this?"

At first, I think she means makeup, but mercifully, Anna turns to explain. "So every Friday, we share the low and the high from our week. Brutal honesty."

"Okay . . . ," I say again, already frantically considering mine. But I know. Of course I know.

"You can go last if you want," Anna adds.

"No, it's okay," I say, trying to sound braver than I am. Something I'm getting really, really good at.

"I'll go first," Simmons says. She has the bottle of alcohol gripped in one hand. "Low: One of my cabin girls, Thuy, is really homesick. She's not engaging with us or the other girls yet. But she won't talk to me about it."

I think of sweet Thuy, who keeps all her possessions neatly contained around her bed. Her suitcase sits on the shelf, ready to grab at any moment. She's always looking down. Not up at the trees, not around at the mess hall. It's like she's not even here, in her mind. A part of me understands. Half of me is a mile around the bend, in a little cabin with my mom.

Simmons takes a long swallow.

"High," she says. "There's a girl in Kiana's cabin this year with a similar background to us, and they're already inseparable."

Before she lifts the bottle to her lips again, she makes eye contact with me, as if daring me to judge her. "The similar background being not ever knowing her mom."

I say nothing. Did their mom leave? Die? She pulls back another mouthful and passes the bottle to Tambe. I mean, Mohan. I have no idea what I'm supposed to call them.

"Okay. Low: snapping at Conrad because he is consistently, *intentionally* annoying." He pauses to drink, then wipes his mouth. "But so was I at that age. High was one of the 5A girls asking to do more boxing after my class. She's a pissed-off kid. So it might be the right outlet for her."

He drinks from the bottle, eyes closing briefly like a quick prayer. "You're up, Lucy."

I take the bottle from his hand. Not because I want to fit in or get drunk. I mean, I'm pretty sure two sips wouldn't accomplish either. It's that sharing in something, even if it's sips from a bottle, feels crucial here. Besides, I need something to do with my hands.

"Low," I say. "Watching Nev go through something so scary tonight."

I tip the bottle back. The liquid is tepid, but it burns, sickly sweet. Saccharine green apples on the front end, but the aftertaste is chemical, toxic. I struggle not to cough. And fail.

"High." I want to say: *All of you. Everyone at this camp who is trying so hard.* But I don't want to be that rookie counselor, the try-hard outsider who overshares. They actually included me tonight, so I shouldn't highlight how separate I am. "Um . . . let's see. Hard to pick."

"Ah, ah, ah," Tambe scolds. "You thought of something. Out with it."

I take my drink before speaking, more of a nerve-easer than a toast. My taste buds try to push it right back out, and my eyes water at the betrayal. "High: Getting to watch you guys be counselors. How good you are at it, I mean."

For the second or two that they're quiet, I feel like I can hear everything: marshmallow sugar melting, leaves detaching from branches overhead, mosquitoes biting into skin.

"Goddamn, Hansson," Tambe says. "That's, like, really sweet."

"Yeah, well," I mumble, bringing the bottle to my mouth—wetness barely touching my lips—just for something to do.

I partake in this strange communion. Truths and graham crackers and straight liquor. When all confessions have been made, we stack s'mores together, gooey marshmallow stretching between crumbly bites.

"This," Anna says, "is revolting with the vodka."

It doesn't stop her or Simmons from drinking it as we each eat at least one more s'more. Tambe eats four and announces he's going to pee, wandering off in the dark woods. Anna and Simmons lie on their backs on the blanket, staring up as they whisper. It leaves just Jones and me on the log, and I realize that on some level, I must see him the way the campers do. Like he's a little larger than life, almost heroic. It feels strange to sit casually next to him when I've spent a week at short distance, watching him with all the kids.

"Water, please?" Simmons asks. Jones pours some from the gallon into a plastic cup, and Simmons crawls across the blanket to take it.

"Jonesy." Simmons presses a hand against his cheeks, squishing them together. Her eyes are glassy, a reflection of vodka and fondness. "You're one of my favorite Homo sapiens."

"Oh, Keels." His smile for her is adoring but, I see now, familial. "I wouldn't change one thing about you."

"Did you know," she says, eyes brightening, "that according to quantum theory, there could be slightly different Keelys in parallel universes, based on scenarios presented but not chosen?"

Anna laughs, a low chuckle, as she glances at me. "She gets really sciencey when she drinks."

"I can *hear* you." Keely whips her head around. "And so do *you*, Annabel. We can't help what we love, and I just love space so much."

"I know." Anna pats the blanket beside her. "Keely? Will you come tell me about other planets again? Please?"

"Okay, okay." She scoots over to Anna, and they both lean back. Keely takes a deep breath, like she's beginning a fairy tale. "Well, Gliese 667 is a three-star system with seven planets. Three of those planets are rocky terrain and possibly habitable. *And* the system is only about twenty-two light-years away. So it's something that could maybe actually happen."

"Probably the thing I'm saddest about right now," Anna muses, "is that it might not be in our lifetime. God, I hope it is. So bad. I just want to know."

I've always thought only in terms of heaven and earth.

In my mind, heaven is somewhere inaccessibly skyward, and hell is somewhere near the molten core of the earth.

Anna twists around. "Lucy, do you believe that there are other life forms out there?"

"Um . . ." I know the right answer is yes, but it would be a lie. "I've never thought about it."

"A nonbeliever," Keely says to Anna.

"We can convert her," she whispers back. They lower their voices more, giggling and occasionally pointing at the sky. I look up, where a patch of dark sky is barely touched by treetops. Stars splattered. If I squint, it's almost like a page of music with the colors inverted. Black page with tiny white dots strewn across.

Tambe returns and joins them on the blanket, happily musing about universes beyond.

I look over at Jones. "What about you? ET? No ET?"

"Ah. I'm an alien agnostic."

"Meaning . . . there may or may not be extraterrestrials, but you don't really care to think about it?"

He taps a finger on his nose and points at me with his other hand. "Got other things on my mind."

"Like trumpet."

"Ha. Sometimes."

"It's very impressive for only 'sometimes.'"

"Eh, not really. I mean, you play the piano."

"Yeah, but pianos have keys . . . I just know what they are and can press them in different combinations."

In the firelight, I can see him arch an eyebrow above his glasses. "What do you think a trumpet has?"

"Well, I know those are keys too, but you only have three! I have eighty-eight! And I don't have to do anything with my *breathing* for my instrument to make sound."

"*Well*, I don't have to use my feet at all."

I guess I do use pedals; they're just second nature now. "How long have you played?"

"Since I was five."

"*Five?* That's early, right?" I don't know when public school kids start playing instruments, but kindergarten seems way early for a brass instrument.

"Yeah." He laughs. "I sounded like a grief-stricken duck because my mouth wasn't even big enough, but I just wanted to play so badly. I couldn't wait. Have you heard of Sean Jones?"

This feels like a trick. "Is that . . . you?"

"No!" This is so wrong, apparently, that he laughs. "No relation. I *wish*. Sean Jones is a trumpet player. One of the best in the world. I saw him play when I was in kindergarten, and I was like: That's it. That's what I want to do."

This feels so awkward, but I have to know. "So, um, what *is* your name?"

"Oh, that's funny that you don't know! Well, maybe it's not. I've always gone by Jones here, even before I was a counselor. You don't want to guess?"

"Rumpelstiltskin," I say, which makes him burst out laughing.

"Henry Morris Jones IV." He holds out a hand, which I shake. His skin is warm across my palm.

"Henry," I repeat. I almost could have guessed it, maybe. Henry: old-fashioned but still cool. Like his glasses and his wardrobe. "Henry Jones. Wait. Isn't that . . . ?"

"Indiana Jones's real name? Yep. But it was my great-grandad's before it was Indy's."

"Four of you with the same name? Isn't that confusing?"

"Nah. My great-grandfather went by Henry, my grandpa's Hank. My dad is Trey."

"That's so nice—a name with all that history, so much meaning." I wrinkle my nose. "I'm named for Saint Lucy."

He shakes his head. "I don't know that one."

"Oh, she was a martyr. Of course. Died for her faith—by eye gouging or sword, the story varies."

"Maybe eye-gouged *with* a sword," Jones offers. "Well, that's . . . charming."

I laugh. "Right? My dad wanted to name me Esther, but my mom thought it sounded elderly. It's my middle name. They couldn't agree on anything biblical, so they branched out to saint names. We're not even Catholic!"

"Me neither. I do like the idea of saints, though. Rhea has a statue of Saint Jude, patron saint of lost causes, even though she doesn't believe in saints or that any cause is ever lost."

If a cause is entirely lost, what's the point of a saint to watch over it? Or to field prayers about it? But I know. I know because, for the first time, I feel like a lost cause—or at least a desperate case. I would want a saint who knows how far gone everything feels.

He tells me more about Rhea, and about her son, Bryan—the tall guy with a beard who I met only briefly. He's always hurrying from one place to the next. I learn that Jones has been at Daybreak since sixth grade, same as Anna. Tambe since seventh, and Simmons since fifth. I don't even feel disappointed to confirm that theirs is an impossible history for me to slide into. I just feel sad— and, okay, a little curious—about all of them experiencing some kind of trauma so young. What sent each of them here?

We talk about the shared lives of musicians—about exacting teachers who pushed us to be better, about the long hours, and nerve-racking performances.

"So, why'd you stop piano lessons?" he asks.

"I don't know," I admit. It felt inevitable, at the time. "I think it's that my mom swam when she was my age, so it's this shared language. Something we both get. With piano, I was the only person at home who played. Plus, I think I wanted to be part of a team instead of all that practice alone or with a teacher."

"I've always thought I want to be a professional trumpeter," Jones says. "But sometimes I think it's too solitary for me. Like maybe I'd be happier with counseling or social work. Not psychiatry—my mom's a psychiatrist, so I'm too close to that, ha. But something where I can help kids the way Rhea and Bryan helped me."

There is a tiny piece of my heart—like rot in an apple—that hopes one of his parents had cancer and made it through. Maybe that's his checked bag. Then he could talk me through it in his highly skilled counselor way. It's so selfish a thought that I stun myself with it, wondering if the devil has sunk his nails into me. I tuck my arms together, leaning forward to look at Jones. "You'd be a natural at that."

"Yeah?" He tilts his head at me, genuinely touched. "Thanks. It's just hard to tell if trumpet is meant to be a hobby I really love—or a profession. All I know is that I better decide before college applications really come at me."

"Yeah. I know what you mean." I never wanted to be a professional pianist. Turning it into work would spoil it. Sometimes I think I'd be a great nurse, like my mom. But I'm not sure if that's me finding a path or simply admiring hers.

I'm about to confess all this when Jones's watch beeps. "That's time, all."

He opens the jug of water and pulls a few plastic cups from his backpack. Simmons reaches her hand back compliantly for a refill, but Anna doesn't move. She's lying on her side, head curled into Tambe's shoulder and blond hair messy across the blanket. Asleep.

Jones hands off another cup of water, and Tambe says, "Let's give her a few more minutes."

We pack up the graham crackers and skewers. When Jones douses the last flames with the remaining water, the branches sizzle and smoke, and Anna stirs.

"Time to go home, Boo," Simmons says, nudging her.

She smiles sleepily, a warm kitten waking up to discover she's still right at home, safe. "Okay."

I offer her a hand, which she takes. Our eyes connect somewhere on the way up, and her smile drops off.

"Hey, Lucy?" Her voice is soft.

"Yeah?"

"Sorry I called the Christian camp around the lake 'crazy' that first day you were here."

Ah, there it is. Sometimes, after people find out I'm a PK, they think back on things they've said in front of me. "Oh. That's okay."

She yawns. "No, I actually do know better—I mean, I'm Jewish! And I shouldn't call other people crazy."

"We're all mad here," Tambe chimes in, with his best Cheshire cat voice.

He folds up the blanket and slings one arm around Anna, and Simmons jumps on Jones's back as they head down through the trees to the trail.

And I want to be one of them. I want to be one of them so, so badly—to fit into this balance, their history, the wolf pack way of them. I see it now, why my mom wants that for me. I see how you can't *help* but want it, if you get close enough to witness a group of friends knitted together like this.

CHAPTER TWELVE *

SATURDAY IS A SPECIAL DAY OF COLOR-TEAM ACTIVITIES, SO I get to spend the morning on the edge of the pier, coaching some older campers on diving. They're unflagging, willing to try again and again. And, I admit, I enjoy their wide-eyed admiration after they ask me to demonstrate.

It's a morning full of lake antics—flashes of orange life jackets in the air, yells that the noodles are *not weapons*, and only one instance of crying after an unintentional belly flop. The sun shows no sign of mercy, and D'Souza returns with an economy bottle of sunblock. While doling it out, I notice that Thuy's hair is still dry.

"You sure you don't want to get in?"

She nibbles at her lip, shaking her head.

"What if we went to the other side?"

"I can't."

"You can't swim? Well, that's okay. You have a life jacket on."

She shakes her head more adamantly, and I glance up at D'Souza, who shrugs.

"Okay," I tell her. "Let me know if you change your mind."

By the end of our time, I'm exhausted in the way that only water can make you feel. Wrung out, like my muscles have turned gelatinous. Something about it makes a cool, dry bed sound like heaven. We towel off at the end of the pier, passing the life jackets to the Green Team.

"Was that the best ever?" Anna calls. A few of the older kids still have energy to whoop, while the little ones pout that our turn is over.

Anna's wearing nylon running shorts and the most appropriate T-shirt after last night: a s'more diagram, labeled "GRAHAM, 'MALLOW, CHOCOLATE, GRAHAM." I'm entirely sure it's a gift from Tambe, connoisseur of the graphic tee.

As we trudge back up, I gather the heavy strands of my wet hair into a pile on top of my head. I'm not intentionally listening to the Blue Team boys chatting behind me, but a name jumps out when one says, "Someone told me Anna, like, used to be a boy or something."

"What?" the other says. "Anna's not a boy. She's a girls' counselor."

"Well, she swims in a T-shirt and shorts."

"So? Lots of people do. My *mom* hates swimsuits."

"But Anna doesn't sleep in the cabins."

That much is true—she has her own little room in Rhea's house on the edge of camp. But only because when her parents wanted her to attend Daybreak, Anna's one condition was a private room—no waking up to panic attacks in a cabin full of strangers.

A surge of protectiveness rises in me. Anna, who took me in without hesitation. I spin on my heel.

"Hey." I stare down at both of them, stopping dead. "Anna's a girl, not a boy—understand? We don't speculate like that."

Their little mouths snap shut.

"Sorry, Hansson," one whispers.

"Yeah, sorry," the other says. "We just didn't know."

"It's okay. But no more talk like that, okay? People are what they say they are."

They nod, running off in front of me, and someone touches the back of my arm. It's D'Souza, complete with an approving look.

"Not bad, Hansson. A lot of first-time counselors shy away from conversations about trans issues."

"Trans?" I repeat.

"Yeah, because—" she says, taking in my confused expression. "Because nothing. Forget it."

I rearrange the pieces of my brief conversation with the campers, but there's really only one thing Souz could have meant. "Because . . . Anna is trans," I guess.

"Right. Whew, you knew. Oh my gosh, I thought I might have just outed her. I mean, I know you guys are friends, and she's out at camp, but I still shouldn't have said that."

Trans. Huh. The questions flood in: *Should* I have known? I mean, I completely unloaded my life story to her that very first night. I thought I knew her really well. Is she not sure she can trust me? But mostly I feel so, so guilty that I know something she didn't want me to.

D'Souza is watching my eyes as if she can see all the questions swimming behind them. Crestfallen, she mutters, "You didn't know."

"Well . . . no. But, it's cool."

She covers her face with one hand. "It's not, though. Do me a favor and don't mention that I told you?"

I shift my weight, surprised that she'd ask me to lie to Anna. "I'm not really comfortable with—"

"I mean, let *me* tell her, so I can apologize."

"Oh. Yeah, no problem."

D'Souza smiles, but it's more of a grimace—so clearly frustrated with herself. "Thanks, Hansson. You're okay."

Am I? That night, I stare up at Keely's bunk as I try to fall asleep, wondering what I should say to Anna if it comes up. I think about Declan, a trans guy in my grade. We chat in class, but I don't really know him well. He's part of the tight-knit debate team friend group. Still, it was a big deal when we were in middle school. Parents can be even crueler than kids—there were meetings, arguments about bathroom policy. I remember being surprised when my mom—never one to criticize grown-ups in my presence—called those parents bullies.

I want to be the same type of friend for Anna that she's

been for me. Safe and thoughtful, ready to listen. Not for the first time, I curse the lack of cell signal here at the lake. The Internet would have tips for this, probably. Or, at least it would have some terminology I could learn.

The night before my first day of freshman year, I remember praying: *Please help me make good friends. Please.* I don't think it ever occurred to me to say the prayer I think tonight as I close my eyes: *Please help me be the good friend.*

On Sunday morning, I oversleep. Yawns accompany my ambling walk around the lake, but I make it just in time. I've been in the chapel for less than a minute when it becomes undeniable: something is wrong. My mom's smile is flattened, stretched into place. She kisses my cheek in greeting, and somehow even that feels terse—like a perfunctory airkiss between political rivals. But otherwise, she looks good. Maybe a little tired. Her complexion, her weight, though—still healthy.

"Do you feel okay?" I whisper. We take the last pew as my dad welcomes this week's church to the service.

"Fine," she replies, not looking at me.

We walk back to the cabin after the service, and I babble to fill the silence. Maybe she's experiencing some nausea from treatment but doesn't want to tell me.

Finally, inside the cabin, I burst out, "Mom. What's wrong?"

"I think I'll have some tea," she announces. "Do you want tea?"

"Um. Sure." I mean, what else can I say?

I sit on the porch, dreading whatever news she might have for me. Maybe the chemo isn't working. Maybe her system can't take any more of it.

When she returns, she hands over my mug. The steam smells like bergamot—the soft, dark notes of Earl Grey. Two teabag tags flutter against her mug, twisting in the morning breeze.

"Two bags?" I ask.

"I need stronger flavor." She waves a hand in front of her mouth. "I have this taste in my mouth, no matter how many times I brush my teeth."

"Is it a chemo thing?"

A nod over her mug. "So. When we were home for a doctor's appointment this week, your dad and I stopped by the grocery store." Her tone is measured, intentionally even. "And we ran into Mrs. Pratt."

She pins me with a look.

Oh crap. I attempt a pleasant, only vaguely interested tone. "Oh. How is she?"

"Well, for one thing, she's very sorry that you and Lukas have taken a hiatus from your relationship. But thinks it's for the best."

Double crap.

"I played dumb, agreeing and *mm-hmm*-ing as your father became very interested in the nearby wine selection. Despite the fact that he does not drink."

I can't meet her eyes. "I'm sorry. That must have been awkward."

"Luce!" she says, pained. "Don't be sorry. I just want to know why you wouldn't tell me something that big."

"I guess I thought we'd get back together immediately and you'd never have to know. I was embarrassed. And I didn't want to worry you, on top of everything else."

She takes this in, frowning at the thought. "This can't be how we do cancer, Bird. I get to set the rules, I think, and my rule is that you don't worry about burdening me. Fair?"

I nod, feeling foolish and unbearably young. "Fair."

"Do you want to tell me what happened?"

My sigh lasts for about thirty seconds. "I don't even *know*. Lukas has been thinking about the future and wants to make sure this is *right*. Somehow he decided that involved 'pausing' our relationship."

"Oh, honey. I'm so sorry. That must be so hard."

That's the troubling thing. Cancer is hard. The problems my campers face are hard. But . . . I'm not really upset about Lukas anymore. "You know . . . I'm actually okay. Which is not at all how I saw this going."

"How did you see it going?"

"I thought I'd be shattered." I thought my chest would ache every time I thought about him. "Part of it is that I'm so busy at Daybreak, I barely have time to think. But shouldn't I be devastated? I thought we'd . . . I mean, I saw us going to college together, you know?"

"I do know." Of course she does. How many nights have we sat on the couch, chopsticks burrowing into cartons of orange chicken, talking about every last one of my feelings?

"I assumed that he was *it*, and now it feels second nature to be happy without him. Which makes me feel insane. Like, were my instincts *that* wrong? Did I just get comfortable?"

Her lips press together, holding off the words for a moment. "Well, you change as you get older, especially at this time in your life. You become more yourself, hopefully. And sometimes that changes the dynamic, even with people you love. So it's not that you were wrong. You were right for that time. But you grow up and you grow out of relationships. Even the ones you thought, at one point, might be forever."

She seems awfully sure of this. Awfully specific. "Did you ever have someone like that, before Dad?"

My ears are already hearing the phrase *Oh, don't be silly*, but her silence goes on for too long. It makes me jerk my head up to study her face, which has a knowing smile. No *way*.

"You know . . . ," she says thoughtfully. "I did."

"Wait, seriously?"

She nods, barely. It's . . . wistful. But I can't imagine my parents' lives before each other. Their love is mythic—a story repeated to me as often as fairy tales. How my dad was working as a chaplain at the hospital where my mom worked. Their first cup of coffee in the cafeteria that she says felt as romantic as being in a Parisian café. I certainly can't imagine her in a framed photo smiling in her wedding dress next to some other man.

"What was his name?"

"Oh, goodness, that hardly matters." She waves this off. "The point is that I thought he was it for me in my younger years. But I changed. Things happened in my life that made me different. They made both of us different. And we both eventually landed where we were meant to be.

"But you know," she continues, "at the time it was ending, I was a disaster. He was such a wonderful guy, and I thought . . . if I can't make this work, I won't be able to with anyone. But God had your dad waiting for me. I just didn't know it then." She turns to face me, her intent gaze full of certainty. "If it's not Lukas, Bird, then it's someone more suited for you. If you want partnership, you'll find it. And in the meantime, you're perfect all on your own."

I take a sip of my tea to hide the tears I'm blinking back. This is what I can't do without. She always knows what to say. She always uncovers my most specific fears and eases them, like salve to a burn. Not fixed. Just soothed. "Thanks, Mom. I hope you're right."

"Oh, sweetheart," she says, almost sympathetically. "I'm always right. Ask your father."

After lights-out, I retreat to the rec room for my evening piano practice. But even my usual favorites can't loosen my worries. I realized on my walk home from Holyoke: I'm seeing my mom once a week. When I'm at college, it'll be even less. That's not nearly enough, and I dread it. And yet, all I want in the entire world is for her to still be here, healthy—even if we're apart geographically.

For a moment, I sullenly decide that the summer before senior year of high school must be the absolute worst time for your mom to get sick. But no. They're all awful, in ways I probably can't even imagine yet.

I'm dancing my fingers through a complicated sonata, still fretting, when I sense movement behind me.

I twist around on the bench to find Anna, who is nearly tiptoeing in hesitancy.

"Hey," she says. "Sorry to bother you. How was your morning off?"

"Pretty good."

"Did you go into town?"

"Nah, just across the lake." I don't necessarily want everyone to know my parents are so close. It's this weird impulse to keep my worlds separate. So I can be Lucy the Daughter and Hansson the Counselor without blurring anything.

"Nice. I love hiking. So, um. Listen. Do you have a second?"

"Sure." I'm about to get up, but she sits right on the piano bench beside me. I scoot over to make room for her.

She inhales, then lets her breath out slowly, calming herself. Preparing.

"Anna? Everything okay?" My pulse beats out an arpeggio—quick taps up and down, up and down.

"D'Souza told me about a conversation you guys had." Anna places her hands in her lap and looks at me head-on. "Where she mentioned that I'm trans."

"Oh," I say. "Yeah. And I'm really sorry if you didn't want me to know. But it's totally okay with me."

She tilts away, almost imperceptibly. "Oh. It's *okay* with you?"

I've never heard her use sarcasm like that, quick and biting. Heat crawls up my neck. Crap, am I messing this up? "I mean, I thought maybe you didn't tell me because my dad's a pastor. But, like, my friend Mallory is bisexual."

Her eyes are narrowed now, the way you watch anything you don't entirely trust.

"Oh, gosh. I don't know why I said that! I'm sorry! I know that's totally different. It's just, sometimes people think that about me because of the church stuff, but that's not what we're about, and, and . . ." Tears fill my eyes because apparently they just live there now. I'm so frustrated with myself and the not-knowing and the idea of hurting this girl who has been good and steady since the first day.

When Anna looks up, her eyes are watery too, and widening with surprise. "Why are *you* crying?"

"Because I don't want to mess this up! I feel like I'm messing it up! You've been such a good friend to me, but I don't know how to do this."

"Be friends with me?"

"No!" Wait, is there a different way I need to be friends with her, in light of this information? "Just . . . this conversation. Say the right thing. That's all. I—"

"Okay," she says. "Let's start over. I'm a trans girl. That's part of me, and my history."

"Okay." I don't even know what questions to ask—or maybe I'm not supposed to ask questions? "And, just so you know, you can tell me anything you want to about it or nothing at all. I don't want to be nosy, but, like, of course I'm interested in your life."

I can tell she's being patient with me, and I'm bobbing around in water wings like a fool. "Do you want me to tell you about it?"

"Well . . . yeah, if you don't mind. I mean, I like knowing things about you."

"Okay. The extremely abridged version: I started transitioning four years ago. My family has always been relatively cool about it. They thought I was a boy and probably gay, but . . . nope. School was whatever. Pretty miserable, sometimes. Part of it was my anxiety and depression stuff, but shit like debates about me being on the soccer team didn't help my health. Um, what else? Camp was almost always safe and good. And, here I am!" She shakes her head, smiling a little. "That's making it seem a lot simpler than it is, but there you go."

"So, did I—" I shut my mouth, lopping off yet another sentence. "Never mind. Sorry."

"You can ask. Not all trans folks want to spend their time educating. But I mean, hello." She gestures around us. "Kids' camp. If I weren't okay with questions sometimes, I probably couldn't be here."

"No, no questions. I just wanted to apologize if anything I said to those campers yesterday was wrong. Thank you for talking to me. You didn't have to."

"Oh, I know." She smiles gently—reminding me that of course it's her business. "But Mohan and Keely and Jones have been with me for everything. I didn't want you to be confused if one of us referenced it. Although I guess we don't talk about it much anymore."

This big, personal thing . . . and she talks to me because she doesn't want me to feel left out. And stranger still, I'm not even surprised. Anna has shown me exactly who she is from the moment she burst into my cabin two weeks ago.

"I think I would have left Daybreak after my first day," I confess. "If it weren't for you, I think I would have bailed. So, thank you."

"You're welcome." I like that she says this simply, sincerely. She doesn't try to downplay her own goodness. "Well, whew! We're okay, right? Mohan thought you were going to *freak*."

"What! Why?" Maybe that's not an unreasonable assumption, but I still feel insulted.

"He's just protective."

"Yeah. I like that about him. About all of you," I tell Anna, smiling a little. "So, speaking of which, do you have any good crushes at home? Or here?" I admit, I ask this because of the way Tambe is with her. He's always funny, but when he gets a laugh from Anna? His grin is triumphant.

"How is that *speaking of which*?" she screeches, her cheeks flushing.

I hold my hands up innocently. "Okay, okay. Maybe it's not. I retract the question."

"Good," she says, scolding. "Because I just told you a big thing. You owe me."

"Well, unfortunately for both of us, my life is pretty boring."

"Please don't take this the wrong way." She places one hand on my arm. "But you got *paused*. That is shitastic. But pretty interesting."

We stay seated on the piano bench as I try to explain Lukas Pratt. But I can't capture what a *presence* he is—more mature than other guys our age. When he speaks in class, it's well-thought-out and logical; everyone takes his opinion seriously. He's handsome in a way that belongs at an all-boys school, one with blue oxford uniform shirts and a rowing team.

"So, what does breaking up for the summer accomplish, according to him?" Anna asks.

I open my mouth to say that Lukas is just cautious. I mean, *all* his running gear has strips of reflective material for visibility. But is breaking up with me really cautious? Or just full of doubt? Especially after my conversation with my mom, I'm lost in the fog of it all. "I . . . don't know. I thought I did, but I don't."

"Hmm. To see if you miss each other? *Do* you miss him?"

"Yes?" I'm just not sure if I miss him in a serious boyfriend way or in the way that I miss my bedroom at home. That is: It's mine, and it's familiar, and I like it. But I'm also fine without it.

"*That* was convincing," Anna says with a laugh. "Okay, okay. I am pleased with your gossip offering, so I *suppose* I will tell you about my megacrush from school. Liam. Liam Teller."

"Liam," I say, testing it out. "That's kind of a sexy name."

"Right?"

My sheet music sits there unturned as we stay up too late, talking about boys and heartache and what we hope to find somewhere in between.

CHAPTER THIRTEEN

ON MONDAY MORNING, I PLANT MY FEET ON THE END OF THE
pier and survey the still-dim sky. I like swimming in the earliest morning light. Stroke after stroke after stroke—arms
cycling, feet kicking. I do a clean freestyle until I'm midlake
and panting. And somehow, on the return lap, I find myself
thanking God for Anna. The quick prayer is as second-nature
as my backstroke. It would be unremarkable, as prayers go—
except that I've been too angry with God to thank Him for
anything in weeks. Maybe it's a start.

Our class after morning chores is supposed to be with
Bryan, but he isn't in the mess hall. Garcia pulls the counselors aside. "Bryan's tied up, so I'm gonna give out the art
prompts. Can you space out and draw with them? And try to
facilitate conversation about what they're drawing?"

On long stretches of butcher paper, we draw our favorite
animals first. It's a neutral enough topic, and we talk about

trips to the zoo and family pets. Thuy doesn't say anything, but she does draw a cat with a bushy tail.

"A group of dolphins is called a 'pod,'" Sofia announces. She's outlined a pod, arcing above the waves.

"Here." Payton hands her a crayon. "It's called 'stone.' A good dolphin color."

"Payton has all the crayon colors memorized," Sofia tells me.

"Is that right?"

Payton nods. "But my *favorite* favorite is cerulean."

She pronounces it "kuh-ROO-lee-un" instead of "suh-ROO-lee-un." I don't have the heart to correct her.

"I like your orange dog." Nadia taps her finger near the fox I'm trying to draw.

I lean against my hand to hide my smile. "Thanks."

Next we draw "Happy": more pets, birthday parties, and stick figures holding hands. I gnaw on my lip. What makes me happy, really? Swimming makes me feel . . . peaceful. Disciplined. And with piano, I *express* my emotion. It doesn't exactly *make* me happy.

I did feel really happy at prom in April. Before everything fell apart. Though it's impossible to capture the crystal detailing, I sketch my dress with a beige crayon. I try to remember how much I loved it before it became forever tied to the worst news of my life. I try to capture my elegant red lip, my hair swept to one side.

Is that the last time I was really, truly happy?

Nadia taps her finger near my drawing. "Is that you as a princess?"

"Not quite. Me at prom."

"Did you go with a boy?" Payton asks.

"Yes," I admit.

"Is he your boyfriend?"

I swallow. Honesty. Honesty. "He was."

"Oh." Payton and Sofia exchange an awkward *oops* look. "Sorry."

"It's okay."

The next prompt is "Sad."

Sad: A mammogram marred by cancer, white webbing over healthy tissue. The idea of my dad and me alone at the kitchen table. An empty seat beside my dad as I walk across the stage in my cap and gown.

Most of the campers seem to be drawing faces with tears bursting out. Nadia is working on flowers beneath a gravestone. Thuy drew a door, a long rectangle with a yellow doorknob.

Sad: Playing the piano at my mother's funeral because it's what she would want. "It Is Well with My Soul," her favorite. How it would break me. Walking home afterward to our silent house. No singing in the kitchen.

Sad: never hearing her voice again.

Sad: *never*.

"I'm gonna run to the bathroom," I say quietly, stepping back from the bench.

I get to the hallway before Simmons catches up, touching my arm. "Hey."

"Hey." I can't meet her eyes.

"You okay?"

I wipe my cheek. Of course it'd be her to catch me being weak again. "Fine."

"Why don't you take a few minutes? Kick back in the Bunker."

"No, I'm okay."

"Lucy." She steps in front of me so I have to look at her. I think it's the first time she's said my first name. I wasn't even sure if she knew it. "We've all been there. That's kind of the point of this camp."

I push a curl away from my face, unsure of what to say. That I miss my mom. That every muscle in my body is trying to push me to Holyoke, to prove that she's real and *here*. That a therapy activity designed for third graders is crushing *me*, an almost-legal adult.

Simmons glances at her watch, which is sporty and mint green. "We've only got a few minutes left here. Just meet us on the Great Lawn in a bit."

By the look on her face, I can tell Simmons is not going to entertain any more protests. "Okay. I will. Thanks."

I'm all set to have a little cry, but when I open the Bunker door, it's already occupied. Jones is on the couch, clutching a bouquet of Red Vines.

"Hey."

"Hey." He lifts the stalks of candy, looking sheepish. "Caught me red-handed. I needed a sugar rush. And a minute alone."

"Oh. No prob." I step back. "I'll just—"

"No! I meant a minute alone from fourth graders. Ha."

My sigh of relief is probably audible. I open the fridge just to look busy. And casual. See? I'm just looking for a soda. You can just be cute on the couch; I'm not even noticing. "What do you guys have this hour?"

"Bocce and beanbag toss."

"That's where we're headed next."

"Rough day?" He motions to the seat beside him on the couch. I wouldn't have encroached on his space, but now it'd be weird if I sat at the table instead.

So I sit with my back against the couch's armrest, far away but facing him. "Not really. Just needed a breather."

"It's good that you took one. That's the key to making it here."

"Breathing?"

"Kind of. You gotta take care of yourself first or you can't take care of the campers. It's the whole 'In the event of an emergency, put on your own air mask before you help others' thing. What? What's so funny?"

"That I have asthma. It's just . . . a good metaphor for my life. And actually, Simmons kind of made me step away."

"Ha." He nods knowingly. "She doesn't back down easy. Best and worst thing about her."

"You guys go to school together too, right?"

"Yeah. My mom got Keely connected with Daybreak back in the day."

He offers me a Red Vine, which I accept. It reminds me of the movie theater. A large popcorn and Coke with my mom. No matter how many times we do that, the routine feels decadent.

"All right. Back into the battlefield for me," he says.

"Yeah, I'd better get back too."

He holds out a hand to pull me up from the couch. His hand is cool and smooth, and I don't know why I even register that.

"So, I've never played bocce," I tell him on our way out. "Any tips?"

"You've never played bocce?" He turns, incredulous. "I thought it was a white people thing. Don't you all play while you drink gin? And wear polo shirts?"

It takes me a second to realize he's teasing me. I do my best attempt at a smirk, shrugging. "Must just be the rich ones."

"Ha. Okay, my trick is: point your feet where you want the ball to go."

I nod slowly, understanding. "Nice. I'm gonna do that."

"You're going to try to beat the little third graders?"

As we walk outside, I turn to give him a faux-withering look. "Well, I'm sure not going to *let* them win."

This delights Jones, but when he glances over my shoulder, his grin drops. We're at the top of the porch, and I follow his gaze to the car at the end of the drive.

Rhea's watching as a kid with red hair climbs into a waiting beige sedan. It's old, with a sagging exhaust pipe. I have no idea who the kid is—the only redheaded camper we have that age is JJ. Did he get kicked out of Daybreak? No way. No lost causes, not at this camp.

"Fuck," Jones whispers, before clattering down the stairs. The car door shuts, and he's sprinting toward it. "No. Wait! No!"

I'm right behind him, spurred by the horrible realization that it *is* JJ. Leaving. Jones almost gets there before the car pulls away, and I can tell he means to chase after it. But Rhea catches his arm in a tight grip. He won't pull against her.

"Come ON!" he yells at the receding taillights. "Are you fucking kidding me?"

"Henry . . ." I'm close enough now to hear Rhea's quiet voice, full of pain. "There was nothing we could do. She got paroled and went through legal channels to get him."

"But she's a neglectful junkie who—"

"I know, baby," Rhea says, gently pulling his arm toward the meeting hall. "But she's his mother. Not here, okay? Come on inside."

I'm standing back, and I don't mean to get involved in something so personal. But Rhea motions me forward, insistent, so I follow them into the meeting hall. In the daytime, the space is beautiful in the way of old things: scarred pine floors, and dust dancing in windowpane light.

Jones faces Rhea just a few feet inside the door. "You know she's only gonna hold down a job for a few months before she starts using again. How many times are they gonna let her *do* this? How is this shit even legal?"

"I don't know," Rhea says. "But Bryan was on the phone with JJ's aunt and the courts all morning. We can't touch this one."

"Do you have any idea how much shit that kid has seen? She's left him at home for days without enough food! He told me that—"

"I hate this too." She settles her hands on his heaving shoulders. "We tried, and we'll keep trying for him the second she messes up. I'm angry too, kid. And Bryan . . . well, he's locked himself in his office with a bottle of whiskey he thinks I don't know about."

Jones sighs, coming down from his tirade. He looks so, so tired. Defeated.

"Go check on my son for me, will you?" Rhea asks.

He heads toward the door obediently, his broad shoulders slumped.

"Goddammit," Jones whispers to himself, shaking his head. Then he slams his palm against the wall as he exits, one last outburst in private.

The pendants of faith rattle on their nails, and I cringe, waiting to hear metal clank against the floor. But they all stay balanced, if precariously.

"It's hard to lose one," Rhea says after a moment. It's a

quiet defense of Jones's explosion and language, but I don't need to hear it. I know where his heart is.

I nod, hoping she senses that there is no judgment in me. Not for Jones or for Bryan or even JJ's mom. Just sadness. Sadness and blistering hope for better. "I'm so sorry."

When she smiles, it's so aggrieved that I wish she didn't even attempt it. "I do try to tell myself it's good that JJ's mother loves him. She wants him with her. But it's a real bad situation."

With a sigh, she steps toward the door, looking back at me. "Could you keep this to yourself for now? I'll break it to the campers at dinner."

"Of course." She seems to be waiting for me to come along, but I don't move. "I think I'll stay here for a few minutes."

"Thank you, Lucy," she says, and I have the strongest sense that she knows I'm staying to pray for JJ and his mom.

I'm left alone with the quiet and the aftermath. The symbols are still askew—crooked on their nails like a collective raised eyebrow at whatever just happened.

Some things are more important than the cold shoulder I've been turning toward God.

So I start working my way down the line, fixing the delicate cross and the Star of David. These are people's precious symbols, their holy tokens. And I don't even know all their names. It's never occurred to me to be interested.

Shame gusts into me, a window opened.

As I straighten the rest of the lineup, I pray for JJ and his aunt who cares for him, for his mom and her disease. I pray he knows he is loved. I pray for Rhea and Bryan and Jones, for peace and strength. Mostly, I pray they know that their love matters in this place. That it moves through the trees like spreading warmth, cocooning the campers inside.

I stand before the wall of faith, a line of talismans representing so much more.

And I say a final last prayer, this one in gratitude that there are people in the world who will protect kids with a fire that makes them sprint after cars, fight systems, curse with rage.

It's enough to make you believe.

Maybe not in symbols; maybe not in gods. But certainly in people.

During afternoon rest time, I stop by Miss Suzette's. I haven't seen Jones anywhere, and I can't get it out of my mind: the look on his face as that car sped off.

"Hey, sugar," Miss Suzette says, glancing up from bandaging a sixth grader's arm.

"Hey. Jones isn't here, is he? A few campers have asked me where he is."

"Not here. But I'm gonna guess he's in the gym. You'll probably want this." She reaches for a first aid kit, nylon-sided and orange. When I frown, she says, "That ridiculous child never bothers to wrap and glove his hands when he's worked up. Stubborn as gravity. You're gonna find him with a punching bag and broken skin on his knuckles, guaranteed."

She's right. I enter the gym quietly. In the back corner, there's the worn-out punching bag and a worn-out counselor.

His glasses are off, and he's in a plain white undershirt—his usual panache stripped away. His eyes focus on their mark, and his fist plows forward. *Thwap, thwap*—the sound of skin against the heavy, swaying bag.

If Jones hears me, he doesn't let on. I hang back, doubting that he'd even want me here.

One balled fist protects his left jaw as the other snaps out. Then the other—*smack, smack*—until he finally stills.

It's the first time he hasn't smiled at the sight of me. He wipes his forehead on his shirt sleeve. "Hey."

"Hey." Indeed, he has at least two visibly split knuckles.

"Miss Suzette?" He gestures at the first aid kit in my hand. When I nod, he hangs his head. "Damn. She knows me too well. What'd she call me?"

"What? Nothing."

"Oh, c'mon."

I step toward him. "Well, the phrase 'that ridiculous child' may have been used."

"There it is."

He sits on the nearby windowsill and slides his glasses back on. It's a Superman to Clark Kent transformation—clearly the same guy. But Clark Kent, you want to care for.

Superman is there to protect you. My hesitation dissipates, and I sit beside him, unzipping the first aid kit.

"I can do it," he says.

"My mom's a nurse."

"I know, but—" He cuts himself off, losing the will to argue. I'm already taking his broad hand in mine and shaking out an antiseptic towelette. He doesn't flinch as I wipe the cuts clean, though it leaves them looking raw. I pad the white medical tape with a bit of gauze and wrap it carefully around the first knuckle.

"When did you learn how to box?"

"Started at eleven." He snorts, shaking his head. "I was really confused and angry, so my parents put me in boxing class."

"That was smart of them, to give you an outlet."

"Yeah, well. They kind of had to." With his free hand, he gestures toward himself. "I'm a black guy, Lucy. It's different for us."

Heavens, I didn't even think about that. I imagine this boy, with his broad smile and good heart, hunched down and scowling in a middle school classroom. Acting out, pushing back. Would teachers have seen past to the core of him, to his sweetness and pain? Would anyone have?

As I start on the next finger, he sighs. "My older sister killed herself when I was ten. I found her. That's my checked bag."

My lungs collapse inside me, breath choked in my throat.

I look up at him, but he's staring down at his hands. "Oh, God," I say.

"Yeah. It's okay. I mean, it's not okay. But I deal with it now. Daybreak saved my whole life, that's for sure."

"I'm so sorry." The words land terribly thin, but they're all I can manage. I try to focus on wrapping the tape. "I'm so, so sorry, Henry."

His name just comes out. Maybe because I heard Rhea say it; maybe because, right now, I don't see all-star counselor Jones, charisma radiating off him like light. I see a boy named Henry, tender souled and tougher than I guessed.

"It was a long time ago. I just wanted you to know why all this messes with me." He shakes his head. "JJ's like me at that age, so much caged up. I thought I could . . . I don't know. Change it for him."

"But don't you think he knows that? And don't you think that counts for something?" When Jones only looks at me, I keep babbling. "Now he has this mental image of a cool older guy who can break up a fight, but who gets that you need to cry and let it out. He knows there are people who will be on his side and see past his anger. And no, maybe it won't change everything. But it sure isn't nothing."

I present his finished hands to him, and he flexes his fingers—soft white tape around four of his knuckles.

"Thank you, Lucy," he says quietly.

"Anytime. Well, not *any* time. If you wake me up from my precious, hard-won sleep, I will come at you with my own fists."

It's enough to make him smile. "I'll wear gloves next time. Though you make a great nurse."

"Yeah?" It's nice to hear, even as I think of my mom patching me up—cartoon Band-Aids and Neosporin, kisses to make it better—and it aches to my core. "Thanks."

I should go to sleep at lights-out, but the piano beckons me. I'll give myself a half hour of alone time with the keys and call it a night.

But when I get to the rec room, Jones is on the couch with a paperback in his busted hands.

"Oh, hey. Sorry, I didn't realize you were in here. I'll just . . ."

He sits up. "No, I . . . Uh, Anna told me you practice in here some nights. Would it bother you if I stay?"

"Oh. No. If you don't mind a little plunking."

"Not a bit."

And plunk I do, revisiting a Debussy that I could never get the hang of. I'm starting to smooth it out when I glance back at Jones.

He's fast asleep, cheek smooshed against taped hands. Do all guys look like little boys when they sleep? As a counselor, he's so capable—so together. But today, I can see him as the ten-year-old he was once, mourning his sister at a camp away from home.

I sit on the coffee table, considering. I mean, I can't leave him, right? I have to wake him up.

"Hey," I whisper, nudging his arm. *"Pssst."*

"Hey." He blinks hard a few times. "Sorry. Wow. That was so good . . . it lulled me away. Like singing lullabies to a baby."

"Guess the book wasn't a page-turner."

"It's pretty solid, actually." He turns it so I can see the cover, which features Einstein and his wild hair. "I'm a sucker for biographies. Rhea always pulls them from donation boxes for me."

"What's your favorite? Like . . . say I've never read a biography. Which one would you—"

"Oh my God. Have you never read a biography? "

I glance around guiltily. "Well, better get to bed."

When I start to get up, he tugs me back down. "No, wait! I have so many recommendations. Most of the founding fathers, Henrietta Lacks, Steve Jobs—obviously."

The next night, he's already on the couch when I show up.

"Hey," he says.

"Hey," I reply.

Somehow, I wind up teaching him the melody line of "Heart and Soul." He picks it up quickly for someone who's never played piano.

"This is maddening," I tell him with a laugh. "You're such a fast learner!"

"Well, you're good at explaining it. Plus, I can already read music. But also . . ." He finds a half-step interval and plays it, a trill. He sounds out the first measure of *Für Elise*—slowly, and in the wrong key. Still. "I am Beethoven."

The night after, he brings his trumpet.

"You have to try it," he insists, holding it out to me.

"I've never even *touched* a brass instrument." But I take it from him, cool metal smooth beneath my fingers.

"Well, now you have! And I didn't say you had to be *good*. Just try it."

"Are you sure?" I hold the silver mouthpiece near my lips. It feels strangely intimate, to use another musician's instrument. "You don't mind my germs?"

Oh, *cute*, self. Honestly.

"We're camp counselors, Luce. I think we've got all the same germs at this point." I glance down, surprised that he'd call me that. It's nice, the familiarity. "Okay, so you want to take a big breath, from deep down, and buzz your lips."

When I try this, the trumpet makes no sound. "I'm a prodigy! Don't be jealous."

"Lips tighter." He demonstrates, away from the mouthpiece. I attempt to do the same, my lips vibrating. We're sitting across from each other—him on the edge of the coffee table, me on the couch—basically just making middle-school fart noises. It hits us both at the same time, and we nearly fall over laughing.

By week's end, I get some sounds out. And not just laughter.

***

On Friday night, Jones holds the bottle in one hand. He's sitting on a fallen log, elbows propped on his knees. Anna leans against his leg from her spot on the red tartan blanket. I wish I could see Jones's eyes, but his gaze is focused, glasses reflecting the bonfire.

"Low." There is no laughter in his voice. "JJ's bio mom pulling him out of camp."

We add murmurs of agreement and grunts of anger as he takes a long swig. His heavy sigh carries across the circle, over the snapping flames.

"High." He lifts the bottle and his eyes to me. It's not the grin that crosses his mouth but something quieter— unspoken and shared. "Lucy."

CHAPTER FOURTEEN

On Monday, instead of a morning chore, the 3A girls congregate around the bags of clean, folded laundry in our cabin.

"Once you're in sixth grade, you do your own laundry," Nadia informs the other girls. All three of us counselors are gently pulling out stacks, trying not to mess them up. "Jones told me. There's a launder-mat in town, and you get to go, and while it's washing your clothes, you hang out at the park or go look in the shops."

Simmons and I exchange glances, too stricken with her cute enthusiasm to tell her it's "Laundromat."

"Okay," Simmons says. "We'll dole everything out. Make a nice stack in front of you, and when we're done, you'll put everything away neatly on your shelf. Anything without a label, we'll figure out at the end."

We pass out polka-dot dresses, thin-striped cotton leggings, soft shorts, and T-shirts with every cartoon character under the sun. It's one thing to see the girls every day, but another to see all their clothes at once. The designs are colorful, patterned, joyous. I tend to like simple outfits, but there's something fun about childhood clothes that I miss.

"Sofia," Simmons says, handing over a loose denim dress with a string dangling. She pulls it back to examine the sagging hem. "Uh-oh."

"It was like that," Sofia says. "It's not the launder-mat's fault."

"That's okay." Simmons leans into her, winking. "I can fix it."

Sofia perks up. "You can?"

"Yep. With needle and thread. You can even watch me do it later."

I examine the label on a pair of denim shorts with a white star pattern: *T. Anderson*.

"Thuy again," I say, reaching out to hand them over. She accepts them without a word or smile, so I keep hunting for clues. All her clothes seem particularly nice—quality fabrics still bright in color.

"Those are cool shorts," I say. "Did you pick them out?"

She nods her head. Simmons shoots me a sympathetic look, because she's been trying too. Thuy does talk—a *yes, please* or *no, thank you*. She has a good appetite and seems to brighten up during crafts and cooking class. Sometimes she starts getting really into games; she loved hula-hooping. But it's like she catches herself, and then she returns to a neutral facial expression.

On our way to lunch, Simmons sidles up to me. "It was a good try, earlier."

She nods toward Thuy, who is walking ahead of us and listening to Brooklyn and Maya chatter. Saying nothing. "Do you think it's time?"

We've been debating when we'll ask Rhea for help. Rhea knows most campers' stories, as they're often referred by her network of psychiatrist friends. There's doctor-patient confidentiality, of course, but a lot of the parents and guardians disclose what's going on so we can help. Rhea prefers that we let the kids tell us in their own time, but I'm about ready to cave.

Simmons sighs, blowing a tight curl off her forehead. "Let's give it till the end of the week. I want to read them a special story and see if it helps at all."

"A special story?"

"Yeah, about a fox and a wolf. It can help with—"

"'Posy and the Dreaming Tree'?" The only story I know with both a fox and a wolf.

She turns to me fully. "Yeah! How'd you know that?"

"It was one of my favorite fables when I was little."

Her frown is not displeasure, just genuine confusion. "Huh. I thought it was only a Daybreak thing."

"Nope." My mom told me the story some nights before she left for an overnight shift at the hospital. She'd add new details here and there, mixing it up for me. I even begged for fox pajamas one year, which Santa delivered on.

"Huh." Simmons tilts her head thoughtfully. "So you've seen our dreaming tree?"

In the story, Posy finds a tree that grows stars instead of leaves. She lies beneath it and dreams of what she wants for her life. And the tree hears her. Or so I always believed. "You have a . . . dreaming tree?"

"Yeah. Kind of. Around the back of the lodge, near the shed."

"Seriously?" She nods, looking a little pleased at my awe.

When Thuy sits across from me at lunch, I take another shot. I talk about my mom and dad a little bit, trying to engage the others. Finally, I look right at her. "Thuy, who do you live with at home?"

"Mommy Sheila and Daddy Pete." She doesn't look up from her potato salad.

Hmm. It's a clue, anyway. I think back to her meticulously clean bunk. She has a stuffed animal—a cat, maybe? "Do you have any pets?"

At this, she makes eye contact. "Bernadette. She's a kitty."

"Cool." I try not to sound too excited. "Like the one in your bunk?"

"Yes. With long fur. But Bernadette is gray, not white."

"She sounds beautiful."

"Yep. And she likes me best." Even spearing the potatoes has become more animated. "I'm going to take her with me if I have to leave."

"Why would you have to leave?" I ask, shocked. Stupid, Luce. Stupid. Overeager.

She looks at me as if I am completely daft. "Because you always have to."

Bingo. I open my mouth to say *Not always*, but I don't know if that's true for her. It's too late, though. Her gaze is downward. I blew it.

But it sounds like Thuy is—or maybe was—a foster kid, like my mom was. Last year, I went to get ice cream with the swim team after practice and forgot to tell my mom, who I thought wouldn't be home till later. I didn't hear my phone as she called repeatedly. In one of the few times I've see my mother furious, she yelled, "Do you have any idea what my life was like at your age? The absolute least you could do is pick up your phone."

Of course, at the time, I yelled back that this was the first time I'd *ever* messed up. But later, lying in bed and feeling mucked over with guilt, I realized I *didn't* know what her life was like at my age. All I know is the timeline: that she moved in with foster parents right before high school, and they adopted her some time after that. When I asked my dad for details, he said, "Oh, Bird. That's her story to tell."

I've figured, since then, that the adoption took a long time. I can't imagine the court dates, the lawyers, the feeling that you have to be worthy enough for a family. That's something no kid should ever have to worry about.

When our girls are settled in afternoon class, I duck into

the Bunker for coffee. Anna sits at the table, reviewing something in a binder and eating Red Vines.

"Hey," she says as I fill a mug. "I thought you were a tea drinker."

"Desperate, is what I am." I dump the nearby glass canister fully upside down. Sugar streams like white glitter for a solid five seconds before I consider the coffee drinkable.

I sink onto the couch and decide I'm giving myself five minutes. Keely's right behind me with the same caffeine goals.

She turns to me. "Did you get anything from Thuy at lunch? I got nothin'."

Sad as it is, our concern about Thuy has been good bonding for us, as we exchange tactics and clues.

"I did, actually." I'm mad at myself all over again, relaying the conversation. "So . . . I think . . . foster care? Or maybe recently adopted?"

She jerks her head back, eyes blazing. "No. Don't make that face."

"Keely," Anna says quietly. A warning.

I'm just as defensive as she is, scowling. "What face?"

"That 'broken family' pity face. Not everyone is lucky enough to have both biological parents around."

So now even my facial expressions aren't right? I can't cry or even *emote*?

"My mom," I say evenly, "was adopted by her foster parents. If I made that face, it's because getting to that point wasn't easy."

"Oh." Her posture relaxes, and she takes a long sip of coffee. "Sorry."

You'd think, based on her tone, that I pried the apology out of her mouth with my bare hands. "It's fine."

"I'll talk to Thuy." She moves to the door, and Anna's eyes follow her, disapproving.

"Tell her if you want." Keely tosses this comment aside without even glancing over. "I don't give a shit."

After the door bangs shut, Anna takes a deep breath. "Sorry. She, um. Well, Keely's mom died not long after Kiana was born. Leukemia."

"Oh, no." The bonfire comes back to me. "Yeah. I remember her saying her mom wasn't around. I didn't know that she . . ."

Anna nods. "It's just complicated because Keely's step-mom is the only mom her sister has ever known. But for Keely? That's not her mom."

I have not considered, until this precise, world-tilting moment, that my dad would ever remarry if God forbid— God, please, forbid—my mom died. I'd want him to be happy. Of course I would. But I can't imagine seeing him with another woman, making a family with her. "Is her step-mom cool, at least?"

"For sure. And Keely likes her. But she's always been con-vinced that Tracy—her stepmom—got stuck with her. That Tracy fell for her dad and toddler Kiana. And middle-school Keely was just part of the deal."

"But . . ." But Keely is so capable, so quick on her feet and good with kids. She's smart and skilled and she shows up. It's magnetic. Anyone would want her as their stepdaughter.

"I know," Anna says, reading my mind. "But you can't talk someone into feeling like they belong."

"Wow." That's . . . a lot.

"Like I said," Anna says, a bit sadly, "some of our checked bags are no joke."

I don't catch up to Keely until afternoon rest time. We're waiting near each other as the girls file into the cabin.

She meets my eyes. "Look, I really am sorry about before."

"I know. But you were right." I've been so angry—at God and the universe and cancer—that I think it's been hard to touch gratitude. That my mom can get treatment, that we have a support system, that I was born into such love. "I am lucky."

Keely nods and turns to walk off, but I call out, "Hey, Keely?"

I don't know if I've ever said her first name out loud. In the cabin, on the clock, I tend to think of her as Simmons.

"Yeah?"

I hesitate, wondering if I'll make things weirder. "You're really good at what you do."

I didn't quite get her approach at first, that my needs—and hers—are secondary to our campers'. Not unimportant, not irrelevant. Just second priority. Because we're in charge of kids half our age who have already seen real hardship.

Keely peers at me, as if waiting for something more. When I simply smile, she says, "I know. But thank you."

That night, Keely holds a copy of "Posy and the Dreaming Tree" in a binder, with illustrations hand-drawn by a camper years ago. The pages are yellowed, but it's surprisingly good art—defined fox fur, beautiful forest scenes, the scary bared teeth of a wolf.

I lie back on my bed while the girls gather around Keely, and I drift off to the familiar story.

Once there was a little fox named Posy who loved her family. Their life in the woods was simple but happy. They ate, frolicked in the snow, and curled up in their cozy den until their red fur felt warm. Posy and her parents cooked meals, picked flowers, and told stories before bed. As Posy drifted off each night, she felt safe and loved.

"Yes?" Keely says, glancing up at Sofia's raised hand.

"A group of foxes is called a 'skulk.' And a girl fox is a 'vixen'!"

"Awesome," Keely says.

But one day, when Posy returned home from a walk in the forest, her parents were nowhere to be found. She waited and waited, until a neighboring hedgehog told her, sniffling, that there had been an accident. Her parents were gone—never to return.

Before long, Posy's aunt arrived from a nearby forest to take her in. With the aunt was her husband, an uncle that Posy had never met—and the largest fox she'd ever seen. He had the pointy ears, the bushy tail, and the russet fur, but he was more than twice the size of Posy's father.

Posy moved into her new den in June, and the summer sun beat down on the forest. Foxes like the snow, so Posy's uncle was cranky from the heat. Posy made herself as small and quiet as possible, to not be in anyone's way. She missed her parents terribly. At night, Posy recited a story her mother used to tell her. It was about a dreaming tree, which sprouted stars instead of leaves. Every moment she could get away, Posy strolled through the forest in search of such a tree.

Winter never came. The heat only increased, and Posy thought she might suffocate in the den with her silent aunt and the uncle who always seemed ready to burst with anger.

It wasn't until late one night, in the third year of summer, that Posy realized the truth. Her uncle came home, and, enraged that Posy hadn't finished cleaning the den, whispered, "You should know better."

He sank his teeth into her arm.

This was no fox. He was a wolf in disguise. And it hurt, though Posy didn't scream. When he saw the fear in Posy's eyes, he whispered, "You brought this on yourself."

In the morning, he was so kind to Posy. He brought her wild-flowers and scones with clotted cream. But outside, the sun melted the world.

It went on like this for years. Posy tried her best, and the wolf bit her every once in a while, but he was always so nice after. Until one day, her teacher, Ms. Bunny, hopped over to Posy after class.

"That mark looks like it hurt," she said softly. "How did you get it?"

Posy knew better than to tell about the wolf. He'd hurt her aunt! She would have no one left. She opened her mouth to give the usual line: that she'd tripped and run into a tree branch.

"Posy," Ms. Bunny said, "I can help you if you tell me."

"My uncle bit me," Posy said. "He's a wolf."

In the months that followed, Posy found it in herself to repeat the simple truth: He bites me. He's a wolf. The details were hard to talk about, but she tried her best.

This time, Posy was taken in by a pair of otters. They said she didn't have to call them Mom and Dad unless she wanted to someday. They worked hard, held hands as they slept in the water, and always had time to play. Posy learned to swim, which she loved best of all.

And in the woods, Posy found it. The dreaming tree. It wasn't what she'd expected—the stars weren't silver. But the leaves were shaped in five points and, in the afternoon light, they glowed above her, yellow as they fell. Beneath that tree, Posy imagined what her life could be.

"A group of otters is called a 'romp'!" Sofia cries out. "Or a raft of otters."

"That's a good one," Keely agrees. "Let's finish the book, okay?"

Under that dreaming tree, she saw herself as a grown-up fox someday. She would go to school. She would help people. She would love the otters more and more, and someday call them Mom and Dad. She would fall in love with someone kind. She would have a fox pup of her own. And someday in the future, when Posy curled around her baby, she would almost feel her own mother's arm around her shoulder. She would almost hear her heart and her pup's, beating: "Mama, Mama." She would almost believe that some things are bigger than time and space and death.

After all, there was once a fox named Posy, who loved her family old and new.

It is not the type of love that ends.

CHAPTER FIFTEEN

AT FRIDAY LUNCH, I REALIZE I HAVEN'T SEEN ANNA ALL DAY—NOT
even in passing.

I'm behind Simmons in the buffet line, and I nudge her.
"Have you seen Anna today?"

"She's staying in. Bad anxiety day."

"Oh, right." Anna's mentioned it, and I know she stops
into Miss Suzette's every day to take meds. But I've never
really seen the effects. "Did something happen?"

"Nope. It just pops up sometimes." Keely turns, considering me. "You should stop by, actually. She's in her room. She
may not want company, but sometimes she does."

"Yeah?"

I don't exactly know how to help someone with an anxiety disorder—or if I even can. But I know Anna would show
up for me. "Okay. I'll make us a plate of food and head over
there. That okay?"

Keely nods. "Yeah. I'll tell Garcia. She has to leave and teach volleyball to the seventh graders."

I've only been in Rhea's cabin one other time, when Anna invited me in to watch a movie after lights-out. Her room is small and on the first floor, and it is full of Anna things: a scuffed-up soccer ball in the corner next to her cleats, a tote bag full of yarn and knitting needles, photos of her family wearing cream-colored sweaters in a backyard.

The door is open, and she's bundled up in bed, gaze locked on her laptop. It's playing a movie or something— young bickering voices in the otherwise quiet room.

"Hey," I say, lingering in the doorway. "Can I come in?"

Her eyes flick up to me. "Sure."

"Sorry you're having a bad day. Can I do anything?"

A shrug, shoulders barely lifting above the bedding. The top blanket is one of hers, knitted in navy and white for her favorite soccer team. Or, as she and Mohan call it: football.

"Anna."

She looks up at me again but says nothing.

"Well, okay. But if you change your mind . . . I'd like to help. You'd do it for me."

This seems to land, and she considers my presence in front of her. "You can stay here for a little bit. If you want to. I might fall asleep, though. I took medicine that's supposed to help me relax enough to sleep."

"Not a problem. You hungry?" I hold out the plate, which is heavy with a turkey burger and sweet potato tots.

"No, thanks."

"More for moi." I pull her desk chair up to the bed and dig in. "You missed quite the breakfast bickering match this morning. There were tears."

"Jones told me. I'm actually *terrible* with confrontation. Poor Manda and Wren. Seventh grade is just a shitshow, top to bottom."

"Right? It's just like . . . a full year of acne and awkward body stuff. And the social cruelty—it's like kids are figuring out how to be truly mean that year."

This makes Anna smile a bit. "You're telling me."

"Oh . . . Lord." I try to imagine navigating junior high as a trans girl. How kids might be.

She laughs darkly at my expression. "Yeah, well. I survived."

"Well, anyway," I say. "If you feel better, do you still want to go into town tonight?"

"Yeah. Jones has that band practice to prep for their July Fourth set."

"Right. And I was thinking I could do your makeup."

"Oh, *really*?" At this, she sits up.

"Mm-hmm. I have some navy mascara that doesn't quite work on me but I think will be perfect with your coloring."

She sighs dreamily. "Excellent. I just need my body to stop gushing adrenaline into my bloodstream before then. Pray for me."

Her tone is flippant—joking. But I would pray for her. I will. I may not exactly be on speaking terms with God about my own life, but I still send up prayers for my parents and friends sometimes. I can't help it; it's like releasing the worries that clutter up my heart. Their names, my holy words, sent heavenward. Which reminds me.

"Anna?"

"Yeah."

"What's your last name? It's not . . . Anna, right?"

"No!" She almost laughs, which feels like a victory. "No one uses it because it's hard to say. 'Meero-suave.' Spelled M-i-r-o-s-l-a-w, though, so everyone says 'Myro-slaw,' like 'coleslaw.'"

"Meero-suave," I try to repeat, attempting to roll the "r" the way she did.

"Polish. It's a first name usually—not sure how it became our last. We've traced it back to Ellis Island, but not much before. It means 'peace.'"

I frown, imagining Anna's ancestors at Ellis Island. I see them in black and white—why do I always do that? The pictures didn't have color, but the people did. They were real, flesh and blood. "You should make people say it. To refuse to learn someone's name just because it's hard to say . . . I mean, it's so narcissistic."

She grins. "Well, the truth is . . . I just like people calling me Anna. Having a hard-to-pronounce last name is an excuse."

"Okay, so what are we watching?" I turn my chair so we're facing the same direction: toward the laptop. "*Toil and Trouble*? Oh my gosh, I *love* this show. Are you getting Wi-Fi?"

"Here? Yeah, right. I have them on DVD."

"Oh my gosh, me too! I'm kind of obsessed. My ex thought it was so stupid." It startles me, that I said "ex" like that. I don't know when I started thinking of Lukas as that. Maybe just now.

"The Pauser hated *T and T*? Yeah, he had to go."

Anna watches the screen for a few moments as the girls conjure a spell in their dormitories. They circle around a bowl, which is wide-mouthed and tarnished gold. Black stone cauldrons are too basic for the ladies of the Bishop School for Talented Young Women.

When the camera has panned to each girl, Anna says, "I'm a total Carolyn."

Carolyn, who is enduringly kind but harbors the pain of accidentally killing someone before she could control her magic. She feels at home with the other witches, but she's often shown on-screen by herself too. An introvert who loves people.

"I can see that. I think I'm an Asher, actually." He's a little too serious for his own good, loosened up by his friendship with adventurous Iris.

"Oh my God," Anna says. "You *are*."

"Right?"

We lie there, watching for a few minutes, until Anna whispers, "Wouldn't you just kill for Zuri's wardrobe."

"Oh my gosh," I reply. "I'd totally be her for Halloween just to wear something that cool."

It'd be a perfect group costume, all the girls and their specific styles. Maybe at college, I'll get lucky and find fellow fans.

"Hey, Anna?"

"Yeah?"

"Can I ask you something weird?" When she nods, I ask, cringing at myself, "Do you have good friends at home? Like, a group?"

She stares down at the screen for a moment, considering. "I'm friendly with a lot of people. But . . . not super close. Not like camp."

"Me neither," I admit, relieved.

"Well," she says, knocking her shoulder into mine. "Good thing we have camp, then. Hey, how's your moms doing?"

"She's . . . okay. Thanks for asking."

"Will you tell me about her? It'll help get my mind away from . . ." She pauses to take a controlled breath inward. "This."

As our favorite witches and warlocks get into trouble on-screen, I tell Anna about my mom, about the swim team, about my house. Eventually, she nods off, lips parted like a little kid's. Good. But I feel strange leaving without saying good-bye. I don't like the idea of her waking up alone.

As I'm scratching a quick note on scrap paper from her desk, Mohan walks in. He doesn't look surprised to see me, but then, Keely probably told him I was here. His T-shirt today reads: I DONUT CARE.

I wave, not wanting to wake Anna with any noise. He points to her sleeping form and gives me a thumbs-up, impressed. Then he puts his hands into a prayer pose, mouthing: *Thank you*.

I want to say, "All I did was chatter to her," but I don't want to disturb the silence. So I just nod.

Without a word, he lies down on the bed in the opposite direction. They look like the grandparents from *Willy Wonka and the Chocolate Factory*.

They look like they've done this a hundred times.

He clasps his hands behind his head, staring up at the ceiling like it's made of shifting clouds. Perfectly content.

She won't wake up alone, but I leave the note on her desk anyway. It's the witch school motto, Latin etched into marble on the floors. A phrase the girls use in the dark moments, to bolster each other to bravery.

Confidimus stellarum, I write. *From one boss witch to another.*

Though I've been here for a month, Friday night is my first time in town. I've been before with my parents, for groceries or an ice cream cone. But I've never been to this street, where we're approaching a freestanding, white-sided building called Tom's. The sign provides no further information about what kind of establishment actually belongs to Tom. A diner? A bar? Sort of both, it turns out, and also a makeshift dance hall.

We enter to a big brass version of the Jackson Five's "ABC." The band takes up most of the back wall, men rocking with trombones and saxes, plus a middle-aged woman on drums. Henry stands in the center of the trumpets, easily recognizable in his Detroit Tigers snapback hat.

The bar smells deep-fried, with a tangy undertone that I think might be beer. It's everywhere—amber liquid in pint glasses, next to chicken tenders and baskets of thick fries. The tension in my shoulders eases as I remind myself: the Cheesecake Factory has alcohol, and I go there with my parents sometimes. I'm not at a *bar* bar.

While I've been busy looking around, Anna, Mohan, and Keely have settled into the last available booth. I slide in next to Anna and examine the plastic menu page.

"Boom! Pay the piper!" Keely slaps a slip of paper onto the table. It's an IOU. "You thought I'd forget. But I *never* forget. Full basket of onion rings, not that bullshit junior size."

"Yeah, yeah," Mohan mutters. With a look of genuine warning, he tells me, "Don't ever lose to her."

"I wouldn't dare," I say. Sincerely.

"There's the entourage!" The man who has walked up to our table has no uniform to indicate that he's a waiter, but I don't know who else he'd be. "How's the summer goin'?"

"So far, so good!" Anna quips.

"I don't know this one." He nods at me.

"This is Lucy, our new counselor. Lucy, Tom."

I give a little wave. "Nice to meet you."

"Welcome. Hope you like fried food because that's what we got. Cokes all around?"

"Yes, sir," Mohan says.

"And a basket of onion rings," Keely adds happily. "Just for me. They go on Mohan's tab. Thanks, Tom."

Mohan rolls his eyes. "Gloat more, seriously."

"And burgers?" Tom asks.

"Yep. Four," Keely says, taking a deep breath. "One with extra cheese, one with no pickle and extra mustard, one—"

"Sans lettuce, I know, I know." Tom glances at me. "And for you?"

I thought maybe Keely was going to order on my behalf. "Um. Burger. Regular. However you serve it."

"Now there's an order I like. No fussiness like these three."

"He loves us," Anna informs me.

I get up to use the bathroom, and the others get up to dance. Henry waves to us, his other hand deftly pressing trumpet buttons. And I think I actually blush from this meager interaction, because my brain gets very, very squiggly around him.

Summer crushes happen all the time, right? Because you feel far away from the real world, everything seems more . . . possible. Every person seems more vital. That's the main reason for these little pangs I feel, probably. Well, I mean—that and Henry Jones's inherent handsomeness. I'm not saying that as a silly, crush-stricken girl. I am saying that as a human with decent vision. He is objectively handsome.

Sad: realizing Lukas will be coming up to Holyoke with our church kids soon. I'll have to deal with that somehow. Unless my mom told his mom, he might not have realized I really did go to Daybreak. Do I even have to see him?

When I return, Anna and Mohan are on the dance floor. Keely's sitting at the bar, where she is being chatted up by a guy whose first name is probably a surname—Bennett or Vaughn. He's tall and lean, with floppy, rich-boy hair. She's entertained by the idea of him—I can tell by her coy smile. And he seems entranced. How could he not be? Keely is beautiful and self-possessed, and you won't impress her. It makes you want to try.

I settle onto a bar stool where I have a good view of the band. Sitting alone at the booth is just a pinch too pathetic, even for me.

A few minutes in, Tom slides another Coke to me. It gives me something to do, which I appreciate.

"Wanna dance?" I glance up to find Henry, arms crossed and expectant.

"Me? Shouldn't you be up there?" This reeks of pity—a dashing gent being chivalrous to a wallflower. "I'm okay, really! I was just working up the nerve to hit on Leather Vest McBiker over there."

Henry throws a glance at the middle-aged guy I'm referring to. He has a handlebar mustache, and he totally, one hundred percent sees us staring.

"Hey, Steve," Jones says as the biker raises his hand in greeting. Whispering only to me, Jones adds, "He's happily married. Guess I'm your only option."

"I don't really dance." It's not true, strictly speaking. Sometimes I do dance around with the swim team girls, amped up in the locker room after a winning meet. *Lukas* doesn't dance, and so I usually don't either.

Henry leans in, divulging a secret. "Well, that's not a problem. Look, I try to stay humble, but I'm a great dance partner."

I don't need convincing now. How long have I been fitting my life into Lukas's without even realizing it?

I appraise Henry, top to bottom. "I'll be the judge of that."

He holds out his hand, and I take it, tucking myself under in a spin. There's always the fear that the other person will hesitate, unsure of your movement, but Henry gets it. In fact, he pushes me out, keeping hold of my one hand to pull me back in.

"How'd you learn to dance?" I ask, laughing. "Did you just pick it up?"

"Well. My granny took care of me over the summer,

and she took lessons once a week. It was either sit there in the dance studio and be bored or . . ." He drops me into a quick dip.

We clasp hands between us, stepping to the side with rapid ball-changes. The name for this move is long gone from my brain, but it's surprising what you instinctively remember from middle school.

"I went to private school until freshman year," I tell him, a bit breathlessly. "Dance was part of our phys ed."

"That's . . . old-fashioned."

"And *mortifying*." Nothing like having sweaty-palmed waltzing be your only contact with boys. I remember panicking that Mitchell Goldwin could feel my training bra.

I tug Henry's arms over our heads, a swing dance move that is cheesy and delightful.

"Stop showing off," Mohan calls.

Henry pretends he hasn't heard. "Grand finale, I pick you up?"

"What? We can't! That's something you have to practice."

"Just run at me, and I'll lift you straight up. It'll still be impressive."

When we part, he flips his hat around so it's backward. And I run right at him, as fast as I can while still feeling safe, and I leap. It's not a fancy lift or anything, just him picking me up as I try to spread my arms gracefully. He turns in a circle, so I see the whole bar from above. People are laughing and clapping, wolf whistles from the band. It's so over the top, such a ridiculous display in a casual environment. I should be blushing, but my cheeks could burst from smiling. I'm so used to solo efforts: only my legs kicking faster in the water, only my fingers pressing the piano keys.

It's fun to have a partner, even for something so silly.

I slide to my feet as the music fades.

"Attaboy, Henry!" someone yells.

"Oh, screw you both." This is from Mohan, obviously.

"Thanks," I say, looking up at Henry. "That was totally fun."

"Anytime. I should get back up there."

I return to a bar stool, which Keely's Nantucket boyfriend has disappeared from. She holds a lime-wedged Sprite, watching the dance floor with a content expression.

"What happened to Captain America?" I ask.

"Left with his friends." She sips from the thin black straw in her drink. "And my number."

"He was cute."

"Not my look," she admits. "But help me, Jesus, I do love a boy who's full of himself."

The band starts in with an old Frank Sinatra ballad with panache. All the older couples are on the floor, cheeks pressed close. Henry, back in the lineup, spins his hat so it's facing front again.

"So," Keely says. She's caught me lingering on Jones.

"So," I repeat, attempting nonchalance.

"You two have been hanging out some evenings?"

"Yep."

She turns fully, arching an eyebrow at me. "Really? That's all you're gonna give me? We share a bed!"

"A *bunk* bed!" This makes me laugh, at least. "I mean, everyone falls a little in love with him, right? The campers, the adults. He's very . . . charming."

"Sure. He just doesn't generally feel the same."

"Oh, I don't think . . . I mean, it's not . . . that way. For him."

"If you say so." She snorts, returning to her drink. I do the same, if only to duck my head and hide my frazzled expression. Is it that way for him?

As we look back over the dance floor, Anna and Mohan sway in the center, hands clasped. They talk, mouths close with small smiles, and they never break eye contact. I was right about the navy mascara and Anna's coloring, but that's not why she's lovely tonight.

I'm so used to the Mohan who is full of smirks and bravado and frenetic hand gestures. How strange to see his face soft, to see him smiling as Anna speaks. How strange to see him standing upright and steady with her hand in his. He's not the jester. He's the prince.

But even when he *is* joking, isn't he always upright and steady with her?

I tip my head toward Keely. "Is that . . . ?"

She hears my real questions: Is that happening? Shouldn't it be? Why isn't it?

"That's a someday." We both watch them for a moment. Anna tilts her head back, laughing loudly at something Mohan says. "Once they go there, that's gonna be it for them. Endgame."

"Do they know?"

"He does, I think. She needs a little more time."

"What about you?" I venture.

"Me? I'm leaving after I graduate. For California." With Keely, I've noticed there are always clues in everything she doesn't say, and I'm learning to read between her lines. She says she's leaving for California. She *means* she doesn't want to be attached.

I think of the starscape above her bunk, the tall redwoods and an Airstream trailer like a silver bullet.

"Why California?"

"I think it's because I saw it in movies so much as a kid. Somewhere along the way, it became the dream."

"So, you'll go to school out there?"

Her smile is wry, almost mocking. "Well, that's the hope."

"Good. You could be the female Neil deGrasse Tyson."

She's disbelieving, if charmed that I think so. "That man is my deity. But out-of-state college is expensive."

We're quiet for a moment.

"So, what will you do in California?"

"Hopefully I get in and get financial aid. But, in any version of reality, I work in textiles or design. I'm really good with patterns and sewing."

I've pieced that together already. "How'd you learn to do that?"

"My aunt, after my mom died. Trying to keep me busy and ladylike." Now Keely's smile is certainly mocking. "I can also do a mean needlepoint. No joke."

"Man, you and Anna are regular Austen heroines. Much more marriageable than I am."

"I really do love sewing, though," she says, the edge of defensiveness creeping in. "It isn't a compromise."

"I get it. I really do love makeup." The truth is, sometimes I think I'd be happier doing that than any job I can think of. "So, you won't want to stay in-state, near your sister?"

"Kiana has a wonderful family." Her voice is brusque enough that I realize I've crossed into treacherous territory. "She'll be just fine. She'll be great."

Kiana has a wonderful family. But Keely doesn't. They're not really hers. That's what I hear.

"So, where in California? LA?"

We chat about her destination, about the hours she's logged on Google Street View and Craigslist, imagining which neighborhood she'll live in. She tells me about the upscale consignment store where she works at home. When designer clothes come in with wear or damage, Keely is the one who patches them. She's even gotten into clothing and handbag restoration, which she's hoping to do more of in LA.

"I'm going to drive out there too. Solo cross-country road trip."

"Alone?" I truly wouldn't feel comfortable driving to Ohio by myself, let alone any farther. "You don't want to experience that with someone?"

"Of course I do." She gives me a smart-ass look. "With myself."

After practice finishes up, the jukebox takes over. Most of the band members hang around, sitting at tables with their families.

Our burgers show up, timed perfectly, as we climb back into the booth—Henry with us this time. He sits next to me, and I stare down at the toasted top of my burger bun.

"Is this mine?" He points to one of the red plastic baskets.

Keely nods. "No pickle, extra mustard."

Based on previous exchanges, I'm shocked when Keely offers me a whole onion ring. A smaller one—but still.

"Here," she says, with the magnanimous tone of a queen knighting someone. "Dip it."

But after a bite, I understand the gravity of the situation. They're crispy and warm and golden. Can something *taste* golden? "Whoa."

"Exactly." She jams one into the dish of sauce.

"Keels?" Henry says.

"What?"

He smiles sweetly. "You're so pretty."

"Do I look like I was born yesterday?" she scoffs. Then she softens, smiling as she turns to him. "But go on."

"Well, you have a naturally great smile and really nice teeth, even when you don't show them. And your hair is looking great since you've been growing it out."

"True." She fluffs her hair. When Mohan snorts, she whirls at him. "It's work! You don't know."

"And you always make lipstick look cool. That's hard to pull off."

Keely nods, looking around the table at us as if we should take note. "Henry Jones? You may have an onion ring."

"For being a kiss-ass?" Mohan shrieks. He reaches across to snatch one, but Keely smacks his hand.

"I know Jones said it for the food, but he was being *truthful* about my beauty," she says, waving her hand in the most dismissively regal way. "And you could have ordered your own."

"I had to order *yours*. I'm not made of money." To Anna he grumbles, "She's like Gollum with those rings."

Keely picks up an onion ring delicately.

"My. Precious," she says flatly, then shoves the whole thing in her mouth.

"Well, now you're just baiting him," Anna says.

Mohan has this particular expression when he is up to something, a little flame-spark in his dark irises. "Fine. You want flattery? Keely Marie, you are the wind beneath my wings."

"Uh oh." Jones snickers beside me. Anna covers her smile with a balled fist, eyes wide.

Keely's expression darkens as she stares down Mohan. "Don't do it."

"Don't do what?" I whisper to Jones. Mohan has his eyes closed, summoning breath or strength—I don't know which.

"Sometimes, when Mohan doesn't get his way . . . ," Jones replies. He doesn't finish explaining because he doesn't have to. Mohan is quietly singing the first line of "Wind Beneath My Wings" and reaching out to Keely. The other hand is clasped against his chest, as if really *meaning* the lyrics.

"Stop it," Keely hisses.

He does not stop it. He sings the next lines a little louder, and Anna sways happily. Keely looks capable of murder.

The faceoff becomes clear to me: Mohan will continue serenading Keely with this cheesy ballad, in increasing volume, until she relinquishes an onion ring. She starts chewing frantically, like maybe he'll stop if the food is all gone.

But Mohan has almost reached the chorus. People have definitely started to look, and Keely ducks down. He takes a deep breath and belts the chorus with total earnestness. The family sitting nearest to us looks *pissed*. If Mohan notices, he doesn't let on.

"Fine, you idiot!" Keely cries. "Take an onion ring. Just stop."

Mohan snaps his mouth shut. He smiles serenely, reaching pinched fingers across to claim his prize, and I join Anna in clapping. Jones laughs, stretching his arm so that it rests on the booth behind us. He's not putting his arm around me, exactly, but I feel tucked into him. Into all of it.

Happy: This. Them.

CHAPTER SIXTEEN

THE PATH I TAKE TOWARD HOLYOKE IS STARTING TO GET WORN in, but it's the first Sunday that I don't feel propelled away from my new camp.

I run into my dad on his way out of the chapel, prepping for the service. "Hey, Bird!"

"Hey." I squeeze my arms around his waist. When I step back, my eye goes right to his hair. He normally keeps it meticulously short, but it's a little shaggy around the ears. "Is Mom in there already?"

"She's going to rest at the house today. I think she has a surprise waiting for you, actually."

"Oh. Should I go now?"

"Yeah, go on. I think you can miss one of my sermons without fearing for your mortal soul." He winks, and something about it wrecks me. Now that I've backed away from my normal life, I can see the whole landscape. Now that I know what some of my campers have going on at home . . . yes, I see very, very clearly. And I'm not sure how I got so lucky. My dad with his steadfastness and his humor.

I bound to the cabin, pausing to examine the car in our driveway. It's new and uncluttered inside. Must be a rental. Who would have a rental car here? The front door clatters behind me, punctuating the loud whirr of the blender.

"Aunt Rachel!"

I fly at her, arms wide open, and she turns to catch me just in time.

"There's the bird," she says, laughing into my hair.

"What are you doing here?"

"Oh, you know. Engaging in a power struggle with your *mother*."

"Where's my milk shake?" my mom calls from the family room. "I drank all my water, so I get the milk shake. Bring more chips, too!"

"She's hungry?" I whisper.

"Yep." She twists the lid back on a plastic container of protein powder.

"How'd you do that? She said most food doesn't taste right anymore."

"Oh, I have my ways." She thrusts a bag of potato chips into my hands. "Take these."

My mom's curled up on the couch, feet tucked beneath her. A loose caftan billows around her, bright blue and embroidered with birds and flowers along the neckline. Rachel's doing, I'm sure.

"Hi, honey." She reaches out to me, clasps her cool hand in mine. "I'm so glad you're here. Rachel is driving me nuts."

"I'd pipe down if I were you, Jenkins!" Rachel has always called my mom by her maiden name, a remnant from swim team in college. "I'm in control of what goes in this shake."

"How was your week?" my mom asks me, ignoring her.

"It was good. Really good."

"Your Highness," Rachel says, tucking the milk shake in the crook of my mom's arm. "She's been a tyrant, Luce. Guilted me into watching *Titanic* last night. Why did we do that?"

My mom twists on the couch so she can reach Rachel's hand.

"I'll never let you go, Rach," she says solemnly. "I'll never let you go."

Then, with no ceremony, she drops Rachel's hand.

Rachel's eyes dart to me. "See how dramatic she's being?"

My mom slurps at her milk shake and shoves a handful of chips in her mouth. "These are the best chips I've ever tasted."

"When you're done terrorizing the snack food, we'll go swimming." Rachel pushes my mom's leg with her foot. "Don't give me that look, Jenkins. I didn't come all the way out here just to cater to your every whim while you whine about having cancer."

I gasp. "Rachel!"

But my mom explodes in laughter. Hands over her mouth, rocking forward with her eyes squinted shut. She's laughing so hard that it's silent at first, but then she lets out a *howl* of it and Rachel does too, both of their faces red and teary.

"Yeah," my mom says, her voice barely held together, "it's just *cancer*. No need to overreact."

Rachel wipes her eyes. "You always were a drama queen."

This sets them off again. Maybe it's more like hooting, I don't know, but it's primal and uproarious. I've heard them do this a hundred times.

"Okay. Swimming it is." My mom shakes her head. "The things I do for you. Sacrificing more of my hair."

The laughter, suddenly, feels very far away. "Swimming will make you lose more hair?"

She smiles sadly. "It comes out more in the shower. On my pillow too. It's okay, Bird. It's normal. It'll probably be all gone by the time treatment's done. We knew to expect that."

"You want me to just clip it down now?" When my mom and I say nothing, Rachel scoffs at us. "What? Why not? I cut the boys' hair all the time."

"It's already so patchy and wispy . . . I guess you can't make it much worse." My mom touches a hand to the fly-aways. "All right. I guess so."

Rachel has this way of nudging her right to the borders of her comfort zone. She won't push her over, and my mom knows that.

"We'll do it later," my mom decides.

"Why not now?"

My mom's gaze flicks to me, then back to Rachel. Like I'm a small child who's not going to notice nonverbal communication.

Rachel understands before I do. "I think Lucy will be fine, Jenkins."

"Me?" I exclaim. "Wait! What?"

My mom folds her hands on her lap. "She doesn't need to see her mother getting her head shaved down. I don't want that memory in her mind."

"Mom, I—"

"Lucy," Rachel says brightly—too brightly. "Can you run out to the car and grab the tote bag out of the trunk? It has my swimsuit in it."

She tosses me her keys. My startled hands somehow catch them, metal nipping my palms.

Mom and I both eye her. We're being played. I'm going to get her swimsuit as a pretense, and she's going to convince my mom it's all right for me to stay. Still, I trudge out to the car in the heat, find the bag, and sling it over my shoulder.

By the time I return, Rachel has moved a kitchen chair to the bathroom and my mom is sitting there with a towel wrapped around her shoulders.

I give my mom a decisive look, one that I hope says: *I'm seventeen. I can handle it.* "Mom, I've thought about it, and I can shave my head too, okay? Solidarity! And we'll both—"

"You," she says evenly, "will do no such thing, Lucy Esther. God gave you those gorgeous curls, and I like looking at them. Besides, your hair will be my beacon of hope as mine regrows."

That is . . . hard to argue with. Rachel chatters as she clips, updating me about her sons—all younger than I am.

"So, Luce," Rachel says, "how's that boyfriend of yours?"

"Oh. Um. He paused me. So, not my boyfriend. But he'll be up here soon when our congregation's kids have camp week, so *that* should be nice and awkward."

"Paused you? Well, sayonara." Rachel wrinkles her nose in distaste. "Any other guys on the horizon?"

"What?" Jones's handsome, grinning face comes to mind, and my traitorous cheeks warm immediately. "Of course not."

My mom's mouth drops open. "Oh my gosh, there *is* another guy!"

"No, there's not!" My voice is a squeal—I am such a *loser*.

Rachel has completely stopped snipping, hair forgotten. "Who is he?"

I cover my face. Two of them against one is a losing battle. "Stop it! No one!"

"Camp boyfriend!" Rachel cries delightedly at the same time my mom huffs, "I can't believe you didn't tell me."

"*No*. Just a crush. Not even a crush. A . . . crinkle." I pinch my fingers together to demonstrate my massive, massive lie. "Go ahead. Tell me I'm a terrible person for liking someone while Lukas and I are paused."

Rachel snorts. "I say glory hallelujah! How dare that kid try to keep you hanging? He's such a stiff, anyway."

"Rachel!" my mom exclaims.

"Oh, tell me I'm wrong, Jenkins." She glances at me, doing a weak impression of penitent. "Sorry, Luce. But the ramrod posture? Always so serious? C'mon. I'm sure he's a nice guy. But that's not for you."

I fiddle with the comb, running my finger over the plastic teeth. "Could have used that information months ago."

"So, the new guy," my mom prods. "What's he like?"

"He's . . . *fun*. And he's so good with the kids, it's unreal. He plays the trumpet. And . . . whatever. Whatever! It doesn't matter! I don't know why I'm talking about it."

"What's his name?" Rachel asks innocently.

"Nope. No way. Because you'll use it against me. You'll be like, *Lucy, how's Joooohn doing?*"

"Ha! His name is John!" Rachel balls her hands into triumphant fists.

"His name is not John. That was a placeholder. I'm not a fool."

Somehow I drive them away from the topic long enough that my mom does, in fact, receive a haircut. Rachel doesn't buzz her hair but trims it close to her skull. I know from studying vintage makeup looks that this is very Twiggy, very Audrey.

"It's not so bad," my mom says. "Although my cheeks look . . . droopier or something."

"Oh, stop it," Rachel sniffs.

"I know. It's silly, to be vain in the midst of all this. But I do wish I had fuller eyebrows. Maybe that'd help."

The idea blooms instantly, a flower in time-lapse. "Aunt Rachel, did you bring a makeup bag? Like, eye shadow?"

"Yeah."

"Can you get it?"

She nods, disappearing from the room for a moment. My mom considers her reflection, smooths her hands over her hair.

"Never imagined myself with short hair." Her tone is kind of self-deprecating, but I know her. She's trying to joke to be brave for me. "I look sick."

"You look beautiful, Mom. And the short hair makes you look delicate *and* tough. Pretty, but like you could beat somebody up."

"Ha!" She flexes a bicep. "Right after I finish vomiting."

"Here." Rachel shoves a vinyl makeup bag at me, polka-dotted and bulging with products. Good. I sift through my options, plucking out a few items. A tawny eye shadow and a thin, angled brush.

"What are you doing?" my mom asks.

"Just trust me."

I swab the tiny brush across the pad of eye shadow. Then I lean close to my mother's face, studying her blue eyes. Her pupils are dilated and the whites of her eyes are a little red—side effects I haven't seen before.

"Close your eyes," I say, sounding more authoritative than I mean to. But she obeys, and I dab gently where her eyebrows begin. The powder clings to the fine hairs she has left, filling the spaces in between. Her eyebrows arch neatly now, fawn colored and subtle.

"Keep them closed. You're going to feel a brush on your cheek."

"What are you . . . oh, goodness." She cuts off as I sweep two lines of bronzer down her cheekbones, then blend upward and add peachy blush to her pale cheeks. With whatever powder remains on the brush, I swipe beneath her jawline and across her hairline.

"Oh, that's nice," Rachel murmurs. She's an art teacher, so this is entirely up her alley. In fact, I think my earliest interest in makeup was after Rachel painted a butterfly on my face. I must have been seven or eight.

"What are you doing?" my mom repeats.

In a singsong voice, I reply, "'Patience is the virtue we use when we must wait. God's timing is impeccable, and He is never late.'"

"Oh, not that one!" my mom groans. It's a Vacation Bible School theme song from when I was in fifth grade. We sang it at morning assembly and before afternoon dismissal; it blasted in the hallways as we walked from activity to activity. Those VBS songs crawl into your ears and embed themselves in your brain. They can go dormant for years at a time, but they're always there.

"Okay." I step aside so my mom can see her face in the mirror.

She touches her palms to her cheeks again. "Well, look at that. I almost look healthy. I bet if I put some mascara on . . ."

We do exactly that. And a nearly nude lipstick. And, just for fun, a smudge of deep brown eyeliner in the corners of her eyes. I explain the idea behind it, how makeup is about playing with shadow and light, drawing people's eyes in different ways. "See, that makes your eyes look bigger, and they're already being highlighted by the dark mascara and accented brow."

"Where'd you learn all this?" Rachel asks carefully.

"The Internet." I say this in the casual way all kids use to get away with something.

The glance she exchanges with my mom in the mirror is quick, but not so quick that I don't catch it.

"You're very good at this," my mom tells me quietly. "Thank you for sharing your gift with me."

Her eyes are a little bloodshot, though she smiles happily. Is that a new symptom? She seems like she's feeling pretty good, just . . . off. I guess that's chemo at work, and I hate that I don't know her experience with it better.

"What's with the stare?" Rachel asks. "Lake time. Suit up."

"My bathing suit isn't here."

"Then swim in your clothes. Or your bra and undies. Oh, don't look so scandalized. We both used to change your diaper."

"Rachel," my mom says. "You're embarrassing her."

"Jenkins," Rachel says. "That's the point."

While Rachel changes into her suit, my mom nudges her shoulder against mine. "I'm swimming in my clothes too. Can't get too much sun."

"His name is Henry." The words splat out, sloppy. "We mostly call him Jones, his last name."

My mom presses a finger against her lips, taps it a few times. She's pleased, considering this new information.

"I didn't tell you because it's honestly so stupid—like, nothing will ever happen. And I know I shouldn't even have a dumb crush right after breaking up with Lukas, but—"

"Oh, Bird." She cups her hand on my cheek. "You're only seventeen."

I flinch. I'm not too young to know my own heart. Sure, it's terrain I'm still learning to map, but I know the landscape better than anyone. I know the unexpected dips and the paths that were not meant for me. "What does that mean?"

"It means that everything changes so fast. It's okay if you change too." Seeing that I still don't quite get it, she smiles ever so slightly. "It means, good for you. Crush away. Get crushed, even. Feel it all, okay? Show up for it."

"I will." The words land like a promise, sealed between us. Maybe they are, come what may.

"Hurry up, you little gossips," Rachel calls. "Don't think I don't know you're telling secrets in there."

We emerge from the bathroom, conspiratorial. My mom

gives her a haughty look. "Chill out, Byers. It's not like anyone's dying."

This makes Rachel laugh again, and I barely disguise my horror.

On the way out, my mom jams a fistful of crumbly chips into her mouth and tucks the bag under her arm. "Chips. My real best friend."

At the water's edge, we survey the lake—our holy ground, our promised land.

"All right, swim team captain," Rachel says. "Let's see a running dive."

"I'm not a *seal*. I do not perform on demand."

"What if I give you a chip?" Rachel digs her arm into the open bag.

"Hey!" my mom says.

I plow into the water, up to my knees. Then I turn back to them, bark, and clap my hands together. Rachel pitches a chip, which I try to catch with my mouth. On my third try, I fall into the water, much to their delight. I give in and pull my arms into a neat, even stroke.

"Look at us," I hear Rachel tell my mom. "Not bad for our midforties after a couple o' kids, eh, Jenkins?"

I wade in farther, walking forward as seamlessly as I would on land. It's not like the ocean, chilled and pushing, pulling. It's bathwater, still and cool. I tip backward, letting the water catch my shoulders and support me. My curls splay out around me, and I think of all the summers spent pretending to be a mermaid.

Pushing my arms out like I'm making snow angels, I almost thank the Lord in my mind. I am grateful for all this, for the feel of water and sun on my skin. For all the years spent here, happy. But with my mom nearby, and her chemo-inspired hair, I'm not quite ready for a truce. He knows what He needs to do.

Nearby, Rachel takes a deep, gasping breath and plunges under the water. Her bare feet pop up, balanced in a handstand, and my mom laughs. That's why she did it, of course—to make my mom laugh. Or maybe because Rachel can still touch the magic of wanting to be a mermaid. She can still play. How can I be seventeen and already feel it slipping from my grasp?

"Still got it!" Rachel announces, wringing out her hair.

My mother dips her shorn head back, eyes closed. When she stands back upright, a bemused smile crosses her face as she runs one hand over her scalp. "How strange. To not have the weight of wet hair."

I should feel like I'm intruding here, a kid with two grown-ups. But I don't. Under duress and ancient trees, I feel older—no, ageless. Three women in waters that have baptized and held so many, including me at all previous ages of my life. In water, I can almost feel cradled by the universe, in the palm of God's own hand. And we float.

CHAPTER SEVENTEEN

WHEN I GET TO THE REC ROOM AFTER LIGHTS-OUT, JONES IS already there. His trumpet is disassembled across the coffee table, and he's dutifully snaking some kind of cloth into the valves.

"Hey," I say, plopping onto the couch beside him. "Is your trumpet okay?"

"Yep. Just routine maintenance."

"Impressive. I couldn't tune a piano to save my life."

"That," he says, picking up the mouthpiece, "would be a weird murder attempt. 'TUNE THIS PIANO OR DIE. DO IT NOW!'"

When I recover from laughing, I watch his careful hands wiping each delicate bend of metal. It's methodical, and a little hypnotic to watch. He glances up, a quick smile at my undivided attention. When he smiles, the apples of his cheeks carve two little lines above his mouth. It's like they're framing that semicircle grin of his.

He looks up again, and I realize I've just been sitting here, staring at his face.

"I like your glasses," I announce. Which is true, of course, but I say it mostly because I've been gawking for a solid thirty seconds longer than is socially appropriate.

"Yeah? Thanks." He adjusts them a little on the bridge of his nose. "My grandpa calls them my Malcolm X glasses."

"Are you close with him?"

"Malcolm X?"

I stick my tongue out. "Your grandpa."

"Yeah. See him every Sunday, for church and then brunch after. He's a trip."

"So, your family goes to church?" I try to say this as if it is any old topic and not fundamental to who I am as a person.

He does this thing—a quick glance-away—when he's trying to deflect his amusement. Apparently I'm not as casual as I thought. "Every Sunday. And we do a kind of church here at Daybreak, you know."

"Really?" I mean, of course I wouldn't know that. I'm always gone at sunup and with my mom until after lunchtime.

"Yeah. In the meeting hall. We do some songs, talk about feelings. Sometimes kids share their traditions. But Bryan also takes some of the kids into town Sunday morning for church."

"Huh."

"You thought I was a heathen," he says happily. "You thought we were *all* heathens."

"I don't think of people as *heathens*." If I did, I might be one at this point. It's a sobering thought, and Henry notices my fallen expression.

"Luce? I was just kidding."

"Oh, no. I know." I figure I have nothing to lose in asking him a question. He's all about honesty, so he'd probably tell me if he didn't want to answer. "Can I ask you something? Kind of . . . personal?"

"Sure." I like how easily he jokes. And I like that he knows not to right now. In fact, he gets up to sit on the edge of the coffee table so we're at eye level.

"Um, after everything with your sister, did that mess with your faith?"

I think of it as this complicated, barbed question, but he seems to be waiting for more than that. When I say nothing, he nods. "Oh. Yeah. Absolutely. Is that it?"

"That's it." Now I feel silly for making it out to be a huge deal. But . . . it *is* for me.

"One hundred percent." He says this with utter clarity, in voice and in assurance. "You know, all these grown-ups were in my face, telling me Nessa was with the angels and that I'd see her again in heaven. Even at ten years old, I wanted to say: *The fuck do you know?* The more certain they were, the more I doubted them. Then, you know, a few real assholes mentioned that suicide would keep my sister from heaven. So, yeah. I was pissed at God and Jesus and probably also Mary and Joseph just because."

I almost laugh, which seems to please him. "But you got it back? Believing in things?"

He presses his lips together. They're kind of distractingly nice, his lips.

That's another tick in the Heathen column.

"Yes," he decides. "Just not in the same way."

I can't bring myself to pry anymore, but he rests his elbows on his knees anyway, settling in. "All that church stuff seemed black and white when I was little—easy. And now it's gray, but I . . . choose it anyway, I guess. And I try to really get the point of it."

And doesn't he, though? I watch him with these kids, being a total servant. Giving over his summers to these campers because he understands them. He's not perfect; I don't even know him that well, and I know that. But he's good. He's deeply good, even without an unquestioned, flawless faith. And so maybe I can be good too. Maybe I can pick faith, even though it doesn't feel effortless anymore. Before I even feel it forming, a tear drops from my eye.

"Oh, Luce. Hey."

I brush it from my cheek. "Sorry. Gosh. Dramatic. Thank you for telling me that. It's what I needed to hear."

"Well, good," he says, hesitant. "And if you need to talk . . ."

"I know." I nod, feeling like an idiot.

He reaches for his now-finished trumpet. "Want me to play you something?"

"Yes, please." He settles the mute into the bell of the horn. "But if you play 'Amazing Grace' right now, I *will* kill you."

Instead, he starts in on a rendition of "Boogie Woogie Bugle Boy," making me laugh. Which I know was the idea.

He holds the trumpet with one hand, using the other to cue me to sing along.

"No," I say.

This only encourages him, jumping up from the couch so he can dance along to his own playing. I'm helpless with laughter, eventually calling lyrics out.

When he sits down, we both notice the familiar silhouette in the doorway.

Keely looks between us and, before walking away, mutters, "Nope. Don't wanna know."

The next few days, I feel so much more at peace. When I try to pray, I don't feel like a crazy person talking to a man in the sky. It feels like me choosing to ask the God I've always known for guidance. Even if one of my prayers is *Please help me stop being so mad at You.*

I keep thinking that I'll report this development to Jones—maybe even tell him about my mom—but he doesn't show up at the rec room Monday night. Or Tuesday night.

When I see him in the breakfast line Wednesday morning, my heart tries to leap toward him. Or at least, that's what it feels like. I've never had such a visceral reaction to someone, been tugged toward them like gravity. He lifts one hand in a wave, but nothing more.

I resign myself to the idea that my questioning must have made him uncomfortable. But I can't take it back, and I wouldn't want to, anyway. If he can't talk about faith stuff with me, then maybe it's better this way.

Still, I'm so mortified that I duck into the Bunker as the third graders file into their shared class. I just don't want him to avoid sitting by me or, worse, sit beside me and feel awkward about it.

But of course, as soon as I open the door, he's there, cracking open a soda.

I blurt out: "Hey. I didn't know——" at the same time he's saying, "Oh, I figured you were——"

We both stop, laughing under our breath at our own awkwardness.

"It feels like I haven't seen you much!" So I guess I'm still blurting things out. But hey, he's the one who's about honesty, right?

He scratches his fingertips through his hair, glancing down. "Yeah. About that. I, um——"

"Oh, it's no big deal!" Great, now I sound like some pathetic girl who is desperate to hang out with him. Which . . . I am. But I don't *want* to be.

"No, I want to explain." He tilts his head up, as if summoning something greater than himself. With a big breath out, he says, "You have a boyfriend. So, I need to step back a little."

My mouth drops open.

Henry's eyes meet mine, dark and deep. "I'm sorry if that's weird for you to hear. But I didn't want you to think I'm mad at you or something."

So he's not mad at me or bored with me. "Okay. But I *don't* have a boyfriend. You know that."

"You have unfinished business, though. Right?" When I don't deny it, he smiles sadly. "I'm not lookin' to get hurt, Luce. That's all it is. Okay?"

As if *I* would hurt him? Is he saying . . . that he . . . that I . . . He needs to take a step back because I have a relationship on pause? Because spending time with me might hurt him?

My time with Henry has shown me what crushes can be: giddy chemistry and near-instant familiarity. With someone who hears me, who will meet me where I am, without discomfort or judgment. Tell me the worst parts of his life without hesitation. And I just can't go back to what I have with Lukas. Not now that I know how much your heart can be into something. Into someone.

It is maybe the bravest I have ever been in my life as I stand before Henry Morris Jones and say, chin lifted to meet his eyes, "Well, I don't think you need to step back. Because I don't think you'll get hurt."

I don't look away or backtrack, even though my nervous system is threatening to ignite on the spot. Henry nods slowly, processing what I mean. And I do mean it.

"Okay," he says finally, with the slightest hint of a smile. "Then I guess I'll see you tonight."

It is no different, that night. Just us, playing and reading and talking. Like he said, I have unfinished business. But when I return to Cabin 3A, I press my grinning face into the pillow and give myself over to dreams.

CHAPTER EIGHTEEN

MIDSTROKE DURING MY THURSDAY MORNING SWIM, I DECIDE HOW to handle the Thuy situation. Not her family life; I don't think I'm qualified for that committee. But I can at least get her more involved. All the activities are geared toward groups, but maybe she'd do better one-on-one. I turn my head to get a breath, and I think of Jones's words. Breathing is the important part. And I think I'm breathing just fine now.

As suspected, during 3A swim hour, Thuy's in the sand, building castles. I taught her how to do drip castles last week, assuming that she'd enjoy the construction element. But now I wonder if she's scared of the water. Normally, at least one other girl builds with her, but today she's on the shore alone.

"Don't you want to get in the water?" I prompt cheerfully. My shadow casts across the foundation of her castle.

"I'm not allowed."

"Of course you're allowed!"

"I can't." She flaps her arms, apparently miming "swim."

"You can't swim? Well, you can wear a life jacket! Or I can teach you."

She looks out at the other campers in the water and slowly shakes her head. "Everyone else already knows how."

I crouch down so that we're at eye level. "Only because someone taught them at some point."

Still she focuses on the castle.

"Did you know that I swim every morning? I get up earlier than you guys so I can practice. I'm on the swim team at my school."

Thuy squints at me, considering. "That's where you come from when we're getting ready in the morning?"

I usually get back as everyone is brushing teeth and getting dressed. "Yep. And if you want, I can wake you up early too and teach you in the morning. Just us."

She dumps a scoop of sand onto the castle base. "No, thank you."

But when my alarm goes off Tuesday morning, Thuy is already sitting at the end of her bed in a swimsuit, ready to go.

She doesn't speak as we walk down to the lake, and I don't try to force it. This is the part where I remind myself how many club team kids I've helped with their stroke form, with their dives. If there's one thing I truly know, it's this.

After I wade in, I turn back to her. "What do you think about getting in to your tummy? You can touch the bottom here."

By way of response, she strides in until the water's at her waist—a burst of bravery. "No farther."

"Deal. How do you feel about putting your head under the water?"

"Well, I can do this kind. Like in the bath." She dips her head back—hair wet but face dry.

"Good!" So, maybe some fear about her nose and eyes in water. Normally, I'd practice breathing, then submersion—getting used to being underwater. In Thuy's case, though, my gut tells me that she needs incentive. She needs to know how great it can be and feel motivated to learn. "Can you try leaning back into my hands? I'll hold you up."

She presses a balled fist against her mouth. "You won't let me go?"

"Nope. Promise."

"Will my eyes get wet? I don't want that."

"They won't."

"Okay." She turns her back to me. "Now what?"

I brace beneath her arms. "Lean back. Your hair will go into the water more, but I'll keep you up."

She leans back a little, still rooted in the lake's muddy floor.

"Okay," I say. "Now let your feet drift up a little."

"No, I can't."

"Okay," I repeat. "That's okay. Can you try to relax and just let me move you, then?"

"Maybe."

I lift up a little, her body easily buoyant in the huge lake.

"Eee!" I take that to mean her feet have left the ground. "I'm not standing! I'm not on my legs!"

"I know. Do you want to kick your feet a little?"

By the time I put her down, my biceps ache. "That was great. Do you want to try floating?"

"No, I don't want water in my eyes."

"I know. We'll be careful," I promise.

She lets me move her toward deeper water. I support beneath her back with one hand, beneath her legs with the other.

"Am I doing it?" she whispers, eyes squinted shut.

"See for yourself."

Thuy peeks one eye open, then both as she takes in the broad blue sky above. It's full of a hundred small puffy clouds today, the ones that look like popcorn. I used to imagine God like a Renaissance painter, rounding each curve of cloud with His brush.

"Oh!" she says. "It's like lying in bed, only it's water. And outside."

And that—the marveling in her voice, it's been just out of my reach. I've been turning over every good thing in my life, searching for cracks in the foundation. But some things—the lake after sunrise, a kid who trusts you to help, the slow rock of cool water—you don't have to doubt.

By week's end, Thuy and I have practiced kicking and arm strokes while sitting on the sand. We've timed holding our breath, complete with noses plugged, to prove how long we'd be safe. We've tried on goggles. No eyes underwater yet, but I'm assembling all the pieces we need to get there.

On Friday, I ditch out of rest time to get my head on straight. Lukas will be at Holyoke on Sunday, so I have to figure out what I'll say. My walk is nearly a stomp, cutting the path from our bunk to behind the lodge. I need quiet and solitude, room for my thoughts.

"Hey!" There's a camper on the porch, watching me hurry past.

"Hey. Tara, right?"

"Yep. The pregnant one." She says it lightheartedly, but I can hear the hurt behind it. I get it: it's easier to own the crap people say about you. "Are you going for a walk?"

"Yeah. Kind of. I was going to walk to the dreaming tree. I've never seen it."

"Oh, cool. Can I come? I've never seen it either."

So much for being alone. But what? I'm going to tell a pregnant fourteen-year-old that she can't come along and dream with me? "Yeah, sure. Of course."

She catches up, surprisingly spry with her basketball belly. "It's insane. Sometimes my back hurts so much that I have to sit. But sometimes my body *aches* to move."

"When are you due?" As if that's going to help me understand her situation. I don't know anything about a baby's development except that it takes forty weeks.

"End of August."

We walk a few paces. "Have you found out if it's a girl or boy?"

"Boy." I feel her looking over at me. "I'll be keeping it, if you're wondering."

I wasn't. Though I admit, I'm wondering what her parents think of this. Was it their idea to send her to Daybreak? Is the baby's father in the picture? Is he also fourteen? I've always heard about teenage pregnancy, but up close—with Tara's soft, little girl cheeks and knobby knees—I can't bring myself to judge. What a thing to deal with. I could barely handle starting at a new school at that age.

Still, walking next to her, I feel off-kilter. Tara's the camper, and she's three years younger than me—only recently a teenager. Yet she's had this major life experience. I haven't even come *close* to having sex, let alone actually doing it. In this weird way, I feel younger than her.

Behind the lodge, we follow a bend in the path. There's nothing this way except for a small shed, but the dreaming tree is unmissable.

Silver stars hang like Christmas ornaments from every visible branch. They're aluminum foil with fish hooks. Years of dreams suspended from the trees. How many have come true?

How many have been forgotten? Or discarded? Or simply lost along the way?

"There's a Tupperware thing by the shed. It has stars and markers in it."

"So you *have* been here before?"

"Nah, Sienna told me."

I retrieve the plastic container of stars and settle onto the plush grass below the tree. Tara's right behind me, but bracing on my arm to lower herself down.

As we lie beneath the tree, staring up at crisscrossed branches and thin-tipped stars, I imagine my mother with gray hair. That's the image that blooms in my mind: her old enough to be a grandmother.

Maybe I should dream of a future where I've rediscovered my faith. Where I have solid footing. Maybe my dream should be that I finally realize what I want to do with my life. But really, I just want my mom here for whatever happens. With all of it.

I'm about to cry when Tara heaves out a sigh. "So, what's this tree supposed to do, anyway?"

"Well, my mom said that if you tell your hopes to the dreaming tree, the tree will pass them on to the clouds. And the clouds will tell the stars."

"And little kids believe that?" She snorts.

I bristle, since I was one such kid who believed this. I mean, it's less ridiculous than a prince kissing you awake from a coma.

"Maybe. But it also can't hurt."

She considers this, in case I'm tricking her or using reverse psychology. "I guess that's true."

"Well, I'm doing it. You don't have to."

I turn over on my stomach, opening the plastic bin. I remove one delicate aluminum star and a thick permanent marker. When I hand one to Tara, she takes it without hesitation.

"What are you writing?" she asks. "Or is it like birthday candles, and you can't tell people what you wish for?"

"Let's not, just to be safe."

Mom will live to be old. I can't even write "Mom will get better." She did that once before, and look where that got us.

I'll need both hands to climb the tree, so I place the star in my mouth.

"I would have held that for you," Tara comments, but I'm already pulling myself up by a sturdy lower branch. The bark etches my hands, transfers its lines to my palms. It takes all my strength to shimmy up, but I manage. I steady myself on the trunk as I stand, then step to an even higher branch.

Just like that, I'm surrounded by a panorama of jewel-green leaves and silver stars, with a dream clenched between my teeth. It's only a little different than I imagined it when my mom told the story. I imagined gold leaves coated in glitter, or maybe iridescent glass.

But I don't need a fancy dreaming tree. I don't have fancy dreams.

I balance carefully as I stretch to hang my star.

"Oh my God, *please* don't fall," Tara says from below. "I can't run for help. I can only waddle."

"I'm good, I promise."

I'm tempted to read the stars around me, but it feels like eavesdropping on a prayer. Has anyone written the exact same plea as mine? I want to believe they have—that my hopes reach back into other generations. That none of us are as alone as we think.

"Here." Tara hands her star up to me, and I crouch down to reach. "Don't look at it."

And I truly don't, as I place her star near mine. They twist a little, settling in. I scramble down, dusting off my hands before surveying my handiwork.

Tara and I stand side by side, looking upward.

"Now what?" she asks.

"I guess we wait."

CHAPTER NINETEEN

I EXPECT HIM TO LOOK DIFFERENT. I IMAGINE THE SCENE DURING my entire Sunday walk to Holyoke, how I'll find him and ask if we can talk. But when I emerge from the forest path, there he is: tall and blond in a lemon polo shirt. He's a beacon of light that does not call me home.

He's pacing, and when he glances up, he stops dead. My parents must have told him I'd be coming over.

I wait for him to remark that I look different. I *feel* different. Tougher and more vulnerable at the same time.

"Luce." He says it like an exhale as he leans in to hug me. "It's good to see you. Your dad told me you went to Daybreak after all."

"I told you that I would." I say this as mildly as I can, with no trace of bitterness. Because I don't feel any, truly.

"Right. Of course." I don't think Lukas could ever look embarrassed; he has too much dignity for that. But he can certainly look sheepish. "Could you . . . would you have time to take a walk? With me? I don't want to steal from your time with your parents, but—"

"Of course." His hesitancy, so reminiscent of when we first met. It dissipated a little over time, as we became sure of each other and fit into a routine.

As we walk toward the rim of the lake, I glance up at him. "How are your parents?"

"Good!" he says. "Good. Dad's in Florida golfing with his brothers. Mom's busy with the garden. She sent up a whole box of jams for you and your parents."

"Ooh, *yes*." My mouth waters at the idea of it. Her strawberry-rhubarb jam is a revelation. "And training is going well?"

He starts in about running, but I can't focus. I know the sound of his voice. I know the reliable khaki shorts he's wearing. I know his combed golden hair and the lines between his eyebrows that form when he's worrying about something.

He's always worrying about something.

Lukas's mind spins constantly. Sometimes I think if I leaned close enough to his ear, I could hear the whir of metal cogs. He ruminates over theology, over morality and the Right Choices. And I love that about him, this immeasurable depth of caring, of trying.

But what makes Lukas happy—like, really giddy happy? We went out for almost two years, and I'm not sure that I know.

I'm working through a lot, and it's easy for me to be serious because of what's going on in my life. I realized that because it's how Keely can be too. She may say blunt things, but her mind operates at subterranean levels. There's so much thinking deep beneath the surface of everything she says.

But people like Jones and Anna wear their emotions like clothes. Jones's happiness might as well be a plaid three-piece suit. Retro and jaunty. Anna's joy is a yellow plastic raincoat. Her anger is a red cape, flashing and spinning out.

And I think that's why I can't get enough of them. They balance me. I don't need another person who is pre-occupied, pulling me further into introspection and worry. I need someone who reminds me to let it out. Someone who reminds me by living it.

We approach a bench, weather-beaten and rusted at its iron joints. Lukas gestures toward it. "Do you want to sit for a minute?"

"Sure." I sit facing the water, happy to soak in the view.

But Lukas turns to me, his face earnest. "Luce, I shouldn't have said some of the things I said before you left. I've had some time to reflect, and I don't feel right about it. I really hope you can forgive me."

"I can. I do." My stomach feels like a hammock—swaying, swaying. I can't believe how our positions have swapped in just a month's time.

How can half a summer shift your whole world? Here's what I am learning: Sometimes, the big changes seem to happen in small, fast moments. A diagnosis. A breakup. A crush. But usually, there was something there—underlying, building up—all along. *C'mon, Luce. Out with it.* "But I do think you were right that we're not the best people for each other."

He looks surprised, chin retracting the slightest bit. "Oh."

It's hard to imagine going home at the end of the summer, back to my little house across the street from the church. No campers running around me, no creaking trees at night, a bedroom all to myself. Something aches in my throat when I think about it. But even when I force myself to think about going back to normal life, I just can't see Lukas as my boyfriend anymore. He was a decision I made a long time ago, and I carried it out happily. But I can't keep making it. "I think we're too alike, don't you? Something just isn't fitting the way it's supposed to."

"Wow. Okay." He's lacing his fingers together. "Maybe, yeah."

"I'd still really like to be friends," I add, though I hope it's unnecessary. "I think we make more sense as friends, actually. I've thought about it a lot."

"Well," he says, and the smile is a little forced. But he's trying for it because he's a good guy. He hears me with grace, and that's not nothing. "That's that."

"I'm sorry. You know how much I care about—"

"I do. It's okay, Luce. I think we both felt something was off." When I nod, he smiles for real. "All right. It's settled. So, tell me about camp. I've been picturing you here the whole time!"

"It's . . . hard. And great." I smile over at him. "The kids are from really different backgrounds, and sometimes it feels like . . . slowly learning a new language for each person. But that's why I love it."

"And you have friends there?"

"I do."

He's studying me, like maybe he can see me now in the light I feel I'm standing in. "I like your hair."

"Oh, thanks." It's wilder in the summer heat; no time or energy to straighten it.

We sit for a while, talking about my life, about this summer.

Lukas was exactly who I should have been with . . . if I was the girl I was trying so hard to be. But I'm not her. I'm not.

And when the morning is over, we part the way we belong: as friends.

The leaves rustle as I stride back to Daybreak, and I can't believe it's settled. Lukas and I ended it . . . because *I* wanted to. A month ago, I never would have believed that.

There are a lot of things I wouldn't have believed two months ago. But then, there were a lot of other things I *did* believe in, without questioning.

Next weekend is the Fourth of July. Independence Day. And maybe a little part of me will be celebrating myself.

Back at camp, my cabin girls are playing tag outside while Keely braids Nadia's hair on the front porch. She glances up at me, my assured stride, hair breezing backward. "Whose empire did *you* just overthrow?"

My own.

After lights-out, I pound a minor scherzo into the piano keys. I'm amped up on my own decisiveness and certainty. I made the right decision for my life today, even though it isn't the safest one.

"So. You okay?" Jones asks, when I come to sit by him. He sets down his biography du jour and angles toward me. "Keely blabbed. Your boyfriend came up to see you?"

"*Not* my boyfriend."

"Right."

"It's really okay. It's nice to have things finalized. Very amicable. Mutual."

"That sounds . . . very grown-up."

I snort. "Lukas is very grown-up. I'm . . . trying."

"But you went out for a while, right?"

"Two years. Yeah." When I say it like that, it seems callous that I'm not upset. "It was hard to realize it wasn't working, because we were really good to each other. Just not good *for* each other. Does that make any sense?"

"Yeah. I've been there. When nothing about the relationship is wrong. But 'not wrong' isn't the same as 'totally right.'"

"Exactly. He's just . . . He's really great, in so many ways. But when something difficult happens, he can't be *real* about it. He can offer advice and be thoughtful . . . but he can't seem to . . ."

"Really feel it with you."

"Yes!" How did he know that?

He smiles sadly, as if hearing my question. "It happened a lot after my sister died. Some people just couldn't get in there. They could be kind. But Keely came over one night that first week and just threw herself down on my bed and sobbed. She really looked up to Vanessa."

I forget, sometimes, that Keely has been in his life for that long. That she knew his sister too.

"Anyway," he says. "I liked that she wasn't afraid to be upset in front of me. She didn't feel guilty, when I had more reason to be upset. She just felt it. That mattered. Because . . ."

"It gave you permission to do it too."

He smiles. "Right. That's it."

"What was she like? Your sister?"

"Nessa?" He considers this, lacing his fingers together. "She was . . . smart. Loved math. But she was also creative, in this precise way. Like, we dyed Easter eggs every year. And she'd always be at the table for hours after the rest of us, experimenting with color fades and stickers."

I love dyeing Easter eggs. Just thinking about it, I can almost smell the sharp vinegar. We sat at the kitchen table every year, fingers stained rose and robin's-egg blue. Somewhere not so far from my family, Jones and his sister were doing the same thing.

"How much older was she?"

"Five years. It's a weird age gap. But I think it was fun for her, like I was an excuse to watch kid movies and play with Legos when it wasn't supposed to be cool anymore." He glances over. "I guess I'm the same way. I think about her a lot when I'm with the campers."

"I'm that way too. I still like Disney movies. Not in an ironic or nostalgic way. Like, I genuinely enjoy them. I've never been too old or too cool for anything in my life."

"The campers sense that, you know—when we're really having fun with them." His smile is wistful, and I know it well. It's the same one my mom wears when she talks about her parents. "Vanessa would have been a great counselor."

"Did your parents ever consider Daybreak for her? As a camper?"

"Yeah. She straight up refused. It makes me wonder, though, if it would have helped. But maybe you've noticed, depression can be a tricky one for campers. Everything at Daybreak is kind of centered around fun. Sensory experiences. Swimming, cooking, crafts. I think maybe it's even harder to be surrounded by all that when you're supposed to feel things and don't."

"I can see that, yeah."

260

"But I still think she would have rocked as a counselor. And she would have done something cool with her life. That much I know. I make it up sometimes, the story of Vanessa. I imagine all the things she'd be doing."

"What's your favorite version?"

"Uhh . . ." He smiles again, thinking about her in this way. "Probably that she runs an art program for kids who have been struggling."

"It's so nice that your parents knew to send you here as a kid, to let you process everything."

"Well . . . ," he says. "Yeah. But now that I'm older, I think part of it was that my parents needed time to handle their own grief. I think me being away that first summer was easier. They didn't have to hide their sadness for my benefit."

I think of my mom, doggedly refusing to be weak in front of me. Did she suggest Daybreak so she could be weak without me witnessing it? "How are your parents these days?"

"Well, you don't ever get over it, obviously. But my mom has forgiven herself, I think. That was a big hurdle." He glances up at me. "She felt like she failed Vanessa, even though she did everything right. Got her into therapy, tried meds, never made her feel ashamed. She still doesn't take on depressed teens as clients—too personal."

I open my mouth, ready to confess that my mom is very sick and very nearby, but a flash of motion catches my eye. There's a camper in the doorway. One with a belly bulging out of her pajamas.

"Hey, Tara." I'm immediately wondering if Miss Suzette is up. If Tara's in labor over a month early. "You feel okay?"

"Yeah. Just heartburn. I wanted a glass of milk."

Jones jumps to his feet. "I'll get it for you. Anything else? Snack?"

"No thanks. Food makes it worse."

Tara looks around the room, a casual Sherlock scanning for clues. "So, you guys hang out in here after we go to bed?"

"Not really. I play piano some evenings, and Jones reads." I gesture to his biography of Cleopatra.

"You play piano?"

"Yep."

"Oh, yeah. From the talent show. Can I hear?"

"Um. Sure." I move to the piano bench and play the first bit of *Solfeggietto*. It's a showy tune, fast enough to impress a layperson. And it's only about a minute long, so it's ideal for briefly showcasing your skill.

"Holy. Shit," Tara says. "How long did that take to learn?"

"The piece? Or playing piano?"

"Both?"

"Many, many hours."

She rests her hands on her stomach. "I wish I could do that."

Jones returns with a glass of milk, which Tara takes from him. "Jones, did you know that Hansson is, like, Mozart or something?"

"Why do you think I read in here at night?"

I smile up at Tara. "I can teach you basics sometime, if you like."

"She's a really good teacher," Jones adds.

She takes a gulp of her milk. "Maybe."

"Can we walk you back to your cabin?" Jones asks.

She looks between us, perhaps snagging on how nonchalantly Jones spoke for both of us. *We*. "I'm okay. Thanks, though. Have a good night."

JULY

CHAPTER TWENTY

ON OUR NIGHT OFF, WE HIKE TO THE USUAL SPOT, BUT NONE OF us can bear the idea of adding to the heat with a bonfire. Instead, we settle in with only the lantern lights.

"Fuck it," Mohan says, opening the backpack. "I'm eating these anyway."

He pulls out the bag of marshmallows, along with whatever alcohol they got hold of this week.

"We're shocked," Anna says, holding out her hand. "Gimme."

When we all have a handful of marshmallows and drinks, Jones lifts his cup. "Another week down. Cheers."

Another week down. At first, I wanted them to rush past—wanted the summer to be over with. Now I'm gripping them tightly, trying to cherish it all. When I examine my cup, there's a small amount of amber liquid. "Mmm. Smells like cinnamon."

"That's because it's cinnamon whiskey." This is from Mohan.

Henry gives him a look. "It tastes like red hots."

"It tastes like Christmas," Keely amends.

My lips tingle before the liquor reaches my taste buds. The cinnamon burns a trail down my esophagus, spreading out in my stomach and back up to my cheeks. As promised, I'm filled with Christmas: spice and clove, sweetness, fireplaces spitting sparks. My mom's snickerdoodles, her favorite holiday potpourri called "White Christmas." How many more of those seasons do I have with her? *Please one more. Please dozens more.* I'll take whatever I can get. In the meantime, I take another swig. My mouth sears with heat and home.

We go around with our highs and lows. High for me: Thuy put her nose underwater for a few seconds. Low: Maya's panic attack during rest time.

"Not your breakup?" Anna asks this with pleasant curiosity—no trace of judgment.

"No," I admit, surprised that I didn't even consider it. "And technically, we broke up over a month ago. This was just . . . I don't know. Finalizing."

"So, you're really okay?" Mohan asks. And with an almost impressive lack of subtlety, he glances at Henry to see his reaction.

"I really am."

When we get to Keely, she looks coy.

"Low: bickering with my sister. High." She pauses to sip

her drink. There is a practiced casualness to her posture, like she knows she holds an ace. "My date."

That's all it takes. Mohan screeches, "EXCUSE ME, BITCH?!" and Anna huffs, "I can't believe you didn't tell us!" while I make eye contact with Henry, both of us trying not to laugh.

As it turns out, Keely's day-off date was with the Kennedy cousin from that night at Tom's. He really did take her boating, and I can no longer restrain my laugh. He let her steer and asked a lot of questions about her life. And listened. All in all, the verdict is Not Nearly as Douchey as He Looks.

"So, yeah," she says, in conclusion. "Then he drove me back to camp."

"And?" Mohan prods.

"And what?"

Anna opens her mouth to portray a sloppy, tongue-heavy make-out session.

"It was good," Keely says, glancing at her nails.

"*Good?*" Anna demands. "A first kiss better be more than good. It should knock your legs out from under you. Right?"

We all nod, if only to pry the details out of Keely. She sighs, resigning herself to being outnumbered. "On the boat, we were laughing. And when I leaned in, he was leaning in too. Like we'd done it a thousand times before. So. More than good."

None of us speak for a few moments. But you can almost hear our shared longing, like an ache between ribs. *If only. I hope.* This is a way I'd like to be kissed, immediately familiar but still exciting.

"So, Lucy," Mohan says. "What was your first kiss with the ex-BF like?"

"Oh, come on. I'm not going to talk about that." I'm sure they think I'm a prude, but really, I just don't want to talk about kissing another guy in front of Henry. Not when I think about kissing him every time I near his orbit. He's sitting on the log, and I'm on the blanket in front of him. I'm glad he can't see my face.

"I bet it was on her front porch after a formal first date," Mohan announces, as if I am not present. "Like, literally dinner and a movie."

It was actually dinner and putt-putt, thank you very much. And he kissed me in the car at a red light. Like he couldn't wait, like he might lose his nerve. Or maybe he was nervous that my dad would open the front door and find us on the porch, who knows?

Keely smiles over her drink. "And I bet it was the third date at least."

Later. We went out for a while, held hands plenty before we kissed. So what? But I make my face blank, shrugging with a kind of smugness. I'll never tell.

"Well, if that's true, it's very 1950s and romantic," Anna, my real friend, says.

"People liked tongue in the fifties too," Keely notes, and the other traitors snicker into their hands.

"Guess all you want," I say, sipping my drink. "But you perverts wouldn't know romance if it handed you a dozen roses."

Mohan cackles with glee, while Keely brushes her hair back, dignified. "I prefer wildflowers, personally. Or handcuffs."

"She only says these things to shock you," Henry says, taking pity on me. But Keely waggles her eyebrows at me, and I really do wonder. "She was singing a different tune when Mr. Yadriel Soto was *wooing* her last year. She *loved* it."

"How dare you bring that up!" Keely swats at his knee, and I lean away to avoid the fray. "Ugh, he was so hot. Do you remember how hot he was?"

"Mmmm," Anna says, and Mohan raises one hand like he is praising Jesus for this guy's hotness.

"Sometimes I get online just to look at pictures of him in his army uniform." Keely sighs dreamily. "He's stationed in North Carolina now."

The conversation shifts to former flames, and I stretch, unfolding my crossed legs.

"You can lean back if you want," Henry says.

"Oh. Thanks." I might think this was weird, except that these four are always in contact with one another—Anna tucked into the crook of Mohan's shoulder, Jones carrying Keely on his back.

When I relax against his legs, my blood speeds up, rushing to inform the rest of my body: *We're touching! We're touching!*

I did not use to be such an embarrassing person.

If you're in a quiet enough room, you realize some light-bulbs make little sounds every once in a while. A zap of energy, an electric hum. When Henry leans forward to whisper something about Mohan's ex-girlfriend, I swear something in my heart buzzes like a filament.

It's the eye contact across crowded rooms, like I'm always the first person he looks for. Our evening routine in the rec room with easy conversation. I collect these moments like gold coins, adding them up in my mind. In the span of ten seconds, I can think both: *This is happening!* and *Am I making it up?*

It's exhausting.

It's exhilarating.

And suddenly, I need to flee. I'm nearly squirming from the way my heart flutters, and I just need to not drink any Christmas alcohol or talk about kissing.

"I'm actually gonna head back," I announce.

Mohan swivels to me. "Say *what?*"

"I'm wiped from this week."

"We understand, Boo." Anna pats my leg, eyes already dreamy from the red-hots whiskey. T minus ten minutes till they're talking about life in other galaxies.

Henry gets up behind me. "I'll walk you back."

"Oh. You don't have to." *But I want you to.* I think I might as well have said it, googly-eyed as my stupid face has got to be.

"Yes, he does," Keely says. "Otherwise we'll worry. And take a lantern."

Henry points up at the full moon, high in the cloudless sky. "We're good, I think. And I can use the light on my cell."

Well, I guess this is happening. "Okay. Thanks. Night, guys."

"Sleep tight!" Anna calls. And then the three of them exchange totally conspicuous glances. *Am I making it up?*

As we begin down the path, I hear Keely start in about how wild things really do happen during full moons. It's *documented*.

"There they go," I tell Henry. "Nerds."

I don't have to look over to know he's grinning. "No doubt. But I like 'em."

"Yeah. Me too."

We're halfway there when Henry pulls out his cell phone.

"The light is much dimmer than I thought," he says, laughing. "Maybe we should have taken a lantern. I just didn't want them bumbling around back there. At one point last year, Anna—"

Before he can finish the sentence, I step into some sort of divot. It only barely disrupts my gait, but Henry is ready to catch me, hand light on my back.

"Whoa. Okay. Do I need to carry you?"

274

"Nah." I steady myself. "Imagine how jealous Neveah would be."

"Ha." His hand drops away, and he goes right back to his rambling walk and his story. *Am I making this up?*

Once we're out of the woods, he keeps walking with me. Now that there are no trees overhead, I can see him clearly in the dove-gray moonlight.

"So, hey. I wanted to apologize on behalf of our idiot friends. They shouldn't have grilled you like that about . . . your ex."

"Oh, it's fine," I say. His expression is skeptical, perhaps even worried. "Really! It didn't bother me."

"Okay. Good. I just thought they might have offended you. Like, maybe you were doing that thing where you don't kiss anyone till you get married. I mean it's cool if—"

"What? No!" I laugh a little under my breath, to let him know that's a silly thought. I know a few people who are doing that, but it's not for me. "*Why?* Because my dad's a pastor?"

He shrugs, with a guilty little grimace. That's a yes.

I shake my head. "I was, in fact, kissing a real live boyfriend until last month."

"Well, I didn't think you *made up* a boyfriend. I mean, Luke and Lucy. It's terrible."

"Lukas. He doesn't like being called Luke."

"That's *worse* somehow," he says, laughing again. "You'd invent a better name than that if he was fake."

"Or a worse one. Like, so bad that there's no way I'd make up something so bad. My boyfriend, Percival."

"Hey! Percival is my grandpa's name."

I whirl to him, free hand over my mouth. "Oh my gosh, I'm so sorry! It was just—"

"Luce, I'm teasing you." He's grinning as I shove his shoulder, laughing. In an effort to keep me from pushing him away, he grabs my hand. "I'm sorry. Couldn't help it. It's cute how literal you are."

It's cute. Cute. Me. Okay.

His fingers, still laced through mine.

"So!" he says cheerfully. "Would it be okay for me to kiss you, then?"

I stop dead. Blink. My heartbeat is a throb, almost painful. "Now?"

That smile, smug and amused. Oh, save me. Literal Jesus in heaven, help me because I cannot withstand it, and I don't even want to.

"Not necessarily," he says. "I know you just broke up with someone. But, you know, sometime."

"Yes," I blurt out. "Sure. Great."

Sure? I said SURE, GREAT?? God, I know You hear me! Bail a girl out!

"Okay, good." His eyes sweep over mine.

He turns to go, even though our hands stay linked.

"Wait, I . . ." My mouth hangs open as I fail to finish that sentence—any sentence. He steps back to me anyway. He's grinning until the split second before he presses his lips to mine.

What was your first kiss with Jones like? they'll ask someday. *Oh, come on,* I'll reply. *I'm not going to talk about that.*

Because how could I ever really explain his sure hands on my neck, tilting my face up to his? How a black ceiling of stars arched over us, pine branches bowing to cocoon us against the earth. How I clung to him because the ground flew out beneath us—or maybe we rocketed upward. How my heart beat so fast that I almost felt like laughing. Because it's giddy to stumble into magic, to realize what this can feel like. Each kiss a phrase exchanged between us: *There you are. There you are.* I wasn't even looking for him, so why do I feel found?

CHAPTER TWENTY-ONE

Is there any stretch of time longer than the space between a first and second kiss? As the girls zip around the cabin, getting ready for the day, I'm goofy-faced and dazed. I keep pressing my fingers to my lips, as if I can hold the feeling there.

"*What* is going on with you?" Keely asks as we herd our campers toward breakfast.

"Me? Nothing. Just excited to have another night off." It's our one Saturday free, thanks to Henry's brass band performance at the Fourth of July festival in town.

When I spot him walking toward the lodge, my heart takes a whole note rest between its beats of percussion. In a crisp white T-shirt, short sleeves neatly cuffed, he's James Dean—but with a leather trumpet case slung across his chest like a weekend bag. Nobody has any business being this cool. Although . . . he did confess to me last week that those tortoiseshell sunglasses are prescription. So maybe not *that* cool.

"Ohhh," Keely says, peeling away to give us space. "Gotcha."

"Shut up," I mumble.

"Hey," he says. We stand there, exchanging the stupid, helpless smiles of having a really good secret.

"Hi."

Gosh, we're dummies.

"So, I'm off to the festival to help set up everything. But I'll see you there later?"

"Yeah."

He reaches for my hand, like instinct, before remembering there are campers all around. The backs of our knuckles brush. Even that tiny touch almost makes me feel fluttery.

The rest of the day drags like a middle-school band tempo, but we're off duty once the girls go to dinner.

I emerge from the bunk bathroom, minimal makeup and hair falling loosely.

"Hmm," Keely says, taking my outfit in. The sound is a pronouncement.

I'm wearing my favorite shorts: pale, cuffed denim. Well, they're my favorite to look at anyway, but I'm always too self-conscious to wear them. This is probably my favorite shirt too. White linen and floaty, so wide-necked that I have to wear a tank top underneath. It slips off one shoulder sometimes, in a way that I think looks casual and soft. So if Keely hates this look, I really don't have a better option. "What?"

She goes back to lacing her boots. "Nothing."

"Oh, come on, Keels. Now I feel like I need to go change."

"Don't." The word is sharp, commanding. "You look like you."

"I look like me?"

"Yeah. This look seems really 'Lucy' to me."

I'm stunned to silence, but luckily Keely doesn't expect a response. She looks, of course, masterfully cool in an olive-green T-shirt dress and her combat boots. The only reason I had the nerve to wear these shorts is because I've been watching how she dresses. The fabric hugs all the round places of her body, and she wears everything like she has quiet knowledge of her beauty, her power. So here I am, exposing thighs that I've always wished were smaller.

Mohan shows up in a Springsteen shirt, Anna beside him in American flag shorts. It feels heady, the swell of excitement that will pop into fireworks.

It's a solid twenty-minute walk into town, and Anna slows us down by picking roadside flowers. She calls them daisies, though I think they might be fancy weeds. My hair rises in the humidity, even curlier than usual, and I run my hands along the white picket fences, nearly skipping.

"Stand still a sec," Anna says. She places the stems of a few flowers into my hair. "Your curls hold them so well!"

The park greets us with swarms of people in aggressively patriotic outfits. I breathe in sparkler smoke and bug spray and the aroma of spicy, food-truck meat. There's a familiar scent on the breeze, floral but tangy. Petunia. They're planted all over the edges of the park, red and white and purple against dark mulch.

My mom plants petunias every spring. In terra-cotta pots for our porch. Velvety petals. From the side, each bloom looks like a Victrola. The smell of soil, hose water in the metal watering can.

In this moment, my senses full of memory, I miss her so much that my chest aches. I briefly consider sprinting to Holyoke, throwing myself onto the couch beside her for a movie marathon. But no. This is what she wants for me, friendships and good summer memories. She made that clear enough.

The park fills the center of town, with a gazebo on the far end. That's where the music is coming from, a spirited cover of "Brown-Eyed Girl."

Anna stops at a free spot of grass on the lawn, one of the last where our blanket will fit. "This is good."

We set up camp, complete with the paper bag dinners Whelan made us. Chicken salad sandwiches, cheese cubes, fresh fruit.

Everyone else sits down while I scan the crowd for Henry. He's lined up in front of the gazebo, standing beside another trumpeter. Like the rest of them, he's wearing suspenders and a flat straw hat with a red-and-navy ribbon. The outfits should be costumey—meant for old-fashioned soda shoppes—but on Henry Jones it looks . . . I don't know, classic. He leans down as the mustachioed trumpeter whispers something that makes them both laugh. The setting sun catches on the tubas and the saxophones and Henry's grin.

Beside me, Mohan is busy picking flecks of feta off a watermelon square.

"You're ruining it!" Anna says. "The mint and feta are the best part."

"*Poison,*" Mohan declares.

The band breaks into a cover of "Livin' on a Prayer," distracting them from their argument.

"C'mon," Anna says, reaching out a hand to pull me up.

Anna leads me into the crowd, her hand warm in mine. We find an open spot near swaying drunk people as a trombone blurts out the first verse. The trumpets come in for the chorus. Anna sings the words to me, laughing as we take turns spinning each other. Keely and Mohan appear by the third verse. We're grabbing at the air above us, pulling it down in passionate interpretations of the lyrics. These are my people. I am so in love with them I can barely contain it in my skin.

I'm not Pastor Dave's daughter right now, and I'm certainly not Lukas's girlfriend. Not Bird or Swim Team Captain or even LucyEsMakeup. But I don't have a name for who I am. Lucy, of course, but a Lucy that I'm only starting to figure out. Maybe I'm a little in love with her too.

"This is his solo," Anna calls to us. Henry has stepped to center, rocking a little to the beat. He takes a deep breath and squares his feet for the last chorus. The notes are sharp, precise. When the key change comes, I wince instinctively, hoping he hits it. He nails the note and slides up a third, wailing in a tone too clear to come from a brass instrument.

The whole crowd claps, and someone whistles near my ear. Jones puts up one hand, modestly acknowledging them as he folds back into the lineup. I grin like the foolish, got-kissed-last-night girl that I am.

"Thanks, folks," the bandleader says into the mic. "We're gonna take a quick break."

Something possesses me, draws me forward. Because I miss Henry Morris Jones. How can that be? It's only been a few hours.

I move through the crowd, dodging little kids playing tag and men sipping drinks. The grass, cool and spiky, tickles the sides of my feet between my sandal straps. I sidestep a group of guys my age huddled around a cell phone. The world blurs over with color and movement, yet I see forward with perfect clarity.

I lean my back against a pillar at the edge of the park shelter, waiting as Jones chats with a trombonist.

When he spots me, his mouth stops midsentence to grin. He touches the guy's arm, excusing himself from the conversation. "Hey!"

"Hey. You sounded great."

"Well, thanks. Wish I could hang with you guys, though." He adjusts the daisy nearest my ear and smiles. "Anna's doing?"

I nod, and his fingers stay in my hair, the heel of his hand light against my cheekbone. *Now?* I asked frantically last night. *Now.* My blood pumps out the message. *Now, now.*

"Look," he says. "About last night. I know you just broke up with someone. I know I shouldn't have——"

Before he can finish, I stretch up to kiss him. To say: *Yes, you should have. Or I would have. In fact, I will.*

Someone from the band whoops, and Jones's hand moves away from my cheek. At first, I think he's backing away. But no. He's taking off his hat, using it to shield our faces from his bandmates. But it's too late. The tambourine is shaking with joyous metal clangs, and we're laughing too hard to keep kissing. I press into his shoulder, somehow both embarrassed and delighted.

"Jonesy-boy got a GIRL," one hollers.

"Yeah, yeah," he says, still smiling as he waves them off.

"I should let you get back to it. You'll meet us at the party later?"

"If you're still there after fireworks and cleanup and all that."

"Good." When I back away from him, our fingers stay linked until the last possible second, and we both laugh at how dorky we are.

I float back to the picnic blanket. Keely looks up from stabbing a fat strawberry with a plastic fork. She glances at me, then narrows her eyes in closer examination. "Man. You're so far gone. Look at your face."

I wrinkle my nose at her, but the smile still doesn't drop. "I can't look at my own face."

"You're an idiot," she says, laughing. The strawberry bulges out the side of her cheek.

"Wait. Here." I grab the whipped cream from the cooler and toss it to her. She sprays the whipped cream straight into her mouth.

She chews with her eyes closed, like this moment of zen in the middle of a crowded park. A happy sigh makes her look delicate. Soft. "I really love summer."

I settle myself onto the picnic blanket, and the twilight clouds shift above me. "Yeah. Me too."

Never quite as much as this one, though. Later, as we walk to the party, the breeze lifts my hair off my shoulders, puffs the curls into the air. I wear them like fireworks.

I've only ever been to two other *high school movie*–type parties. That's how I think of them, at least. Parties with my friends at home are, like, board games with the swim team, movie marathons, and church stuff. Anything that has a keg feels like I'm watching it from a distance, not really a part of it.

But here I am, standing next to Anna and a big silver barrel of beer. I wonder if all parties are like this, if they just bleed together. Obscenities yelled as Ping-Pong balls whiff over red plastic cups. Sloppy kissing under bad lighting, sticky linoleum in overcrowded kitchens.

No one but me seems to wonder where the host's parents are.

"So we're staying? You sure?" Keely asks.

I assume the question is for me, but Anna answers sternly, "I said I've got this."

Anna's anxiety has clearly eased a good deal since this morning, but Keely still frowns as she hands us drinks.

A half hour in, we squeeze together on a high-rise deck to watch the fireworks.

"These are my favorites. The drippy golden ones." Anna sighs, tracing one finger against the black sky.

"Yeah," Keely says. "Like a glittery weeping willow."

The grand finale starts, burst after burst—white and green, red and purple circles expanding over each other like a kaleidoscope view.

"I wish Jones was here," Anna whispers. "All five of us."

All five of us.

Mohan presses a kiss against her temple, and I feel like I'm intruding on a personal moment.

"Simmons, Tambe!" a voice yells from the kitchen. "Game time! Defend your title or forfeit it."

"So," Anna says once they've left. "You and Jones?"

"I think so," I admit. "Yeah."

Her smile is almost smug. "Good."

She wrings the details out of me—how helplessly I like him and last night's kiss. The memory is only twenty-four hours old, and it already feels precious, like I have to whisper it. So as not to disturb the magic. I thought I wasn't ready to tell anyone, but . . . it's Anna. She's been my person here since the first day.

We're on our way to get some water when a voice calls out, "Hey, ladies. Why don't I know *you* two?"

Anna pauses, and I can tell she's debating whether or not to turn her head. Before she can, a girl's sharp voice replies, "Oh my God. Don't bother with that one. Fully crazy."

Only then do I turn. By the staircase, there's a girl with dark hair standing between two guys. Her eyes are on Anna, and I step forward. It's a useless impulse—as if my body will block my friend from this girl and her blazing eyes. I've heard Anna call herself crazy, but this is different. It's nasty. Intentionally nasty.

"Good to see you too, Greer." Anna's voice, from just past my shoulder, is over-the-top saccharine—totally sarcastic.

"Oops, we better be nice." The girl's laughter trills through the air, still directed at the two guys as if we don't exist. "Don't want to witness a freak-out."

"Like some kinda mental breakdown?" one of the guys asks.

Anna tugs at my shirt, but I am not letting this girl get away with it.

"Yeah," the girl—Greer—says. "She's actually—"

"*Don't*," I cry out, holding up a hand as if I can stop whatever words come next from entering the air. "Ugh. What is *wrong* with you?"

Anna's fingernails dig into my arm. I've floated outside my body, pulse thumping and palms sweating with the foreign, poisonous feeling of confrontation.

"Excuse me? This is my best friend's party, bitch." The girl retracts her head, but not even her darkened expression will stop me. She glances between Anna and me. "And who the hell are you, her *girlfriend*?"

I'm about to say . . . something, I don't know what, when Keely wafts in, settling between me and this minion of Satan. The coconut scent of Keely's leave-in conditioner and her sandalwood perfume drift in too, and I realize how much I associate these with our cabin, with the peace of going to sleep. I breathe in, glad to have broken my gaze with the girl.

"Hey, ladies," Keely says to us, in a singsong. "Let's get going."

Keely's eyes cut over to the girl. If I didn't know her, this would seem like a casual glance. But, oh no. It's measured, calculating. "Oh hey, Greer."

I watch the little posse take Keely in, dark curls to scuffed-up boots. The outfit that made me feel like I was trying too hard by comparison. Her build—somehow both full and compact at once, beautiful and strong. Her lip color has worn off a bit, now a rubbed berry color across her mouth. She's a presence. Everything about her says: *I'm cooler than you, and yet I care less than you.*

"Keely," Greer says icily.

"Thanks for the booze. You all have a good night." Keely takes Anna by the hand and they're gone, moving through the hallway crowd.

Before I follow them, I turn to the girl, hands trembling. "You're . . . *mean*. And, just, like . . . incorrect about *several* things. Which makes you seem stupid." I hold out my hand to number off these accusations. "So, to summarize . . . Mean. Wrong. Stupid."

Well then. Not as clever as I'd hoped. But, hey, it's my first party confrontation. I barely register the look of utter revulsion on her face before turning to leave.

She calls after me. "Don't bother ever coming to another party because—"

"Great," I say, barely glancing back. "I literally don't care at all."

"Oh, burn," one of the guys says, laughing.

"Shut up, Cal," she snaps. She says something else, her tone slashing at me like razors, but I'm not listening. My back is to them; I'm as good as gone.

I go numb to any feeling but my thumping pulse. Fortunately, my feet keep moving down the front porch and the lawn, to where everyone waits for me on the sidewalk. Anna's face is tear-streaked, her hair wild—as if she's tugged at it in agony. She and Keely are half-talking, half-ranting under a yellow streetlight. Mohan's arms are crossed, like he's refereeing.

When I approach, legs shaky, I open my mouth to ask if Anna's okay. But she beats me to it.

"What the *hell*, Lucy?" I almost look behind me, as if there is another Lucy she could possibly be mad at. "You *know* I hate confrontation. I tugged at you. I wanted to *go*."

"I—I'm sorry. I thought that meant . . . I wanted to . . ."

"Well, you shouldn't have. I don't need a savior. You don't get it!"

She bolts away, down the street and toward the woods and home, and Mohan goes off after her.

Protect you. I wanted to protect you. Those are the words bouncing around inside my throat. But maybe it wasn't my battle. I should have gotten her out of there. I misread the whole thing.

"Did I . . . oh my gosh." I turn to Keely, tears filling my eyes. "Did I mess up? It happened so fast—they were just so horrible!"

She turns to face me beneath the pale lamplight. "We do the best we can in the moment, yeah?"

"Yeah." It's not agreement. It's helpless resignation.

"Greer . . ." She sighs, glancing up at the dark sky above us. I can't tell if it's filled with shifting clouds or clearing smoke from the fireworks. "Greer lives in town, but she was a camper with us a few years ago. Just one year. She and Anna have a history. You couldn't have known."

From Keely, it's the closest thing to absolution I'll ever get. I bob my head up and down, arms crossed tightly over my chest.

Keely tilts her head in the direction of camp. "C'mon.

Let's head back. Text Jones that we skipped out on the party. While we still have cell signal."

We walk in silence, passing other parties here and there as we reach the edge of town. Kids flinging cherry poppers against the concrete, adults still in lawn chairs laughing between sips of beer. I want to ask Keely if she thinks this will ruin my friendship with Anna, but I honestly can't bear to hear the answer.

Finally, when we run out of sidewalk, Keely glances over. "I would have done the same thing. For what it's worth."

I snort, brushing my palms over the tall grass on the side of the road. "No, you would have gotten us out of there gracefully. Which is what you did."

"Uh-uh. I only did that because I could see, walking up, what was happening. If she'd surprised me? Oh no. No one gets near Anna with me. No way."

The forest looms beside us. "Really?"

"Really." I can feel her glance my way, surveying my disbelief. "You know we've all fought with each other over the years, right?"

"You have?"

"Of course. We've gotten *into* it, all of us. Mohan and I didn't speak for over a week during eighth-grade summer."

Camp is surprisingly quiet. It's after lights-out, but I thought maybe they'd be riled up from the festivities. Maybe they wore themselves out. Mohan's sitting on the lodge steps, elbows on his knees. "Hey. She's in the Bunker. She's fine— just needed to have a little cry."

Keely turns to me. "You're up."

"But . . . she'll want one of you. Right? I mean . . . ?"

They exchange glances, debating whether my question is even worth responding to.

"Go on," Mohan says. "Chop-chop."

I hurry inside, and everything sounds loud—my breathing, my feet on the wood floors. What will I even say? I guess "I'm sorry," which I am. I just wish I knew what I did wrong. All I know is that I've never had a friendship so immediate and natural as Anna's and mine. The horror of messing it up rolls through me like nausea. At the Bunker, I stop short. Push the door open only a tiny bit. Anna's stretched out on the old plaid couch, facing me.

"Hi," she says in a small voice.

It's enough to know I'm okay to enter. I curl up on the floor in front of her, leaning against the couch. Even after a confusing fight, it would feel weird not to sit right beside her. "I'm so sorry, Anna. Are you okay?"

"I'm okay," she says, sniffling into a tissue. "I'm not mad at you. I shouldn't have yelled."

"Not important," I say. "At all."

"Like, it's not that I'm upset that you said something. I'm upset that anyone would be that awful to me in the first place. It's like, I don't know. Sometimes I'm ready and okay to fight the good fight, and sometimes I'm so exhausted and beat up and sad."

I reach up to the couch and thread my fingers with hers. "That makes so much sense, Anna."

"And, I just *hate* that she got to me like this. I wanted to be tougher."

"Well, letting yourself process hurt *is* pretty tough, I think."

At this, Anna almost smiles—a twitch of her cheeks. "Spoken like a true Daybreaker. Listen to you."

"Well, that just tells me that I'm right." Internally, though, I can't help but feel a flash of pride, warm through my chest.

"Yeah, I know. But, ugh, Greer using parts of who I am like they're bad, like they're weapons against me," she whispers. "It makes me *sick*."

"That girl is awful. She chose to be awful. And you know what?" I look around as if my parents will materialize out of thin air to yell at me, simply because I thought the word. "Fuck that."

I try to say it with ferocity, but Anna laughs. "Oh my God. Is that the first time you've ever said that word?"

"No!" I scoff, offended. "Like, second or third. And she deserves it."

"You know, she came to Daybreak the summer we were twelve, before I really started transitioning. We were good friends, but she had a crush on me. Which I didn't reciprocate." Anna's face clouds over, moving from hurt to thoughtfulness. "She has a lot of problems. At home, I mean."

I narrowly resist growling. "That's not an excuse."

"Yeah. I know." She looks down at me. "Camp is generally, like, this bubble for me. Home *is* usually pretty okay these days. I just really hate this."

"Do you want me to go back and mess her up?"

"Ha! Yeah, right. You're totally a turn-the-other-cheek type. Or you'd, like, slap-fight her."

"Hey! No way! Hair-puller. Ruthless." I mime ripping at a big clump of my hair. "But which of us do you think would be the best in a fight?"

"Lucy Hansson, I'm surprised at you! We have a non-violent philosophy here at Daybreak."

I roll my eyes at her. "So, Mohan?"

"Oh, totally." She squints, imagining it as she laughs. "He's so quick and scrappy. He'd get it done."

"Not Henry? He's no joke with the punching bag, either. Or Keely?"

"Jones has too much *honor*." She pronounces the word like she's mocking it, even though I know she loves that about him too. "Mohan would fight dirty, which you'd need with Greer. And Keely's the queen of shit-talking, but she's not gonna throw a punch. Gentle, that one."

"Oh my gosh. Wait. If we could send anyone from Daybreak to fight Greer, I totally know who I'd pick as tribute. She'd probably volunteer."

"D'Souza!" We both say it at the same time and lean forward in laughter, almost knocking heads.

"Oh my gosh. I bet she'd be like a superhero, all choreography and business."

"Wait, wait," Anna says through her giggles. "I bet Rhea would be like Yoda. Like small and wrinkled but ready to defend everyone."

I can't get out words. I wave my hands in front of my eyes as if this will dry the laughter-tears that are forming. "ANNA. We're not going to be able to look at her tomorrow."

Anna can barely speak through laughing. "What if, at breakfast, she says to us: 'Hungry, you are.'"

"Stop," I gasp out, wiping at my eyes with one hand.

"What if . . . oh my God. What if Bryan busted out, like, formal karate. Wearing one of his polo shirts."

As the moon peeks through the windowpane, we imagine all of our co-counselors as opponents. My stomach muscles feel stretched out from laughter. My hand stays locked with Anna's the whole time.

"Hey, Luce?"

"Yeah?"

"Did you say anything to Greer after I left?"

I tamp my lips together, hesitating. "I told her she's mean. And wrong . . . and stupid."

Anna busts up laughing again. "Wait. So you basically called Greer a meanie-head stupid-face? The third graders are rubbing off on you!"

My arm is propped up on the couch, and I lean my face into it, giggle fit taking me over again.

"You're like a kitten trying out her tiny, little claws tonight."

"Oh my gosh," I howl, laughing at how ridiculous I am. We recover after a few seconds, but it feels so good to be okay. It's tinged with relief, as we patch the first rift between us. Maybe we'll even come out stronger.

"Hey, rock star." Anna's looking over my shoulder.

Henry leans against the door frame, straw hat gone and top buttons undone. We must look quite the scene—Anna flat across a couch with a fistful of tissues, me curled up on the floor beside her, our eyes glittering from laughing so hard.

"Hey." In the Jones Encyclopedia of Smiles, this one is somewhere between "amused" and "relieved." "You guys okay?"

"Yeah," Anna says. "We'll be fine."

And you know what? We will.

CHAPTER TWENTY-TWO

THE NEXT WEEK, HENRY SHOWS UP FOR OUR REC ROOM EVENING with his trumpet and a sheaf of papers in hand.

"I have a favor to ask," he says.

I spin on the piano bench, trying to look like someone who drives a hard bargain. "Oh, *really*?"

"My cousin Laura is getting married in two weeks and, of course, she just told me she wants me to play trumpet for the wedding. There'll be a band the night of, but could you practice with me for it?"

"And what do I get in return?" I ask, smiling as I look up.

"Funny you should ask. Laura said I could bring a date. So . . . an evening with me? It comes with the condition of having to meet my crazy family."

"Sold." I take the music from his hands, and he kisses the top of my head.

I smile like a moron for the first few measures of "La vie en rose."

We're a few attempts in when the rest of the crew shows up, carrying snacks from the Bunker.

"Sounds good in here, music nerds," Mohan says.

When we practice "Trumpet Voluntary," Anna pretends to walk a faux-weepy Mohan down the aisle, where a stoic Keely awaits. They are *ridiculous*.

And later, while Henry piggybacks me back to Cabin 3A, I think maybe I am ridiculous too.

It almost seems too easy, me and Henry Jones. Until the next week, when I'm on my way to swim hour and I stop into Miss Suzette's for some aloe vera.

She hands it over, looking at me more seriously than usual. Like she's disappointed that I let myself get sunburned. "I'm glad you stopped by."

"Oh?"

"I wanted to check in: Are you okay on protection?"

"Oh, yeah! Thanks. This was my fault." I tap my pink nose. "But I have plenty of SPF50 back in the cabin."

"No, sweetie. I meant . . . I mean." She clears her throat, recalibrating her approach. "Rhea mentioned that you and Jones have been . . . well, that you're seeing each other. And it's vital that you're prepared for any possible . . . intimacy that—"

"Whoa! Oh my gosh! No! I don't need that . . . kind of thing!" My face could start one of our Friday night fires.

"Well, you may not think you do, but sometimes in the moment—"

"No, you don't understand. I don't do that. I'm not doing that. Why would Rhea think that?"

"Oh, it's not about you, sugar. She doesn't want to forbid counselor relationships, but over the years, there's been a pregnancy or two."

"Seriously?"

She cocks her head at me, like she's honestly confused that this is a surprise. I just—*what?*

"Well, I appreciate the consideration. But that's not something I'll be doing. I'm a Christian, and it's—"

"I am too, baby. You don't need to explain your choices to me or anyone. But if you change your mind . . . no judgment here."

"Thanks, but I really won't."

I hurry right to the lake's edge, where I grab Anna away from one of her fourth graders. I drag her to a private-enough spot.

"What's with the drama?"

"I need to talk to you." I cross my arms, leaning close.

"Okay." Her face drops the teasing look. "What's wrong? Is it your mom?"

"No! No. It's just that . . ." It's tortuous, trying to get the words out. "Miss Suzette just asked me about . . . protection."

Anna nods, waiting for the rest of the story. As if this is merely a lede line.

I fling my hands out. "Why would she *do* that? We've been together for a week! Do people think we're doing that? Does he think we're going to do that? Because I'm *not*! I just . . . I . . ."

"Whoa, whoa, whoa." Her hands find my arms, trying to contain the emotion. "I'm sure it's what they do if they know there's a relationship happening. If there's any chance at all. They just want everyone to be safe."

"But do you think he . . ." I drop my voice into a nearly inaudible register. I can't believe I'm asking this. Like, what insane turn has my life taken that this is a question? It would never have been a question with Lukas. "Expects that?"

"Oh, God, Luce. No. This is Jones we're talking about." She corrects herself, straightening up. "I mean, I shouldn't speak for him. You should talk to him about it."

"I should talk to a guy I've kissed a few times about"—I drop my voice to less than a whisper—"sex?"

"This is really not my department." She shifts uncomfortably. "But, I mean, just articulate your boundaries. Right?"

"Okay, but not everyone grew up here at *Talk About Your Most Honest Feelings* camp!"

She bursts out laughing, though it doesn't sound unkind. "You mean they don't emphasize communicating about sex in Sunday school?"

"Ugh." I cover my face with both hands and whisper to myself or to God or possibly Satan: "What is happening right now?"

It's Anna who answers, gently. "You're figuring things out with a second boyfriend. Not everything's going to be like the first."

"Yeah, you can say that again." I sigh, twisting my hair

up into a big knot. "Okay. Thanks for dealing with my crazy. Being religious can just make things hard sometimes."

"Aw, sweetie." She leans in to hug me—really hug me. I rest my chin on her shoulder. "I think most things that matter can be difficult sometimes."

"Yeah, you're right." Of course she's right. The night of the Fourth, I watched exactly how awful people can be just because Anna exists as herself. Heck, her ancestors emigrated from Poland. A huge part of her history is made of faith and difficulty, and I'm blabbering like I invented it. Over something totally harmless. I pull away to look at her face. "Oh, my gosh. I'm so sorry. Of course you know that."

She lifts one shoulder, not denying it. But her smile is easy—forgiving. And I'm not even surprised. If I'm learning one thing at my hippie camp, it's that we're all trying, and we're all messing up sometimes. I'm grateful when grace is extended to me.

"I'd be lost without you." I give her arm a playful push.

"Oh, you're still lost, for sure," she says. "But I am too, and at least we're together?" We both lean back to make grim faces at each other and then burst out laughing.

I think that issue is settled, blissfully far away from my actual reality. Until the next night in the rec room, when Henry drops a bomb.

"So, I was thinking . . . Would you like to go camping Friday night? We can't stay the whole night, but it might be fun for a few hours."

I sit back, defensive. What the heck?! It's like the whole universe has conspired to believe I am interested in doing the most intimate possible thing within a few weeks of knowing a person. "Okay. Um. No, thank you."

I turn to get up and leave, but he touches my arm, gentle. I shrug it off. "Whoa, whoa, hey. What did I do?"

"We just started going out!" The words burst forward.

He ducks down a little, trying to get onto my level. Trying to find me. Something connects, his eyes and mine—like he found what he was looking for. "Luce, two sleeping bags. I just meant that we don't get a lot of time alone together. To hang out! I wasn't—oh man. No, I really wasn't trying to . . ."

My arms are crossed, blocking myself off from him. "I mean, you know I have religious beliefs."

"Of course. And I do too."

"I know, but. I mean, what would people think?!"

His eyes narrow. "Did Miss Suzette talk to you?"

My cheeks answer for me.

"Ah. I thought it was only me she cornered."

"She talked to you too?"

"Yeah. And I told her it's not like that. Though I appreciate her looking out." He lifts one shoulder in a helpless shrug. "Look, there's always been a rumor that a counselor got pregnant years and years ago."

"Seriously?"

"Yeah. I once even heard someone speculate that Bryan got someone pregnant when he was a teen. I don't know if it's true, but that's why they're like that."

"Bryan? Ew." I mean, no offense. I guess he's good-looking for his age, but no one wants to think about a middle-aged dad doing . . . that. "Really?"

"Nah. Just gossip. I think I'd know if it had actually happened."

Okay. So it's not that anyone made assumptions about me or about Jones and our relationship. They would have spoken to any of the counselors about this—probably campers too. "I didn't realize. Geez. Okay. I'm sorry. This is . . . mortifying."

"Hey. This?" He gestures between us. "Belongs to us. We make the rules. So how about Rule One is that you never apologize for telling me when you feel uncomfortable?"

"How about Rule Two is that I actually tell you instead of freaking out first?" I reach my arms around him and nuzzle into his neck, safe now.

He presses a kiss to my temple. "Just be honest with me. We'll figure everything else out."

Footsteps enter the rec room, and it's just my luck that I hear Keely's voice. "Ugh. Get a room. A different one."

We don't even look at her. I tilt my chin up to smile at him head-on, and I think this is what it means to be starry-eyed. I feel like I'll never get sick of looking at him.

And we do go camping, or something like it. It's pretty much a usual Friday night, only just the two of us. Mohan was very salty about it.

"So, is this just how it's going to *be* now? You two going off on your own?" he snipped, looking back and forth between us. "I don't support it."

Henry clapped him on the back. "It's one time, man."

And for this one time, we sit beneath the stars, laughing over s'mores and swapping stories about our cabin kids.

"So, here's a question," he says. "Where are you planning on applying to college?"

"Not that question." I groan.

"Okay, okay." He puts his arms up in surrender. "I just felt weird that I didn't know. But if you don't either, I'm happy to not know with you."

"I don't know," I confirm. "And I feel sick thinking about going home to senior year. I don't want to leave."

"Well," he says, reasonably. "Some things aren't camp only. You can take me with you—and those other crazies we call friends. In fact, you better."

I grin at the thought of driving the fifteen minutes between his town and mine. Maybe homecoming together at both our schools. Maybe Anna and Mohan could come down for the weekend and crash!

I'm so giddy with ideas that I second-guess myself, smile dropping. "Is this stupid?"

"Is what stupid?"

"This. Us."

"For me? No. For you?" He shrugs, unbothered. "I can't make that call. You did just break up with someone."

"But it's not stupid for *you*? What if you're a rebound?"

"I'm aware of the possibility. I'm just willing to risk it."

"We don't live in the same town. How will we even see each other? I mean, if you want to still see each other!"

"Okay, two things. Yes, I want to still see each other. And to answer your first question: cars. Automobiles? We have a few in Michigan." He pretends to maneuver a steering wheel. I refuse to laugh.

"I'm serious, Henry! I'm really busy during the school year! It'll probably be difficult to actually be together."

"So what?" His smile is easy, unencumbered. "You scared of difficult things?"

"Yes!" I say, laughing. But maybe I'm not—not with him.

For some reason, this unwinds me. He's not trying to deny that we'll have challenges, but that doesn't mean we'll fall apart. It's a nice perspective, I think.

So maybe I don't know what'll happen. But it's nice to have someone to not know with you.

I could use this time to tell him my biggest unknown: about my mom and chemo and how that might be a really big, difficult part of my year. But he leans in to kiss me, and I just want this happiness for a little while longer—this happiness that feels safe and entirely mine.

CHAPTER TWENTY-THREE

"You were offsides," someone yells.

"No one knows what that means!" one of my Blue Team kids yells back.

D'Souza blows her whistle. "Bickering penalty!"

"That's not a thing!" the kid howls.

"It is now! It means someone has to substitute in for you."

Soccer against the Red Team is going *great*. It's sweltering hot, which is messing with all of us. The humidity feels like something building in the air—a visible cloud packed around us.

As if the pressure has hit its peak, an ambulance siren shrieks, getting quickly louder. The campers stop everything—bickering, kicking, sulking—to cover their ears.

On pure instinct, I look around for any obvious distress. D'Souza mouths the numbers as she counts us off. The siren is nearing, and the counselors exchange worried glances.

"I'll go check." Tambe jogs toward the lodge and Miss Suzette's cabin.

"Could it be Tara?" I whisper.

D'Souza grimaces, looking at the path Tambe took as if she might run after him to investigate too. "I hope not. She's a few weeks away from full-term."

When Tambe reappears, he's walking. I exhale. If it were bad, he'd run.

"It wasn't for us. Drove right past," he said. "It's probably for the church camp that's another mile 'round the bend."

Holyoke. Mom. My hand flies to my mouth. "Oh, Lord. No. *No*."

"Luce? What's wrong?" Tambe asks.

"My mom. Shit. Shit!" I take off in a sprint, sneakers slamming against soft ground. I've never run so fast in my entire life, the world distorting as I tear past the lodge, past every cabin, past every person who calls something out to me. I can't hear any of them; I have to get to her. I plunge through the trees, and there's no sound but the huff of my breath and the crunch of the leaves. A branch stretches into my path, and I can't dodge it in time. It digs a line into the skin across my upper arm. I feel nothing.

My leg muscles move easily into a long stride, like my whole body knows that now is the time to perform. I could run for hours, for miles, for days.

What if I don't get there in time? What if she's scared and she needs me to be there and I'm not?

I push my legs harder, pumping my arms. I'm moving so quickly that the sweat on my forehead cools. What's a fast time for a mile? Six minutes?

I burst into the clearing and up the path, where I see a crowd has gathered by the chapel. *I'm coming, Mom. Whatever happens, I'm going to be there with you.*

The ambulance sits with open doors, belligerently red in a world of oaks and evergreens. I can't see through all the kids and adult counselors waiting in a wide circle. I can't see her. Two people in navy blue EMT clothes are crouched low, strapping a gurney.

"Mom?" I call, trying to duck through people.

Every head snaps up, staring at the crazed stranger who just emerged from the woods. But it's not my mom on the gurney. It's a man with salt-and-pepper hair and a sheepish look on his face.

It's not her. It's not her.

My mom steps forward, arms crossed. I didn't even notice her standing near the third EMT. "Lucy? What's wrong, honey?"

It's her. It's her. With her dangly earrings, with her face creased in concern. She looks sicker than last week—her face a little puffy, her hair thinner.

"Oh, thank God. You're okay." My panting turns into sobs of relief. "We heard the ambulance, and I thought—I thought—"

I clutch onto her, needing both comfort and affirmation that she is really in front of me. Fine. Whole. Here.

"Oh, honey." My mom rubs my back. "Everyone's fine. One of the pastors from Conley Lutheran threw out his back doing relay races."

In response, I sob into her shoulder. *It's the adrenaline,* I hear Miss Suzette say in my mind.

"You ran here? Oh, Bird. I'm fine. Just fine." She watches as I feel around in my shorts pocket for my inhaler. Of *course* this is the morning I forget to grab it. "I've got a spare in the cabin. Let's go inside, okay?"

"Okay." My legs tremble beneath me, and she wraps an arm around my waist. Everyone is still gawking, but only now do I feel a twinge of embarrassment. My heavy breathing sounds more like a panic attack than an asthma attack, but honestly, in this case? They're one and the same.

"They must think I'm insane," I breathe. "I'm so sorry."

Back at our cabin, the inhaler helps relax my throat and lungs, and my mom puts the kettle on. I slump at the table, where my elbows can barely fit between the stacks of Tupperware.

She kisses the top of my head. "I'm gonna give Rhea a quick call. Have a few muffins."

On our tiny kitchen table, there's a pile of food: Miss Rosa's muffins, zucchini bread, brownies. I crack open the nearest container and stuff a mouthful of banana walnut goodness into my mouth. The cinnamon crumbles are the magic part, I think. Miss Rosa brings them to every church event: retreats, Bible studies, funerals. With my second taste of buttery muffin, I almost expect to smell her powdery perfume, hear the *click-click* of the low heels she always wears to church.

Of course our church family would be sending food back with my dad on Sunday. Or maybe leaving it at the house for when my parents stop by after doctor appointments. So many people know the code for our front door—honestly, it's probably not safe. But we've never been robbed, only gifted.

I'm on my second muffin when my mom returns. She makes two mugs of ginger peach tea, and I follow her to the living room.

"Is Rhea mad?"

"No, no. Of course she understands. She said to stay a bit."

"I'm so embarrassed. I just . . . panicked. I didn't even *think*. I left my fellow counselors and all the campers. I probably scared the heck out of them."

She blows on her tea, thoughtful. "Having an almost-adult daughter is new to me, you know. Once, when you were quite small, I was watching as you explored the playground at the park. And I felt it in my bones that you were going to fall. I was there like a flash of light, hands out to catch you. You'd already caught yourself, so you just smiled at me. But that was the first time fear gave me this super-human mom speed and heightened instincts."

I sip my tea, confused about where this memory came from. Where it's going.

"It never occurred to me that one day you'd be almost grown and sprinting toward *me*." She smiles happily, as if flattered by my crazed appearance here. "Motherhood and growing up, full of surprises. Highly recommended."

She says this lightly, but I burst into renewed tears. I want her to live to see me grow up all the way. And how could I ever, ever be a mother myself without her around?

"Oh, dear," she says, taking my tea from me to set it down. "I've moved us in the wrong direction. Though I have to admit, I'm a little relieved."

"Why?" The question comes out in a ridiculous, whiny tone. My own third-grade campers wouldn't dissolve like this.

"Because, Birdie, this is the first time you've cried since before my diagnosis. We've been a little worried you weren't processing it."

I wipe my eyes. "It's not the first time."

"Ah," she says. Her voice is gentle and slow with understanding. "I see. You just haven't cried in front of me or your dad."

"I didn't want to make it worse."

"Honey, nothing about you has ever or will ever make things worse for me." She pulls me close. "Well, your all-night screaming during the first year of your life wasn't my *favorite*. But even then, I was so grateful for a healthy, if angry, baby. Usually."

It almost makes me laugh, but nope—I just cry more as she rocks me there and tells me about when I was a baby.

It's hard for me to imagine her as a nervous new mom. There's something comforting about imagining her calling my grandmother at 2:00 a.m. to ask a question. There's something comforting about knowing my mom needed her mom too.

"I wish I could remember Nanny and Pops," I whisper.

"Me too," she says, smoothing my hair. "I wish I'd had more time with them too. But they were in their sixties when they adopted me. I was just glad they got to meet you at all."

I fall asleep on my mom's lap, sprawled out and cried out.

By the time she drives me back to Daybreak, it's late. I soak in the feeling of being in the car with her. It was how we spent so much time for the first sixteen years of my life—her driving me between piano and swimming lessons.

"Well, I'm so sorry you had a scare." She stops the car right where she and my dad dropped me off weeks ago. Time is so slippery these days, gone like water through my fingers. "But I think the Lord knew I could use a little extra Lucy time."

"I'll accept any explanation that makes me sound less unglued."

She laughs and leans over to peck my cheek. "Love you, Bird. See you Sunday."

"Love you too."

I watch as she reverses out, waving back at me. Then it's just me and the humming porch lights and the faraway flapping of insect wings.

And Henry, sitting on the lodge steps.

"Hey," I say, moving toward him.

"Hey." He nods at the flash of headlights pulling away from camp. "Was that your mom?"

I nod. How strange. He and my mom live in two different parts of my world, but they were just yards away.

"Are you all right?"

"Yeah. Listen, I—"

"Rhea told me. I'm glad you're both okay." He nods, businesslike, and stands up.

When he starts off toward his cabin, I follow stupidly—surprised by his terseness. I would have expected a bear hug.

"Are you mad at me?" When I catch up and touch his back, the look he gives me over his shoulder is hurt. Raw, undisguised hurt.

"I just need a minute, Luce. And you should get some sleep."

"Oh, yeah. Like that's going to happen when you're clearly pissed at me."

"I don't want to do this right now. We can talk in the morning. I just wanted to make sure you were okay."

"Well, I'm not okay! Not if you're mad at me!"

"Let's just sleep on it, Luce, okay?" He sounds wearied.

We're near the spot where he first kissed me, and this feeling has to be the opposite of that. My voice is graveled with uncertainty. "Let me make sure I'm clear here. My mom has cancer, and you're mad at me? That *sucks*."

At this, he turns fully. "No. Your mom has cancer, you see her once a week a mile away, *you didn't tell me. That's* what sucks."

I swallow. Oh. Right.

"I've told you everything. But you hide this major thing from me? After I ask you for honesty?" He crosses his arms like he's protecting himself from me, and I'm crushed—I am *crushed*—that he has reason to. "I mean, how do you want me to feel about that?"

"What do you want to know?" My lip trembles, betraying me.

"I don't know, Luce! I just wish you'd talked to me! Even if we weren't . . . whatever. You're my *friend*. Do you not trust me?"

"I wanted to pretend it wasn't happening, okay?" My hands fly out, as if I can push away the pain of it. "Like, when I was here, if no one asked me about it, life could feel normal for a split second."

"Well, that's not a healthy coping mechanism."

My jaw drops before I can hide my shock. "Don't you psychiatrist-mom me!"

"Well, I'm sorry! I told you I wanted to sleep on it so I could get my thoughts together! I'm not—" He pauses to take a few measured breaths, hands on his hips. "Damn, Luce. I just . . . You may have been able to pretend, when I didn't know. But that meant I couldn't support you."

"You have been supporting me! By having fun with me. Letting me be free from it."

This seems like a perfect explanation to me, but he looks even more hurt. Disappointed, even. "I don't want to be comic relief, Luce."

This pulls tears to my eyes immediately. "Well, maybe I do want that. Maybe being with you is the only time I can escape all the worries. Because those worries? They invade nearly all my thoughts—every good thought catches on something sad."

"Like what?"

"Like what sad thoughts do I have?" Now my arms are crossed, and here we are—facing off.

"Yeah."

"You really want to do this? Fine!" I throw my hands up, flinging my frustration outward. "When I was just over there, and she made tea, I was thinking about how she talks back to the kettle. When it starts to steam, she says, 'Hold on a minute!' or 'Just a second!' like it's an impatient child."

His anger falls away, hunched shoulders drooping. But I'm just getting started, and it feels good. To be ranting about it. Not because I'm mad at myself or at him, but because I'm just *mad*.

"She signs her text messages 'xoxo' like it's a handwritten letter. She is doggedly kind except when it comes to red carpet fashion. She can eat a large movie theater popcorn before the movie is even halfway over." I come up for air, panting as my mind plays the tiny details of my mother like a highlight reel. "And these things don't even matter in the big scheme of who she is. But I don't think I can live without them."

"Luce," he says quietly, but it's too late for that now.

"And it feels like anything could hurt me. My mom's own cells are trying to kill her." My laugh pierces the air between us, jagged and unkind. I'm gesturing passionately, helplessly, like a fire-and-brimstone pastor. "Bones can snap. Skin is like paper. And I just want to go back. I want to go back to when it felt like nothing could hurt me."

His wince isn't quick. It stays, a pained expression of true understanding. "I know, Luce. I really do. And I wish I could fix it."

He does know. He has known for years. The world that is safe—full of bedtime lullabies and solid ground—was gone for him at age ten. In the most horrible way imaginable.

"I'm so sorry that I didn't tell you," I whisper. I step forward, taking a chance as I wrap my arms around his waist. My hands barely touch, and I feel comforted by the warmth and solidness of him.

"No, don't apologize. You told me when you were ready." He rests his chin on top of my head. "*I'm* sorry. I shouldn't have made you feel bad that it wasn't sooner."

"So, we're okay?"

"Yeah, of course."

"Can I still go to the wedding with you?"

"I *guess*." He smiles, to prove he's joking, and I lean up to kiss him.

I never fought with Lukas like that. Not once. And only now do I wonder if maybe we just weren't feeling enough. Or expressing enough. I don't want to compare everything, but he's the only other relationship I've had.

And this one? This one feels easy, even with voices raised as we try to understand each other. It occurs to me, not for the first time, that maybe I was always supposed to end up right here.

Back at the cabin, I find Keely sitting on the step, arms curled around her knees in the weak porch light.

"You waited up for me?" I ask, with embarrassingly transparent hope.

She shrugs, brushing off her shorts as she stands. "Just in case."

Just in case. Just in case I came back to a dark, quiet cabin and it felt like the sadness would consume me. Keely startles awake if a camper so much as whimpers in the midst of a dream. If I came home upset, she'd sense it from the top bunk. And that means she's sitting out here just in case I needed to be sure someone was with me.

"You could have told me," she says. "You could tell me now."

I knew that. I know that. It just seemed unfair to take my pain to Keely, who lost her mom even younger. "Could you tell me about your mom too?"

She sits back down, patting the space beside her, and I settle in.

CHAPTER TWENTY-FOUR

Saturday morning, I get ready for the wedding while the campers are swimming. I go for subtle makeup—sheer foundation, plus a soft, peony pink on my cheeks and lips.

Henry is waiting outside the cabin, wearing his usual button-down and shorts. We don't have formal clothes here, of course, so I'm changing at my parents' cabin. Henry and Keely will have to change when we get to their hometown.

"You ready?" I ask Keely.

She sticks her head out of the bathroom. "You think I'm crashing Jones meeting your parents? Yeah, right. Pick me up on the way back. I'll wait at the end of the drive."

Rhea's letting us borrow her car, and I fidget nervously as Henry drives us down the short stretch of road to Holyoke.

"They're really nice," I tell him for the thousandth time. "And my mom does look pretty sick. I just . . . don't want you to be surprised."

"Luce." He gives me an encouraging smile. "I know."

It's a good thing Henry sounds sure, because my dad is waiting on the porch like a sentry. Lord, help me.

"Good morning, sir. Henry Jones." Henry sticks out a hand.

"Pleased to meet you, Henry Jones." His voice is a little lower than usual. I don't think he's trying to intimidate Henry. But he's not trying to make him feel too at ease, either.

My dad leans in to peck my cheek. "Hi, Bird. We brought you a few dresses from home. They're in your room."

"Please tell me you remembered shoes."

"Oh no! I didn't." He looks horror-stricken, then breaks into a grin. "But your mother did."

I swat his arm as we walk into the living room. My mom's camped out on the couch, looking exhausted.

"Hi, Mom."

"Hi, baby." She looks my date up and down, smiling. "You must be Henry."

"Very nice to meet you, ma'am. I've heard a lot about you."

"Likewise. Lucy, you'd better go change."

I let go of Henry's hand, moving toward my room. I give my dad a pointed look: *Don't let Mom grill him!* But my dad just waves me on.

When I return, they're talking about Henry's musical roots. My dad has relaxed enough to sit down, a good sign.

"Lovely choice," my mom says, eyeing my floaty dress.

"Very pretty," Henry agrees. He barely glances at me, though. Pastor Dad is a powerful force.

"So, Henry," my mom says. "You're playing today, right? At the wedding?"

"Yeah! 'Trumpet Voluntary' and then a part of the first dance."

"How wonderful. So you have your trumpet with you?"

"In the car."

"Can you play something for me? Do you have time? If not, I—"

"Mom."

"What?" she asks, all feigned innocence.

Henry smiles. "Of course we do."

He runs out to the car for his trumpet, and my mom smooths my hair. "You look beautiful, honey."

"Thanks."

"Are you nervous to meet his family?" She doesn't even let me answer; she knows I am. "They'll love you, Bird. Just be yourself."

"Okay." Henry opens the instrument case on his lap. "Any requests?"

"Oh, anything. Anything you like to play."

He puts the mouthpiece to his lips. The mute keeps the sound from piercing too loudly as the first notes play out. I know the words. Did I tell him about this song? Or did he just know?

When peace like a river attendeth my way, when sorrow like sea billows roll . . .

Henry takes his time with the rhythm, letting each tone resonate. His high notes soar upward; they raise goose bumps on my arms.

Whatever my lot, thou has taught me to say, it is well, it is well with my soul.

The hymn is not difficult musically. But meaning the words and playing like you mean them—that's the trick. Henry plays with the true, slow emotion of someone who has known pain. He plays this psalm—a hallelujah cry from the depths of despair—to my mother, and I will never be able to articulate what it means to me. I wipe a stray tear from my face.

It is well, with my soul. It is well, it is well with my soul.

"That was perfect, Henry," my mom says. Her voice cracks twice, but she holds it together. "Just perfect."

One set of parents down, one to go. I have the whole drive to fret about what the Jones family will think of me. Will it bother them that I'm white? I didn't even think about it until now—should I have thought about it?

We drop Keely off at a nice little house with dark green shutters. Her stepmom is waiting on the porch, waving excitedly as we pull up. She looks like a cereal commercial mom, in capri pants and a pressed shirt, and she opens the door to call to Keely's dad.

"See you at the church," Keely says, bailing out.

Before we drive away, I see her stepmom throw her arms open, waiting to embrace my friend.

The church we pull up to is small and lovely, and my palms start sweating when I see how many people are pooled outside, exchanging hugs and greetings.

"Ready?" Henry flashes the grin—no trace of nervousness. In fact, he looks proud to have me with him. And for the millionth time, I wish I had inherited my dad's social ease.

"There he is!" a booming voice yells. Henry's family envelops him, all back claps and cheek kisses. For just a flash, I imagine them in funeral black, mourning his sister. What a thing, to be a family—together from the solemn suits to the wedding day florals. Once you survive the former, days like this must be all the sweeter.

I hang back shyly, glancing down at my pumps and second-guessing my dress. Too plain, maybe? No—I'm a plus-one. Simple and subtle is good.

"You," a clear voice says, "must be Lucy."

The speaker is a woman in an iridescent dress—violet, with a matching jacket. Her smile is deeply genuine and entirely familiar. "I'm Michelle Jones. Henry's mother."

"So nice to meet you." I hold out my hand, which she shakes—failing to hide her amusement at my formality. Maybe I should have hugged her?

"It's very nice to meet you too. My son's manners have gotten lost in that wild bunch." We both glance back to where Henry's grandmother is talking to him, her hands placed adoringly on his cheeks. "I trust his manners held up for meeting your parents this morning?"

"More than held up," I report. "They were *charmed*. Very impressed."

"Ah, yes. He'll do that. Partially his nature, partially coping mechanism. *I* am impressed that he has dropped the charm for you so quickly."

The images play in my mind: Henry angry at the punching bag, Henry expressing his frustration at me, Henry nodding off as I play étude after étude.

"My son is very easy to love," she adds. "But quite difficult to truly *know*."

"Well," I say, carefully, "I like what I know."

Over her shoulder, I spot Keely, tugging at the straps of her dress.

"Hi, honey bun." Keely lets Mrs. Jones squeeze her into a hug. "Don't you look like a dream."

"Hi, Miss Michelle."

Henry's mom pulls back, examining Keely's face. "Can't wait to have you all home soon. Everything been good?"

"Yeah. Real good."

"Tracy says Kiana's doing great."

"So great. Starting in on that tween attitude a little early, if you ask me. But great."

"Everyone," Henry says, motioning me forward to the crowd. "This is Lucy. Go easy on her."

I'm in front of a panel of aunties and grandpas, little cousins and probably family friends too. I don't even see who steps forward to hug me first. I'm drawn right into the crowd—exclamations about my dress and my hair, and, over an auntie's shoulder, Henry grins.

His family makes sense to me—demonstrative and buoyant, like him. It feels, instantly, like somewhere I want to belong.

Henry's cousin's wedding turns out to be the most thoroughly purple event I have ever attended. It starts with the bridesmaids' processional. They're draped in amethyst chiffon, sheer straps across their shoulders. The bride's bouquet contains every shade, bright anemones and soft hydrangeas.

And my eyes overfill as Laura walks down the aisle in a cloud of gauzy tulle, as the groom glances upward, blinking back his own tears. During the prayer—a beautiful entreaty that the couple be blessed with good times and strengthened in the bad—Keely presses a tissue into my hand.

When the couple floats out for their first dance, I'm not prepared. I'm not prepared for "La vie en rose" amid their life in lavender, for Henry to front the band with his trumpet in perfect blasts. His grandfather sings the words in English, though I barely register them. The words don't even matter. The melody tugs something inside me, some deep, reverberating part of my soul. How can a grandfather's voice and the snap of a double bass and the brassy call of a trumpet sum up everything? Nostalgia and hope. Romance and loss.

"Sap," Keely mutters at me, though she brushes beneath her lower lashes too.

As soon as the bandleader invites everyone to the dance floor, Henry is beside me.

"Let's do it," he says, and taking his hand feels something like relief.

We have to squeeze onto the black and white tiles, jammed as it is. But he leads me through the crowd, turning back to grin. The bride rustles across the floor in her confectionary dress, pausing every few seconds to hug someone. When she stops to talk to her mom, I have to look away. I can't watch a mother fix a crystal pin in her daughter's hair on her wedding day.

Instead, I sway and I lean toward this boy I like so much, and I shimmy my shoulders in a way that is probably very dorky. The dance floor is full enough that we bump into people, so full that my toes only narrowly dodge a stiletto stomp. But still, I only see Henry Jones, his cool-guy nonchalance as he breaks it down.

The first slow song is a crooning oldie, one that always seems to be playing while my mom and I shop our favorite antique mall.

Henry sweeps my hand into his, clasping my waist with an air of gallantry that makes me grin. And I just know that every time I hear this song, I'll come back to this moment—when the world is hazy with lilac and old love songs and safe arms.

Or will I just remember that everything made me think of my mom? That I spent this day—someone else's wedding day—squinting into an unseeable future, refusing to let myself hope *or* mourn for it. Why does every part of my life feel like waiting?

"Hey," Henry says quietly. "What is it?"

"Nothing," I say, tilting my chin up to smile fully. "I just like you, that's all."

"Liar," he says affectionately. He knows what I'm feeling—the pangs of confusion when your life is magic and tragic all at once.

"I can't believe we have to go back to real life soon," I whisper. I can't imagine moving home, into my room with no bunk beds or Keely or bubble of giggling girls. That's what Sofia decided a group of third graders is called: a bubble.

"Ah, Luce. I don't know how to break it to you." He leans close to my ear, his cheek warm on mine. "This is real life too."

A few hours in, I kick off my heels beneath our table. I scrape the last bit of icing from my plate. And I check my phone for the thousandth time. I'm sure—because irony is cruel—that I'll hear bad news about my mom as the band blares "Celebration!"

Instead, I watch from my seat as Henry twirls his grand-mother. They're near his parents, who talk quietly, hands linked. I know it's painful for them all, to imagine the ghosts of a milestone his sister will never hit. A wedding in a poufy dress, hair wound up and cheeks aching from all the smiles. What grace it takes—to be on the dance floor all the same.

Keely returns to check her phone too, but she frowns while scrolling. "Anna wants to know if we've seen Tara."

"Tara?"

"She says they can't find her."

"Can't *find* her?"

She shoots an annoyed look at the echoing. "As I understand it, yes."

"Like she ran away?"

"I have no idea." She's tapping at the phone.

"I'm sure it's a misunderstanding. Did they check the dreaming tree?"

Henry finds his way to us as the song ends, immediately reading the concern on our faces. "What is it?"

Keely shows him her phone and announces, "I'm going to head back."

"Luce, you should go with her," he decides.

"But—"

"Tara likes you." His eyes search mine. "You should be there. My parents will drive me back after the reception. They won't mind at all."

He's right.

His family is gracious as I try to convey how lovely it was to meet them all. I'm seized with the bizarre urge to thank his parents for raising this kid who looks at me with lit-up eyes. Like I'm the toy in a cereal box. Like I'm what he was most hoping to find.

Who walks me out and kisses me on the cheek with more sincerity than anyone else has ever kissed me on the mouth. "Drive safe, okay? Text me if you hear anything about Tara."

"Thanks for inviting me. It was nice to . . ." *Remember that you can still dance at your cousin's wedding, even though you'll never get to at your sister's. Be reminded that you can be okay and also not okay.* "You know."

"I do know." He brushes back a curl with soft fingertips. "See you at home."

The drive feels quiet, despite the soft tones of a nearby indie station. All my attempts at conversation are summarily shut down with "uh-huhs" and "yeps." Keely scratches her thumbnails down the steering wheel.

"I'm sure she's fine," I say.

"Mmmph," she replies.

Silence it is. A singer warbles on about darkness and cigarettes.

When we finally pull down the lane toward Daybreak, Anna is sitting on the porch with a walkie-talkie. D'Souza is right behind her, arms crossed.

"God," Anna says. "Finally."

"Any news?" Keely asks.

"Not yet."

"What *happened*?"

"We don't know." Anna chews on the inside of her lower lip. "Tara went to use the bathroom before dinner and didn't come back. At first, her friends thought maybe she went to see Suzette. But she's not there. She's not anywhere."

"Did you call the police?"

"Well, yeah," D'Souza says, annoyed. "But she's been gone for three hours. That's not exactly a concern to them."

"Shit," Keely mutters. "And her friends?"

"They don't know anything," Anna says. It's so unlike her, this defeated tone, that I'm starting to legitimately fear for Tara. "They're as upset as we are. All they said is that she's been a little teary the past few days. They thought it was hormones."

"Look," D'Souza says. "We've been over this. We called local hospitals. We've got a counselor in each cabin trying to keep kids occupied and calm. Mohan and a few counselors are in town, asking around. Rhea's on the phone calling every contact she can think of."

Keely grabs a flashlight. "I'm going to push out farther than the camp grounds, search around the lake."

D'Souza nods. "Good. Take a walkie-talkie."

"What do you want me to do?" I put my hands on my hips, ready for action.

"Actually." Keely picks up a second flashlight. "Go put some walking shoes on. I'm gonna need you to come with me."

Keely's theory is that Tara might have been walking around the lake but stumbled. Twisted her ankle and got stuck somewhere.

"You're sure this is the path you normally take?" Keely asks.

"Yeah." I point my flashlight beam into the woods, calling out hopefully, "Tara?"

"Tara?" Keely echoes into the darkness. "It's Simmons and Hansson!"

No response. I move the light back to the ground, to guide my steps. "You really think she would head toward Holyoke?"

Leaves rustle near us—something moving—and I yelp, jumping back.

"Tara?" Keely calls, unconcerned. Her flashlight illuminates a squat raccoon barreling away from us. Oh my gosh. Possibly rabid. Why is this walk so lovely in the sunrise and so terrifying at night?

We make it all the way to the clearing where Holyoke begins. The chapel lights glow brightly, and I'm relieved to see a light still on in my parents' cabin. As long as we're here, we might as well stop in. Maybe my dad can help look too. Drive around.

But Keely whispers, "This way."

She's hurrying toward the chapel, not looking back to see if I've followed. The doors open with an *oomph* sound, and I'm rushing in behind her.

"Tara? Tara!"

"Simmons?" a small voice calls from the front.

We don't even glance at each other before we rush up the aisle. Our flashlights aren't necessary in here, so I'm not sure why we both keep grasping them so tightly. They illuminate a scared-looking pregnant girl leaning against the front pew.

I crouch in front of her. "Are you okay?"

"I don't know." She wipes the back of her hand across her cheek, looking so impossibly young. "Something hurts."

"Near your belly?" I ask. "Does it feel like contractions?"

"I don't know. It just *hurts* down there."

"Do you feel wetness? It could be your water breaking." Or blood.

"No, I'm dry."

"Good."

Keely presses the button, walkie-talkie to her mouth. "Souz? We've got her. She's okay."

I don't even hear the rest of the conversation as I take Tara's pulse—high, but not dangerously. I'm not sure if we should call 911, but I know who will know.

"I'm so sorry I scared everyone," she whispers. "I was feeling upset about some stuff, and I wanted to go for a walk to calm down, but then it started hurting. Feels like my hips are going to split apart. I'm—sorry."

"No one's mad at you." I squeeze her hand. "Keely's going to stay with you for a minute while I go get my mom. She lives next door, and she's a nurse."

"Your mom?" Tara whispers.

"Yep. She and my dad own this camp."

"Okay," she says. "Okay. Can you help me up first? My back hurts from sitting now."

Keely and I haul her to her feet.

Of all the things I expected at the beginning of summer, opening our cabin door late at night because of a pregnant ninth grader is not one of them.

"Mom?" I call. "Dad?"

"Luce?" My dad's eyes are wide, panicked as he jumps from his easy chair. He's rumpled in his pajama pants and a gray T-shirt. "What is it? What's wrong?"

"It's a camper. I'm fine. She's pregnant and walked over here from Daybreak. She's in the chapel right now, says something hurts. I need Mom."

"I'll get her."

"I heard." My mom emerges with a robe wrapped around her thin body, head covered. "I'm coming."

"Mari," my dad says. "Let me see if the girl is well enough to walk, please."

"Oh, don't be ridiculous," she scoffs.

"She is," I insist. "She's up and moving."

My dad follows me, gesturing for my mom to stay inside.

"You're going to pay for that later," I tell him.

"You're telling me." His hair is a shock of white in the darkness outside. For the first time, I wonder if my mom's hair will grow back in the same color, with the same curl.

"Is she doing okay?"

He's quiet for a moment. "Yeah. Hanging in there."

Once we hit the threshold of the chapel, my dad's strides lengthen until he spots the girls. Keely has an arm around Tara's back, and they're pacing the center aisle slowly. Tara's legs are spread hip-width apart as she lumbers forward.

"Hi, sweetheart," my dad says. "I'm Dave, Lucy's dad. Can I help you to our cabin for a quick checkup?"

"Yes, please." Tara puffs out a few breaths, and I second-guess my call that she isn't in active labor.

"Good. My wife is a longtime nurse, so she can help you. Everything's going to be fine."

There's some strange collision of worlds, my dad introducing himself to my bunkmate as they both support a pregnant teen camper. I trail behind them to the cabin, feeling useless. Tara's steps are heavy, and it's impossible to imagine the weight that she carries.

My mom's waiting by the door, looking frail in body but determined in stance.

"Hi, honey," my mom says, smiling at Tara's surprised expression. "Oh, don't worry. Just a little cancer. I'm not as sick as I look."

For the first time, I don't believe her. She's gaunt in the porch light, even her once-full hips slim in silhouette.

"Come on back to Lucy's bedroom. You can lie down, and we can talk about your symptoms." My mom holds out one arm, and Tara goes to her the way any child goes to a good mother: instinctively. "Dave, some tea, maybe?"

"On it." He disappears into the kitchen, calling, "You girls take a load off. Do you need anything? Are you hungry?"

"We're okay," I decide, but I know he'll bring us short-bread cookies anyway.

We settle on the couch, and Keely looks around the room. I wonder what she sees. She's always taking people in, getting a read on them. How does the cabin, this living room, my family add to her impression of me? I have no idea.

Keely's gaze goes past me, toward a family picture on the side table. "You look like her."

"Yeah." Less and less, as her face thins out. But I can't think about that—not now. "So, how'd you guess Tara would be in the chapel?"

She shrugs, brushing her hair back. "I walked there once, when I couldn't sleep."

"When you were little?"

"Yeah. My second year at Daybreak." The snort she gives is self-effacing, the admission of an embarrassing moment. "Back when I thought you could ask for things like God was a genie."

I don't let myself ask what she wished for.

Keely is still looking at our family pictures. She leans toward a picture of my mom and Aunt Rachel, arms over each other's shoulders. "How does your mom know Rachel?"

My head jerks back. "How do *you* know Rachel?"

"She helped us paint the mural on the side of the gym one summer."

"At Daybreak?"

"Yeah." Keely looks confused by my disbelief. "She knows Bryan. They were at camp together as kids."

"No, they weren't. Rachel—" I begin, but I cut myself off. Rachel went to camp with my mom. That's where they met. "She went to a camp called . . ."

"Donoma?"

My mouth goes slack. How could Keely know that?

"Yes," I whisper.

"Yeah, Daybreak had a different name the first few years after Rhea started it. Camp Donoma." Keely's looking at me like I'm the one who's crazy. "The people who owned the property before Rhea called it that. She changed it once she learned the name might have been appropriated from a Native American language."

My mom went to Daybreak in its early years? Not possible. She'd have told me that ages ago—or at least early this summer, when she first tried to sell me on being a counselor. But if—*if*—it were true, no wonder Rhea helped my parents buy the Holyoke property. It makes so much sense if she knew my mom as a teenager. Did Rhea assume I knew that?

"Lucy?" Keely asks, quiet.

"All right!" My dad's too-chipper voice blares in the silence. "Two cups of pomegranate green tea. That okay with you, Keely? It's Lucy's favorite."

"Perfect," she says, and takes a cookie to be polite.

"Luce?" my dad prompts.

I hold my hands out to accept the mug. My mind can't form rational thoughts, so I stare down into the tea as if it will spell out the answers. I don't want to say anything in front of Keely. It feels wrong to interrogate my parents, given the circumstances. Or maybe it's just that I don't fully believe it.

We sip our tea, and my dad valiantly makes small talk. I swear, there must be classes on this in seminary.

I nibble four cookies like a nervous squirrel, barely making eye contact as I wait for my mom and Tara to emerge.

When they do, Tara has my mom's Sherpa blanket over her shoulders like a poncho, her stomach jutting out almost comically.

"Braxton Hicks contractions," my mom reports. "At least, I think. Nothing to suggest she's in active labor, though we'll want to get her to a doctor just in case."

"You need anything before I drive you back?" my dad asks Tara. "Something to eat?"

"No, thank you," she says. "I just really want to go to bed."

"Well, then, let's get you back."

My dad ushers Tara out, offering his arm to steady her. He's being so solicitous to this very young, very unwed pregnant girl. But then, of course he is. Why did I ever think my parents would turn someone away for having premarital sex? It's such a trivial concern in the face of cancer, abuse, drugs—all the things Daybreak sees every summer.

If my mom was at Daybreak in its first years, why? I know she was in foster care, but did something happen?

"She's gonna be just fine, baby," my mom says, thinking that my stunned expression is about Tara.

"Thanks, Mom," I manage, in a whisper.

When she leans in to hug me, I almost flinch, wondering what else she's kept hidden from me. She no longer smells like her shampoo because, of course, she no longer has hair to wash. "I have loved you since before you were even born, Lucy Esther."

I pull away to look at her, confused.

"Seeing Tara . . . it just takes me back, that's all. You are the gift of my life. Okay?"

"Okay." My voice cracks, tears spilling over. She's crying too, and it doesn't even feel weird anymore.

With a ruffle of my hair, she puts on her brave smile. "See you Sunday, little bird."

Back at camp, I watch as my dad drives away from Daybreak. June, when he did this the first time, feels like a lifetime ago.

"Will you walk me to Rhea's cabin?" Tara asks. She's looking at me.

"Of course." When I offer my arm for support, she shakes her head—steady for now.

Keely squeezes Tara's arm. "Hang in there."

"I'm really sorry for all the trouble," Tara replies.

"I'm not."

I amble down the dark path, hand ready to brace Tara at even the suggestion of a stumble. When Keely's footfalls are out of range, Tara says, "Your parents are nice."

"Yeah." My eyes itch, threatening to flood. "They are."

"Your mom told me about giving birth and everything."

"Oh, yeah?"

"Yeah." Her voice is reverent, almost awed, as she touches the swell of her belly. "She seems like a really brave person."

My mom's body is riddled with mutating cells and the toxins meant to kill them, and yet she still cares for others—gently, nimbly, with such great love. "Yes. She is."

"She said that this will always be part of who I am, but that I can move on too."

Of course she did. Of course my mom could empathize with someone so different from her—enough to say the perfect thing. "She's right."

When I glance over, Tara is wiping her cheek. "She prayed for the baby. And for me. She asked if she could, and I said yes. It felt real."

"Oh, Tara," I whisper. I stop walking and open my arms. She rests her chin on my shoulder as her stomach presses into mine. I almost ask what she meant—that it felt real. But I know what she means. Prayer used to always feel, for me, as real as sending a letter.

"I thought I'd want to keep the baby. My mom said we don't give babies away. But I still don't feel anything. I thought I would by now."

"That's okay," I say stupidly. How the hell would I know? "Oh, Tara, don't cry. It's all going to work out."

"I'm only crying because your mom made me feel better. I want the baby to be adopted. She said my gut feeling counts, and I'm just . . . I don't know. Relieved."

We stand there, near Rhea's cabin, hanging on under the moonlight. I'm not sure how long Tara sniffles on my shoulder before I hear Rhea approaching.

"Hi, sweet girl," Rhea says. Without a word, Tara transfers to Rhea's arms. "It's okay, honey. It's all okay."

"I'm sorry. I'm so sorry I worried everyone."

"I know you are. It's okay." Rhea cradles her close, and I wonder if she ever comforted my mom in hard times. Part of me wants to interject with all my questions, but now is not the time.

Over Tara's shoulder, Rhea mouths, *Thank you.*

CHAPTER TWENTY-FIVE

THE NEXT NIGHT, I'M STARING AT OUR CABIN'S THICKET OF SMALL children. Somehow, the bedroom routine seems to make them double: little girls everywhere. They bound around, through the routine. Pajamas on, teeth brushed, bathroom squabbles broken up before they escalate to tears.

"Well, we're done with *No Flying in the House*," I say when they've settled. "Who wants to pick the next book?"

Thuy raises her hand. "Can you read 'Posy and the Dreaming Tree'?"

"Oh. Sure."

She scampers over to hand me the hand-drawn book. She's been keeping it on her neat little shelf.

I stare down at the cover in my hands. At Posy's fur, sketched with thin strokes of autumn red. Posy wears a flower behind her ear. It's familiar, like a daisy but with slimmer, purple petals. An aster. Rachel taught me that.

Rachel. My hands go cold. Rachel illustrated this.

When I was little, we would draw together for hours. I tried to emulate her delicate flowers—the curved arcs of tulips, the dotted centers of sunflowers. And asters just like this.

I'm still studying the pages, heart thumping off-beat, when the girls gather around. They look expectant in their soft pajamas, and my mouth feels too dry to read aloud.

But I open to the first page. "'Once there was a little fox named Posy who loved her family.'"

A fox named Posy whose parents died. Who went to live with extended family. Who was eventually adopted by yet another family. Who longed to care for people, to be brave, to be a mother.

It's a story I've been told my whole life. I thought it was a fable, but no. This is my mother's story, illustrated by Rachel. My lips won't move to form the words on the next page.

"Hansson? Are you crying?" Brooklyn asks. "Are you sad?"

"It's just a very sad and beautiful story," I manage. "Isn't it?"

They all murmur their agreement.

"Sorry. Silly me!" I wipe my cheeks and turn to Garcia. "Can you take over?"

In the bathroom, I weep as quietly as I can. I cry into my hands, back leaned against the door. Because once there was a girl named Marianne, who grew up to be my mother. And I never knew she lived with a wolf.

In all the times I wondered what happened to put my mom in foster care, did I ever truly consider this? I don't think I wanted to. I don't think I could have.

By the time I emerge, nose red from crying, Garcia is holding the book open to the final page.

In a softly decided voice, she reads the final words: "It is not the type of love that ends."

I slide the book into my backpack the next morning. It's still dark, the girls asleep in their various postures: Thuy in a fetal position, Payton with one arm hanging off the side.

On the walk over to Holyoke, I practice what I'll say. I barely slept last night, trying to figure out which questions, in what order. I'm not exactly angry that my mom didn't tell me about her time at Daybreak. Confused is more like it. And . . . hurt, beneath the confusion.

But when I walk into the cabin, my mom isn't waiting for me. I'm a few steps down the hallway when I hear it: what sounds like the final coughs after retching, the flush of the toilet. My foot launches forward, the first step in running to her, but I freeze. She may want privacy. I've always thought of myself as inside her bubble—like I could never be intruding. The faucet turns on, the creak of running water that I know so well.

"Mom?" I start toward the bathroom, thinking better of my hesitation.

"Oh, hey, Bird," she says, turning the corner. She's gray-faced behind a pleasant smile. "I thought you'd be along later after such a long night."

"Are you okay?"

"Of course!" She just looks so *sick*. I'd almost gotten

used to her bare head, but I realize: it's that her eyebrows are almost gone. In the new daylight, it's undeniable. "Sit! How's Tara?"

"Fine, I think."

"Good." She moves toward the refrigerator, gripping the handle tightly, steadying herself.

I'm still frozen near the doorway. "What are you doing?"

Her laugh is just thin air forced out of her throat. "Making you breakfast."

So, I guess what we're doing this morning is pretending she's okay. I slink to my seat at the breakfast table, unwilling to play my part in her charade. I want to insist she go to bed, but I don't want to insult her. I don't want to be the mother.

As she arranges the carton of eggs and a package of turkey bacon on the counter, leaning to put a pan on the stove, my mind moves to Jesus washing the feet of his disciples. It's such a strange practice, but I get the point: total devotion to service, humbling yourself before someone to the extent that you'd wash their dirty feet.

And here, my mother—with her kerchief and her trembling hands—is still trying to wash my feet. Still trying to serve me, to meet my most basic needs.

She opens the turkey bacon and jerks her head away from the smell of raw meat, her face dimming further in color.

"Mom. Here." I leap up, reaching for the handle of the pan.

"Sit, Luce. I've got it."

My hand closes over her bony one. "Let me. Please? Just

today. One of the girls' classes this week was on cooking. We learned crepes! I can show you."

I feel her tense, her body gone stony with betrayal. Her eyes flood with tears as she lets the pan drop onto the stove. "Fine. You want crepes? Do whatever you want. I'll be in bed."

I can tell she wants to huff away, but she's too sick. Instead, she braces one hand against the wall, hobbling against what I know must be nausea. My arms move to steady her, but I don't want to upset her again. I can't read the situation: Should I go after her or give her some space? Is she just tired, in need of some privacy and rest? Or does she want me to apologize?

Instead, I stand at the stove crying. This was my exact fear this summer: that I would stop feeling like an expert on my mom.

Because I don't know what else to do, I wind up melting butter and whisking eggs with milk and flour, making perfect circles on the hot skillet. Either the warm batter smell will draw her out or I'll have an excuse to go into her room.

Inside the refrigerator, I find two items I knew would be there: strawberries and whipped cream. My mom picks up baskets of strawberries every week at the farmer's market in town and could eat them for every meal. She buys peaches, too, cuts them into broad slices, and covers them with whipped cream. Her favorite summer dessert. At least I still know her this well.

I lay the crepes out and arrange strawberries on them, spray whipped cream as artfully as I can. Then I pull my shoulders back and march the plates into her bedroom, where she's curled in a ball on the bed, facing the door.

She sits up, and I set the plate on her bedside table. Her face is unreadable to me, but I won't let myself back down. I pull a chair up, taking a bite of my own crepe as if making a point.

"Mmmm," she says, through a mouthful. After she swallows, she looks up at me innocently. "There was chocolate syrup in the fridge, you know."

It almost makes me laugh, remembering the year she gave up chocolate for Lent. *I know Jesus died for our sins,* she said on Day 6. *But this is* horrible, *Lucy*. I retrieve the chocolate syrup, which she adds to her crepe, and I do too.

"Thank you, Bird." My mom closes her eyes, leaning against the headboard. "This tastes as good as anything has in quite a while."

"You're welcome."

"I know that I'm acting bananas," she whispers. "But I can't surrender motherhood to cancer—not with grace, anyway."

"Mom. Motherhood isn't . . . making me breakfast."

She scowls at me. "I know that. But I *hate* feeling compromised. I hate it, Luce. I'd rather feel healthy and capable and die in a hundred days than feel this sick and die in two hundred."

Die. A hundred days. My stomach almost turns the bites of crepe upside down onto the quilt. That's an arbitrary number, right? "So . . . are you . . . going to stop chemo?"

"No! Oh no, sweetie. Because it's not the difference between a hundred days and two hundred days. It might be the difference between a hundred days and thousands." She sets her fork down. "I'm sorry I said it like that. I'm just rambling."

"But you won't keep anything from me, right? Any news?" My tone is the opposite of what I'm going for. I sound like a little kid, begging. "It's just . . . I can take it, okay? I know I'm not a grown-up, but I'm tough. I am."

I'm not sure if this is true. I just want it to be so badly. And my mom, for her part, looks touched—by my boldness or naiveté, I'm not sure. She brushes my cheek with her thumb. "Oh, I know you are. So much like your namesake in that way."

"I'm like a martyred saint?"

She snort-laughs. "Heavens, no. Oh, dear. Who told you that? Your Memaw?"

Come to think of it, maybe she did. In my memory, I taste lemon bars dusted with powdered sugar. The musty smell of old rugs that need to be aired out. It *was* my grandmother who told me. My father's mother. "Yeah."

My mom leans forward. "Oh, Bird. I'd never name you after a dead saint. But your Memaw was insistent that her grandchild have a religious name. So we told her 'Lucy' was after Saint Lucy."

It snaps together, a silent connecting of two obvious parts. "Lucy Pevensie."

"Of course!" my mom says, as if any other option is silly. Of *course*. "The first time you kicked inside my belly, I was rereading *The Lion, the Witch, and the Wardrobe*. And I wanted you to be curious and loving, sensitive and full of belief."

Well, three out of four ain't bad. "You never told me."

"Well, I worried you might mention it to your Memaw. Then I suppose I forgot you didn't know!"

Named after Lucy Pevensie. It's inconsequential, really. My name is Lucy regardless of where it came from, and I don't know that my name has affected much of my life at all.

Still. I feel more like myself than I ever have. And it's this added tie between my mom and me, all of our hours spent reading and watching The Chronicles of Narnia.

"You used to call me Queen Lucy the Valiant," I muse, thinking back. "But I never knew that's *why* you named me Lucy."

My name means "light" or "light bringer"—that much I know. I looked it up once. In Greek and Roman times, Lucius and Lucia were popular names for babies born around dawn.

Around daybreak.

And there's no going back. It's like God Himself unfurled a red carpet to segue me from this conversation to the one I need to have.

"I'll be right back," I say, though I doubt she'd follow me. She looks too unwell to be on her feet for long.

When I return with my backpack, I place the "Posy and the Dreaming Tree" binder on her lap.

Her eyes widen, and I know. I know I have not made this up in my head.

She reaches out a tentative hand, touching the pages like they are museum documents under glass. And this *is* a historical document—hers. "I'd forgotten all about this. It was a camp project, like creative therapy. Rachel drew the pictures. The summer we met."

"Mom," I whisper. "Why didn't you ever tell me?"

"That I went to Daybreak as a girl?" She scratches the back of her neck. "Well, at first it was because I wanted you to go to church camp. Ironic, no?"

"You didn't want me to go to Daybreak?"

"It was a different part of my life, Bird. Lifesaving, but . . . very hard in some ways. I just wanted my adult life— my family—to be separate from it."

"So, that's how you knew Rhea? And Bryan?"

"Yes." She opens her mouth to say more, but thinks better of it, searching my eyes. I don't know what she sees there.

I place my palm on the cover of the handmade book. "You never told me about your uncle. The wolf."

"Telling you this story was my way of sharing that with you." A tear spills over her eyelid, one quick streak until it drops from her chin. "How do you tell your daughter something like that? I promised myself I'd tell you when you were eighteen. But I'm not sure I would have, if I'm being honest."

"Mom, I'm so sorry." Her crying makes me cry too, and I don't even bother to clear my tears. "I'm so sorry you went through that. I'm sorry he . . . existed."

"Well, he did die in prison," she says. "Heart attack. And, God forgive me, I felt no pity. No mercy."

"Good," I say darkly. "Saves me the trouble of breaking the sixth commandment."

She almost smiles at this. "You sound like your father."

My dad has threatened to kill the man who hurt my mom? "So he knows? Everything?"

"Your dad knows everything there is to know about me."

"And now I do too?" I ask hopefully. When you're faced with your mother's mortality—when her withered hand is in yours—you can't help longing for more pieces of her story.

"Well," she says, patting my hand. "Let's save a *few* things till you're older. Now while we're at it, anything *you* want to tell *me*?"

She seems to be referencing something specific, but I have no idea what. "No?"

"You sure about that, Lucy Es?" My heart stops beating for a moment. It's a reference to my online channel name, LucyEsMakeup.

"You know?" I whisper.

She snorts, without a trace of anger. "Oh, please. I've

known for ages. Since Mallory's mother raved about your 'smoky eye' tutorial."

"Mallory's *mom* knows about it?"

"Adults use the Internet too, child of mine."

Well, *this* is mortifying. Possibly the only thing worse than someone finding out your big secret is realizing that they've known all along. "And you're not mad?"

"I mean, I wish you'd told me, of course. But your dad and I thought it seemed harmless enough. We're glad you have passions, you know, even if we don't share them. We're not monsters."

That warrants an eye roll from me. "Of course you're not. I guess I just . . . wanted something that was mine? If that makes sense?"

"It does." She settles in more, adjusting her back against the pillows. "So is that it? Any other secrets from me? Better tell me now in case this is my deathbed."

I recoil, horrified. "Mom!"

"Sorry! Sorry. Dark humor. It keeps coming out because . . . well, I'm so angry, Bird." She reaches for my hand, a wry smile on her face. "It is not well with my soul, Luce. I want it to be. But damn it, I want to see you grow up all the way. There are things I want to tell you, experience with you. I want to help you through college and life out on your own. I want to see who you spend your life with, if you have kids. And I'll just be so . . . *pissed* if I get cheated out of that."

"I'll be so pissed too."

She sighs, wiping my tears. "Don't say that word, Luce—it's ugly."

"You just said it!"

"Well, I have cancer."

We laugh in a way that feels . . . yes, dark. But as necessary as all the rest of it: our clasped hands, our mirror-image faces, our seventeen good, good years together.

I stay longer than I'm supposed to; I stay until my mom nods off. Sundays are slow, even at Daybreak, and my cabin can live without me for a bit longer.

My dad walks me out. In the warm noonday sun, his hair looks almost blond and his face, by contrast, even younger. He's wearing his most awful, beloved jeans—worn thin and faded to near-white—and a T-shirt from his alma mater.

And all I can think is that I haven't noticed him enough. My whole life, my mom and I have been attached. Sure, our family of three has always done pizza nights and the movie theater, trips to the beach, dinner table conversations. But my mom and I have spent so much time en route to swim team or piano practice, talking about boys and school and every feeling that I've ever had. I don't think I've ever really appreciated what a loving, steady father he is to me.

I have always felt loved. But I have only recently learned just how lucky that is.

And now I feel left out—the two of them here, dealing with the worst of the cancer and treatment.

"It feels wrong, leaving."

"I know it does, Bird."

"Dad." My voice drops, not wanting even the trees around us to hear my worst-case scenario. "If it gets really bad and I need to leave Daybreak for the summer to be with Mom . . . you'll tell me, right? Because if you didn't, and—"

"I would tell you." His solemn face shows me he understands. If she's not going to get better, I would never forgive him if I wasn't here, getting in every moment I could. "But for now, she likes knowing you're at camp. And she can't seem to let herself be sick in front of you. She always tries to buck up."

"That's so *ridiculous*, though."

"I have expressed that same sentiment to her." He gives me a sardonic smile. "It was not very well received."

I think of my dad writing sermons on a legal pad in the car as he waited for my piano lesson to end. I think of him in the stands at my swim meets, wearing more White Hills High School logos on his person than the actual mascot.

Never looking annoyed when I showed up in his office at church, wanting him to check my English homework.

Apologizing so earnestly when church member emergencies got in the way of something we'd planned.

I throw my arms around him, nearly knocking him back with unexpected enthusiasm. "Love you, Dad."

Unstartled by my dramatics, he hugs me right back. "Love you too, Luce."

On the walk back around the lake, I try to recount the smallest details of life with my parents. The Easter egg hunts in patent Mary Janes, the Christmas mornings with shiny wrapping paper, the birthdays with striped pink candles. But it's not the holidays that matter most, I think. It's the nights my mom stayed up listening to how Carly Battista hurt my feelings in sixth grade. It's my dad stopping by Dairy Queen after I flubbed the hardest part of my eighth-grade recital piece.

I try to stuff these details into the pockets of my memory.

I try to keep my eyes dry and on the road ahead.

CHAPTER TWENTY-SIX

THE NEXT WEEK, THUY—BUG-EYED IN BORROWED GOGGLES—SWIMS with her head below the surface of the water.

I burst into tears and make it weird.

"I'm so proud of you," I blubber. "Oh my gosh. Thuy. You did it."

She's pleased, if a little taken aback by my display. "It's okay, Hansson."

But my floodgates are open now. I'm helpless as I remember swim lessons with my mom. My first real dive, arms straight in front of me. How proud I was, how she leapt up from the lounger by the pool, cheering. I acted embarrassed in front of the other kids. I was thrilled.

"Sorry!" I wipe my eyes, trying to laugh at myself. This is why Simmons warned me not to cry: freaking out these poor, innocent children. "I'm totally fine! I just cry when I'm happy sometimes."

"It's okay to be sad," Thuy says. She's so earnest, with

those blue plastic lenses stretched over her eyes. "Mommy Sheila tells me that all the time."

"Yes. It *is* okay," I agree. "It's okay to be sad."

On Friday, a bonfire is out of the question. I don't even want to be outside in this heat. We wind up making a too-long, sticky-hot walk to town, where Tom's has ice-cold soda and air-conditioning.

"Oh my God," Anna says, somewhere near the gazebo. "It's too hot to *live*."

Keely wipes at her brow. "This is truly disgusting."

"Detour?" Mohan asks, jabbing his thumb toward the nearby playground. "Swings to cool off your face, Keels?"

"The sign says it closes at dark," I say, squinting to make out the white letters.

"Aw." Mohan gives me his most patronizing smile. "You're so cute."

He shimmies up the nearest ladder, whooshing down the slide by the time Anna gets to the swings. I sit beside her, wondering when the last time I did this was. Years, I think. I kick my legs out experimentally and that giddy, little kid feeling comes right back.

"Want a push?" Henry asks, fingertips on my back.

"Yes, please."

He's gentle at first, with Keely beside us pushing Anna. Mohan races back, fitting his slim hips on top of the swing for babies.

"You're going to break it, you idiot," Keely says.

"Because I'm so heavy due to my well-developed muscles?" Mohan calls. Still, his energetic kicks get him going fast. "Bet I can swing the highest, even without backup."

"Oh yeah?" Anna asks. Keely pushes her harder, purposefully, and I turn to glance at Henry, nodding.

"Whoa," I whisper as a firm push sends me up, up, up. "Ahh! Oh my gosh."

"And now for the dismount!" Mohan yells, leaping from the swing. He lands on his feet, then stands with his arms raised. "The judges give it a ten! Full marks! A huge day for Mohan Tambe's career!"

Anna flies off from my other side, landing just a hair farther than Mohan did. When she straightens up, she uses her best announcer voice. "Guess that means . . . it's an eleven for Anna Miroslaw! Wow, folks. Truly a historic day in swing-jumping."

"All right, Luce," Henry says. At this point, he's backed up so much that his hands are basically on my butt every time he pushes me. "Gonna take 'em down?"

I open my mouth to say: *But you're not supposed to jump off!* That rule is, like, explicitly stated in elementary school. Only the bad kids do that.

Truth is, though, the line between the good kids and the bad kids is so blurry that I'm not even sure it exists anymore. I think maybe it never did.

"C'mon, Hansson," Keely calls. "Show 'em up."

"I don't know . . . ," I reply from so high up, whooshing back. But then, maybe it's not the height or the drop that scares me. Maybe it's the idea of letting go.

"Live a little!" Mohan demands.

My mother's cells are dying halfway around a bend in our lake, so maybe the least I can do is keep trying to live a little.

"You've got this, Luce," Anna calls.

And this time, I agree. With a salute, I yell to her, "*Confidimus stellarum!*"

I swing forward, tilting toward everything that is still to come. I am okay, and I am not okay.

I let go.

AUGUST

CHAPTER TWENTY-SEVEN

FOR ALL MY WORRYING THIS SUMMER, I NEVER REALLY IMAGINED
what it would be like, the moment things got worse.

As it turns out, it's like Bryan pulling you aside during
afternoon kickball.

It's like the world warping into slow motion. Like floating
away from yourself.

It's like picking up the landline in Bryan's office, hands
shaking.

"Dad?" I whisper into the phone.

"Hey, Bird. Listen. Everything's okay, but I'm at the hospital with your mom."

That could be anything. It could be for chemo; I don't
know her checkup schedule.

"Dad." Tell me. *Tell me.*

"She's got an infection. They need to keep her to monitor
everything, but I'm sure it'll be just fine."

He's not sure. He's lying to me, or maybe to himself. "I need to be there."

"I do think you should come, yeah."

Tears slip down my cheeks. He promised he would tell me if it got really bad. If he's telling me to come home, it's gotten really bad. "Will you come get me or . . . ?"

Bryan points at himself, then mimes using a steering wheel.

"Never mind. Bryan says he can take me."

"Put him on the phone, please. It's going to be okay, Bird. Your mom's a fighter."

"I know." I hand the phone over, the world a blur around me. My hands find the desk, steadying myself. Trying to touch something solid, immovable.

"Dave? Yeah, hi. I'll bring her now, if that's okay with you. Yeah. No problem. Can I bring you guys anything? Sure. Okay. See you soon."

I wipe my face, uselessly. The tears are falling faster than I can clear them away.

"Hey." Bryan reaches for a tissue and presses it into my hand. "Why don't you go pack up a few essentials in case you stay overnight? I need to call my wife and then let Rhea know what's going on, but I'll meet you right back here in about ten minutes, yeah?"

I'm already hurrying off, wondering where Henry's campers are at this hour. I don't have time to go looking for him. "Bryan!"

He turns back.

"Can you ask Rhea to tell my friends that—"

"Yeah," he calls. "Of course."

I race back to Cabin 3A, and jam my toothbrush and a stack of my clean laundry into a tote bag. I don't know or care which clothes I've grabbed. Nothing matters but getting to my mom.

Bryan isn't back yet when I return to his office, panting. I can't stand still, so I pace across the floorboards, end to end. There are built-in shelves on the left side of the room, and I spin a decorative globe with one finger. It gives me tactile proof that I'm in reality. This is happening. My mom's in the hospital.

I skim a fingertip along a picture frame, along the plastic leaves of a fake plant, along a glass award with dust on its base. I run my hands across book spines.

Toward the end of the lowest shelf, my fingers find books with no jackets or titles. Except . . . they're not books. They're picture frames, three of them shelved in a row. The same picture frames used for the hallway display of every Daybreak class of campers. I slide one out, expecting a sliver of broken glass up the center—damage that caused them to be taken down.

How do I know? How do I know, in that moment, who I'll see?

My mother's young face, bright-eyed and full-cheeked. It's like looking at myself in outdated clothes. Rachel, her same sneaky smile like she knows something you don't. And Bryan, tall and thin-faced behind them.

But Bryan took these photos of my mother down. Why? *Why* was she so intent on hiding her history here?

In the third picture, my question is answered.

My sixteen-year-old mother is sandwiched between Bryan and Rachel, arms wrapped around their waists. Bryan is looking down at her with total affection.

And a pregnant belly strains her counselor shirt into a huge sphere.

A chill raises goose bumps to my arms. This is a cruel, bizarre use of Photoshop—why would someone *do* this? To teach me a lesson about judging pregnant teens?

Oh, dear Lord. My *mom* tried to teach me a lesson about judging pregnant teens. That first Sunday I walked from here to Holyoke. Sitting on our front porch, I used Tara as an example that Daybreak was a bad influence for me. And my mom scolded me—not because she was being magnanimous but because she *was* Tara all those years ago?

Her total obsession with abstinence or at least information about safe sex. What if it's not just a Christian nurse's perspective? What if it's from her own experience?

Your mom told me, Tara said to me, *about giving birth and everything.*

It can't be. This cannot be. If she had a baby as a teenager, I would obviously know. I know her better than anyone. Or do I just think that because she knows *me* better than anyone?

Do I know *nothing*?

There was a man she loved before my father; she told me that.

You've never mentioned him, I said. *It was a hundred years ago*, she replied.

"You ready?" Bryan's voice comes from the doorway. The first time he saw me at Daybreak, he nearly jumped back. But not because we ran into each other, like I thought. He was startled to be looking at my face. To be seeing my mom's face.

I look up without raising my head. Just my eyes, leveling him.

He's adding it up in his mind: me by the bookshelf, holding a photograph. When his eyes widen, I know he's hit the equals sign.

"This is some kind of joke, right? It's a joke?" I wave the frame at him.

The gulp in his throat is nearly audible. "I, um. I think it would be best if we got you to the hospital, and you can talk to your parents."

All the rumors that there was a pregnant counselor years ago. That Bryan was involved. The way he looks at her in this photo. There is absolutely no way.

I don't budge, not even the tiniest facial muscle or twitch of my finger. I stare, completely unmoved by his suggestion. No way, man. I will stand here until I stop feeling so utterly, impressively lied to. "Was it yours? The baby?"

"I . . . Look. Lucy. It's—it's a long story, and it was a very long time ago." He squeezes his eyes shut as if he's trying to disappear. "For the record, I did tell her. I *told* her you would find out sooner or later. It was just hard for her to——"

"Yes or no," I snap.

"Yes," he answers, almost reflexively.

"And she miscarried? Or what?"

He looks only momentarily puzzled before his face softens. "No. The baby was healthy. Beautiful. She was adopted."

"Wait. What?" I feel physically jolted, my worldview shifted one degree to the left. Everything I see looks a little different. My mom had another daughter. A baby that would be my half sister? Not a baby, now.

A grown-up half sister somewhere. Half sister. Sister. No. How can that be true when I have gone seventeen years without hearing a word of this? Without even knowing her name. When I spent half my childhood wishing for a sibling, until I was old enough to realize that asking my mom for one made her sad. "And has my mom seen her since then?"

"No, she hasn't. Look, let's get on the road, okay?"

Even with Bryan pushing the speed limit, I have about an hour to process this news. I calm down just enough to do mental math, arms crossed and rapping my fingers. My mom was sixteen; now she's forty-five. That makes the baby twenty-nine now. My half sister is twenty-nine. Does she look like my mom at all? Like me? Or more like Bryan, his dark skin and slender cheeks and lanky build? I bet she's beautiful. Under my breath, I laugh darkly, but Bryan says nothing. *Why* wouldn't my parents tell me?

But the moment I truly consider this question . . . of course I know why. As a young girl, I would have been upset to learn my mom had another daughter but we don't know where. And by the time I was old enough to understand, it would have felt shocking, like a betrayal.

Which it does.

Really, though, does it matter? That's what I keep wondering. We're barreling toward my mother, who is hospitalized with cancer complications. Is it that big a deal that her younger years were different than I had imagined them? That her life is more complex than I thought. Harder. So what?

"Did you love her?" I can't bring myself to look at Bryan, but I ask loudly enough that he can certainly hear over the music and open windows. "My mom?"

In my peripheral vision, I see him glance over to gauge my reaction. "I adored her. We were together for a long time."

This, I suppose, is not a shock. Bryan is a good man, smart and patient. And nothing is a shock compared to having a long-lost sibling.

"Was it a closed adoption?"

"Yes."

"So, you have no idea where she is now?" It's a question with a simple answer, but he remains quiet. I twist in my seat while he attempts to strangle the steering wheel. "Oh my gosh. *Do* you know?"

"She could legally reach out and look for us once she turned eighteen. But she didn't, until she was twenty-five. She was getting married, and—"

"But my mom hasn't seen her, right?" I feel sick. I turn my face to the open window, gasping in the air that pushes against my face. It's poisonous, how proprietary I feel toward her.

"Lucy, this is . . . not a comfortable position for me to be in. I shouldn't be the one who discusses this with you." When I glance over, he looks tortured.

"Well, *someone* needs to tell me. I just want to know and get over it before I have to deal with her being *hospitalized*."

My point is taken. "No, your mom hasn't seen her. When I told Marianne I was open to hearing from our daughter if it happened, she said she couldn't. She had to leave that part of her life all the way behind."

For all the times I wished for a sibling, I never once considered that I already had one. She's real; she's an adult. She's married. And some hideous, deep-down part of me wishes she didn't exist. I want to be my mother's only daughter. I hate that it wasn't me who came first. How petty. How entirely, cruelly beside the point.

Maybe even more than that, I want to see her face. I want to hear her voice. Does it sound anything like my mom's?

Was anything ever as simple as I thought it was?

CHAPTER TWENTY-EIGHT

WHEN WE FINALLY ARRIVE, MY DAD'S WAITING OUTSIDE THE hospital, squinting in the unclouded daylight. Bryan pulls up to the curb, and I spring out.

I throw my arms around him, relieved by the familiarity of him. He was an accomplice to all the lying, I assume, but I can't bring myself to be mad at him.

"Hey, Birdie," he whispers. "It's okay. She's all right."

When I release him, he ducks down to look Bryan in the face. The strangeness gnaws at me: the fathers of my mom's two daughters, face-to-face. How can they stand it?

"Thank you for driving all this way," my dad says, nodding at him. "Why don't you come on in too?"

Bryan shakes his head resolutely. "No, no. I wouldn't want to in—"

"She asked for you." I know that tone in my dad's voice. It says: *This is not up for discussion.*

"She . . . Okay." Something in Bryan's face changes—from determined to bewildered in one second flat. I wonder when they last saw each other. "I'll go park, then."

"Room 2200."

"Well!" I say brightly, as Bryan pulls away. "That'll be nice! A big family reunion! Everyone who's been lying to me, all in one room!"

My dad's face, I swear to heaven, turns gray. Like wet clay, tinged with green.

"Yep! I found a picture of Mom at camp when she was a teenager! Pregnant. That was a *super* fun way to find out, by the way."

After a moment, he clears his throat. Apparently he's collected himself, gathered up the pieces of surprise and discomfort. "I imagine that came as quite a shock. But, Luce, there's a lot to the story. And right now we need to focus on your mom's health."

"I agree. But can you just tell me this one thing? Have you guys hidden anything else from me? Any other siblings? Please just tell me and get it over with right now."

"Nothing else. Truly."

I survey his panicked face. He's suffered enough, I think. Too much. "Okay."

"Okay?" Based on his tone, I don't think he believes me.

"Yep. I just want to see Mom." I step toward the hospital doors, but he remains frozen in place. "I'm okay, Dad. It was a long time ago. I just wanted you to know that I know."

I wonder if anything feels as grown-up as not blaming your parents. Understanding where they're coming from instead of waiting for them to see your side. We walk briskly to my mom's room, where a nurse has me scrub my hands and arms with antibacterial soap. *She already has an infection!* I want to yell. *Just let me see her!* But of course I'd never do anything to put her in danger.

Rachel leaves the room as I enter, swooping in to peck my cheek. How did she get here so quickly?

My mom is stretched out on a bed by the window. It's a muted-over scene—the off-white walls and beige plastic hospital bed and the dull blue blankets. My arms feel chilled even though I dried them off. And any anger I felt on the car ride dissolves like mist.

"Hey, Mom."

"There she is." Her smile curls up beneath the nose tube. "I was just thinking about you."

Is this how it happens? So fast, one summer later, in an anonymous hospital room? It can't be.

"Bryan drove you?"

"Yeah. He's parking the car, but he'll be in to . . ." Rehash the sordid details of your shared past? Discuss the daughter you mutually created? "Say hi."

I glance away, overcome by my awkward pause, and her grip tightens. "You know, don't you?"

Only after I nod can I look her in the eyes. "Since about an hour ago."

Her lips make a small circle, whistling out air. It's a sound equivalent to the phrase *Oh boy*. "How mad are you?"

I think I want to be mad; it would be easier. But hospitals shift things into perspective. Nothing in the outside world really matters now. "I'm not mad."

"Would you be mad if I didn't have a nasal cannula and a central line?"

"Maybe."

"Fair enough. Bird, I wanted to tell you. But there was never a right time. You always seemed too young, and then by the time you weren't . . . it felt unfair to drop it on you."

I've gone over this in my mind, enough that I can truthfully say, "It's okay, Mom."

"I'm glad you know." She runs her thumb across my hand. "No more secrets. Okay. Now, cheer me up. Tell me about your campers, will you?"

I obey. She's smiling—even laughing—at the updates on Thuy's swim lessons, about Sofia's animals, Payton's colors.

"It would be petty of me to say I told you so," my mom says. "But I knew you'd be the most wonderful counselor. You're a natural teacher, Bird."

Am I? I do like helping people learn things—swim strokes and makeup contouring and simple piano chords. Teaching is what everything I do has in common. How did I not see it before? Leave it to my mom to drop a casual epiphany into a conversation meant to cheer her up.

I can tell the moment Bryan walks in because her gaze moves over my shoulder. The smile falls into lips-parted surprise.

"Bry?" She sounds so young, even in that one syllable.

"Hi, Mari."

He's standing with Rachel, hands clasped like a suppliant. Bryan, who knows my mother. Who loved my mother, once upon a time.

My mom reaches her hand out to him, her eyes filled with tears. In front of him, she crumbles. All this time, I've begged her to be real with me, but I confess: seeing her overwhelmed is gutting.

I step back to give them room. Or to give myself room. I don't know. I don't know anything anymore.

He goes right to her, taking both hands in his. At first they don't speak, just look into each other's older faces, wide eyes glistening.

"I changed my mind, Bry," she says. "I need to know about her. Just in case I don't—I mean . . ."

"It's okay." He sits on the edge of the bed, so they're closer to eye level. "She's okay, Mari. She's *great*."

Tears dribble down my mom's cheeks. "She found you?"

"She lives in Chicago with her husband." Bryan's breathing stutters, as if he's crying too. "She works at a nonprofit and just finished her MBA. Great relationship with her parents."

My sister, the businesswoman. I badly wish that I had a

mental image. Will she want to meet me? Would we get along right away or would she feel like a stranger?

"What did they name her?" my mom chokes out.

"Elena," he says. "And they kept our name too. Elena Grace."

"Elena." My mom whispers it, a fervent prayer. "Elena."

"Come on, Bird," Rachel says quietly. She clasps my shoulders to guide me out. "Let's give them a minute."

"But—" I begin. But I want to hear more about my sister. Elena. I have a half sister named Elena. Haven't I been kept in the dark long enough? But I know my mom deserves privacy. Is this—being able to consider your mother's feelings above your own—what growing up is?

There's a bench outside the room where my dad is sitting, staring into nothing. I sit beside him, exiled from our own family.

Wow, am I working up a flair for drama.

"How 'bout I track down some decent tea?" Rachel asks.

I nod blandly and assume my dad does the same. Once she's down the hall, I glance at him, at his linked hands and wrinkled button-down. "Are you okay?"

"That's supposed to be the dad's line." He looks over as if he's going to try to smile. He can't quite manage it. "I'm so sorry about all this, Bird."

"It's all right, Dad. I mean, I assume you'll pay for my therapy into adulthood . . . but."

The joke fizzles, even as my dad huffs out a laugh.

"Your mom worried that it would be harder to guide you, morally, if you knew her past. She carries a lot of guilt from that time in her life." His gaze pushes hard against mine. "*Very* misguided guilt. She didn't do anything wrong, you understand?"

"Yeah. I do. Must be weird for you, though."

He shrugs, not exactly denying it. "I've known about Grace for almost as long as I've known your mother."

"So, it doesn't bother you, Bryan being in there with her?"

"No, honey. Your mom's life is with us. But Bryan's a big part of her story, and he was always so good to her." He looks over with a mock grimace. "Though, I admit, it would be easier if he'd aged poorly."

I laugh—half at his honesty, half at the absurdity of having this conversation. It's the closest I've ever felt to sitting at the grown-ups' table. Half of me is delighted; half of me is terrified that my easy childhood days are already gone. Did I even appreciate them?

My dad wraps an arm around my shoulder, and I lean into him. "I need to ask you something, Bird."

"Okay . . ."

"Will it be okay with you if . . . if your mom wants to see Grace? If Grace is willing to come here. Just in case your mom . . ." Dies. He can't say it. Neither can I, and I hate my traitorous brain for thinking it.

"Elena. Her parents named her Elena," I tell him. "And

yeah, it's okay. Bizarre but okay. I mean . . . I'd like to meet her too, of course."

"You're the best kid in the world, you know that? To take all this in stride."

"I feel like I know Mom better," I say. "That's a good thing."

"It is," he agrees. "Never fails to amaze me. All the good things that spring from the difficult things."

I pull back so I can look at him. "You writing a sermon or . . ."

He rolls his eyes. "Stinker."

Who would call me Bird? I wondered at the beginning of the summer. He would. And it wouldn't be the same, but we would have each other.

"She's going to be okay," I whisper. "Right?"

He considers his answer for a moment, lips pressed together. "I believe that, yes."

But that's not exactly a real yes, is it? Maybe it never has been. My whole life, my dad has been a font of answers. Of truths. Right at this moment—beneath fluorescent hospital lights and the fog of doubt—I wonder if I imagined it. If every kid sees their parents as certain. When really, we're all just trying our best. We're all just slowly deciding what we believe.

We sit there for a few minutes in the quiet, until a nurse stops outside the door. "How we doing? Have you guys gotten some coffee?"

"Someone went to find tea, yes. Thank you."

"Can you explain what's going on?" I blurt out. "I know it's an infection. But what does that mean?"

My dad turns to me, opening his mouth to say . . . I don't know. That the nurse is busy. That I might not want to hear the response. "Luce, she—"

"No, it's okay," the nurse says to him. "A number of things, including your mom's organ function, need to be monitored, which is why nurses keep coming in and out. She's on antibiotics, and we'll see how she responds. We may try other kinds."

"So, it could get much worse," I say, "or much better."

She nods, somehow portraying empathy in even this. "Like most things."

My dad says something else, thanking her. I stare at everything, at nothing, watching the hospital staff move around us in scrubs. Bright blue. Patterns. A few in this deep red-pink color. What would Payton call them? Dark mauve. Muted pomegranate. Dusky rose.

I remember my mom's scrubs so vividly. When she worked at the hospital, sometimes she'd be leaving for an overnight shift right as I went to bed. She'd tell me a story, lying on my twin bed beside me in her scrubs. A falling-leaves print in October, ice cream cones in the summer. I remember especially loving her Mickey Mouse scrubs. I thought that kids must like her best, out of all the nurses.

The instinct to pray comes like a pull in my chest. Insistent tugging.

"I'm gonna go find the chapel," I tell my dad, and he starts to stand. "No, I'm okay solo. Really."

He studies my face. "All right. It's through the waiting room, then down the hallway to the right."

All the late nights my mom and I stayed home, watching movies. Sometimes he was here. Sometimes he was sitting by bedsides, clasping hands, offering prayer. Offering people peace as they slowly left this world.

"What?" he asks, since I'm still standing there. Taking him in. Understanding a little bit better.

"Nothing. Come get me if there's any news?"

"Of course."

The waiting room is full, which I didn't notice when I entered the hospital. Elderly people with age-spotted hands clasped patiently, a flushed-face toddler in his mother's arms, and—from somewhere in the sea of people—a persistent, hacking cough.

And a few feet before me, a handsome young man with his elbows propped on his knees, fingers laced together in front of him.

"Henry?"

He jumps up. "Hey! Are you— Is she— Is everything okay?"

"For now. It's an infection. It's a wait-and-see kind of thing." I'm blinking up at him in the too-harsh light. "How did you—"

"Rhea."

Right. Of course. Henry holds his arms out to me, palms up—offering comfort if I want it. And I do. I step inside and let myself be held.

"What can I do?" he asks, his voice a rumble against my chest.

"Um. I'm okay. Although . . . I don't know when my dad ate last. Maybe I should go find something to—"

Before I can finish that sentence, a familiar voice catches my ear. ". . . and if Lucy doesn't want the Boston cream, *I'm* eating it."

"I'd like to see you try."

Anna almost drops the box of donuts when she spots me. "Luce! Hey. How's the moms?"

I'm stunned at the sight of them—Anna with her hair in a chunky braid, Mohan in an Alexander Hamilton T-shirt.

A fever of stingrays, a bouquet of pheasants, a charm of hummingbirds.

What is a group of friends? A relief, a scaffolding, a safety net?

"You're here," I say, bewildered.

"Durr," Anna says. "And Keely's around here some-where."

I can't quite get out the words "She is?" but Henry catches my eye, nodding.

"And you brought donuts," I add.

"When in doubt!" Mohan chirps. "Donuts never hurt, you know? I wanted to write on the box: DONUT PANIC,

380

LUCY, IT WILL BE OKAY, but *someone* thought that was insensitive."

Anna, unperturbed, says, "I have no problem admitting *someone* was me."

"You want one?" Mohan asks. "Sprinkle, maybe? Cinnamon sugar?"

"Yeah, when I get back. I need to . . . make a stop."

"You want company?" Henry asks.

I glance down the hallway, where the sign is directing me with a simple cross. I frown at it, thinking of the many other symbols hanging in Daybreak's meeting hall. "No, thanks. I just need a few minutes."

The hospital chapel is empty but for one person in the front. She's staring up at the brass altar cross, arms crossed. Washed in low lighting, Keely looks almost heaven-sent. She'd snort at the thought.

"Hey," I say, sitting beside her.

"Hey."

She doesn't ask if I'm okay. Of course I'm not. But she sits here—in a hospital, in a chapel—like it is no big deal to her.

"Any news?" she asks gently.

"Not really. It's wait and see."

My friend nods slowly, considering this.

"Okay," she says simply. "Then we're waiting."

It's only then that the tears come. I came to barter for my mom's life, and maybe God knew I needed Keely. Someone to wait with me. She reaches to hold my hand on the seat between us.

"What if I can't survive it?" I ask, face pressed into my palm. "What if I'm never, ever okay again?"

Her hand stays clasped on mine. "Yeah. I asked myself that too. More than once. But here I am."

It's a fair enough point. Hasn't Daybreak shown me, day after day, that people can outlast unbelievable pain? That human hearts are like noble little ants, able to carry so much more weight than you'd expect. Hasn't my mom shown me that, every day of my life?

"It changes you," Keely says. "You can be okay again. Just a different kind of okay than before."

"Well, that's something," I mutter, wiping mascara from my cheeks. "I just wish it were still easy for me, to believe. In all of it—in heaven and prayer and . . . I don't know."

Keely is quiet for a moment, but she doesn't flinch or move away from me. "Did you know that energy can't be created or destroyed?"

Confused, I just wipe my face on my sleeve.

"It means that people may die but their energy doesn't. It gets redistributed." She settles back in the pew a little, looking up at the cross. "I like that what we know—about everything—is only a fraction of what's really happening. You can look at the unknown parts as scary. But personally? I like the mystery. I mean, of course I want to know about other galaxies and other life forms. But I also enjoy the wondering."

We are on a dark, twisting road that she knows so well. Of course Keely, who believes people are made of stardust, would know how to light the path. If her astronomy is about divine unknowns, about pushing for more understanding, about hoping for new, hard-won revelations . . . can't my faith be the same? About trying to enjoy the wondering.

So I pour out my heart in silent prayer; I pour out my tears in steady streams. *Please don't take my mom from me. Please not yet. Please don't let me be alone.*

You're not, a voice inside me whispers.

My dad is eating donuts with my friends in the waiting room. Mohan has a few sprinkles flecked down his T-shirt, so I guess Anna won the Boston cream battle. Or, more likely, Mohan ate two donuts. Minimum.

"There you guys are." Henry's smile is hesitant; he's reading my expression and body language. It's strange to see him sitting next to my dad. In any other circumstance, I'd be nervous that my dad is telling "endearing" stories about me. But right now, I'm just glad to have a full team.

"Did you get a donut, Bird? There's a sugar twist left." My favorite. It's simple, with a curl to it, freckled with cinnamon. I have really narcissistic taste in donuts, I guess.

"Hansson? Mr. Hansson?" A nurse is standing by, looking around for him.

He's on his feet in a flash, and I'm right behind him. "Yes."

"If you could just come with me. The doctor needs to update—"

"What's going on?" he asks.

I trot alongside them, and I don't care if I'm not supposed to. She's my mom. We're through the swinging doors, and the nurse turns back to me.

"Sweetie, maybe you should wait—"

"No!"

"Luce," my dad says, weary.

I am unmoved. "*No!* What's going on?"

The doctor outside my mom's room has a neat ponytail and a hand clenched on the chart. It is not good news. You can feel it in your bone marrow, that heavy certainty. Mom.

"I'm Dave Hansson," my dad tells her, breathless. I stand back, but only a little. "I was just in here five minutes ago— she was fine, she—"

"Mr. Hansson," the doctor says, as softly as I think she can muster. "Her vitals show a move to sepsis. We're moving your wife to the ICU. We need to get her on dialysis and keep vigilant watch."

As if on cue, hospital transport wheels my mom out. We both reach for her hand, but they're at her sides. Rachel is right behind the bed, face drawn.

"We love you!" my dad calls, his voice frantic as they race my mom down the hall. Flashbacks to her surgery, her being wheeled away from us. The hollowness and dread. "We'll be right here!"

She raises a hand to her mouth. Blows us a kiss.

I manage to mime catching it.

Then she's gone—around the corner, out of view, and I sob, "*No.*"

Rachel, though, looks too stunned to cry. "I'm so sorry. I should have run to get you. But it happened so fast, and I didn't want her to be alone, and—"

"No, me either," my dad says.

"But she's going to be okay, right?" I'm asking this half of my dad, half of the doctor who is still nearby, leaving us some space. This is happening too fast. I can't process. Septic: that's something to do with an infection and the bloodstream. My mind races too quickly to recall what else. Dialysis? "Does she need a kidney? You can test me. She has another daughter too!"

"It's okay, Bird," my dad says quietly, and I can hear how insane I sound, offering up my organs. Offering up a stranger's organs! But my knees threaten to buckle, loose hinges bending, bending. I wrap my hand around the inhaler in my pocket.

"We're going to do everything we can," the doctor says.

"Thank you. Please update us as soon as you can," my dad says.

That's it? I turn to stare at my dad in horror. I don't know why a part of me expects him to fix this.

"Dad?" It's a question and a plea, spoken in a whispered tone.

"Your mom knew it was a possibility. People do recover from it. She's young and strong." It sounds like he is reciting from something.

"I shouldn't have left the room," I whisper.

"It was easier for your mom that you weren't there to see. I promise." His tone is calm, but his face is ashen.

Rachel wipes her face, gesturing back into the room. "I'm just gonna pack up her things real quick. In case she can have them in the ICU."

"Thanks, Rach. That helps." He glances around, disoriented. "I should . . . I need to go to the chapel, I think . . ."

"I'll stay in case there's news," she says.

I walk out beside him to the waiting room, where Anna jumps up first. The others stay seated, nervously trying to read our faces.

"Septic," I whisper to her. "They're moving her to the ICU."

"Okay," she says, nodding. "Okay."

"If you could just excuse me," my dad says thinly. "I . . . need to . . . uh, call Pastor Dana. While I have a moment. I'll be right back."

Anna keeps her arm around my shoulders as my dad hurries through the waiting room. It registers too late: he's not calling Dana. Dana already knows my mom's here.

"Dad," I say, but not loud enough. The automatic exit doors slip open, swallowing him up.

"I'm just . . . I think I need to be with him," I tell Anna.

"Yeah, go," she says, clearly trying to read my expression. "We'll be here."

I follow my dad outside, into the fading daylight. I don't want him to be alone any more than I want to be alone in this.

Sure enough, neither hand reaches for his phone as he walks to the car. I trail behind him because yelling seems too loud, too brash. This is a sadness for whispers.

I'm about to call out when he throws open the driver's door. Where is he going? He wouldn't leave me here. I stand on an island of mulch and saplings in the parking lot, staring from a distance. Something anchors me here, an inner voice insisting that I stay where I am.

And I watch as my father beats his hands against the steering wheel. He hits the roof of the car, slaps his palms at the windows—mouth open in wails I cannot hear.

I watch his teeth press fiercely against his lower lip and pull open into a swearword I can make out from here. He screams it, using all his air until his face turns red. His balled fists hit the dash again and then he leans over the wheel, shoulders heaving.

But I back away one step, then two. I won't go comfort him. Because I know my dad, and he would never forgive himself for letting me see this. But I do see him. My dad—the pastor—is only a man. Staring down loss, and blinking.

Inside the car, he props his head against his hand. One last time, I see his mouth spit out the word—lips against teeth for the "f," the guttural *uhh* of the vowel, the crisp "k."

If I'm going to believe, it has to be in a God who would forgive my father for this word.

I have to believe in a God who knows how much my father loves my mother.

I have to believe in a God who would sit beside my father in that car, place His hand on my father's back.

And maybe it took me until now—until this horrible moment—to realize, but I do.

I believe in nature, in science, in jazz, in dancing.

And I believe in people. In their resilience, in their goodness.

This is my credo; this is my hymn. Maybe it's not enough for heaven, and maybe I'm even wrong. But if I can walk through the fire and, with blistered skin, still have faith in better days? I have to believe that's good enough.

So I turn back inside, shoulders squared. Not because I'm Saint Lucy or Queen Lucy the Valiant or even particularly tough. Because I'm me, and I'm trying, and I have a family of friends who wrap around me like clouds. Because there are surely other names for grace, and mine are Mom, Dad. Rachel. Henry. Anna. Keely. Mohan. Rhea. Bryan. Lukas. Our congregation and my swim team and, somewhere, a half sister who might someday become a whole one.

In them, my sense of holiness only grows.

It's not the Bible or the light bending through the church's stained glass or the rafters filled with glorias. Although it is still those things.

It's the white light that fills you, wide and glowing, expanding your seams. And maybe you find it in the smooth lake water or piano chords, so lost in them that you sway back and forth. In brassy hits of trumpet, playing until you pant, breathless. Maybe you find it somewhere beneath the tall pines, during a summer that changes everything. Or in an Airstream trailer on an open road that you earned. In every dance move that sets you free. In the hands that mend your split-open knuckles. In the people who teach you, who forgive you.

I found it on Adirondack chairs, in cups of tea, as my mother was laughing and telling the truth and dying. I found it at a camp where love falls like leaves.

And under the dreaming tree, I see a girl who can be okay and not okay all at once. So, I guess I'm just grateful to be here for all of it, for the mess and the ache and the unknowing.

After all, once there was a girl named Lucy who loved her family, old and new.

It is not the type of love that ends.

ACKNOWLEDGMENTS

I'm ever grateful for Bethany Robison, Taylor Martindale, and Mary Kate Castellani—the three wise, thoughtful women who help me shape my stories. Never wiser or more thoughtful than with this one.

To Erica Barmash, Beth Eller, Jessie Gang, Cristina Gilbert, Courtney Griffin, Melissa Kavonic, Linette Kim, Cindy Loh, Donna Mark, Lizzy Mason, Linda Minton, Sally Morgridge, Emily Ritter, Claire Stetzer, Katharine Wiencke, Brett Wright, and the entire sales team: you are unparalleled. Thank you for shepherding my work into the world.

This book was an extremely collaborative process at every stage. I'm indebted to a motley crew of saints, for everything from quick questions to existential conversations, from early reads to micro-level final edits. You are appreciated beyond measure.

My sanity, too, is an extremely collaborative effort, and for that I owe my family and friends. Thank you for keeping the faith.

I'm grateful to the community of readers, to the librarians and booksellers and educators who do hard and worthy work, to the teachers who are my friends and the friends who are my teachers.

And to J, who makes it easy to believe.

Jawbone Lake

Ray Robinson, an award-winning short-story writer, novelist and screenwriter, first won attention in 2006 with his debut novel, *Electricity*, which was shortlisted for both the James Tait Black Memorial Prize and the Authors' Club First Novel Award. The film adaptation of *Electricity*, starring Agyness Deyn, will be released in 2014. Robinson's other novels are *The Man Without* (2008) and *Forgetting Zoë* (2010). *Forgetting Zoë* was a winner of the inaugural Jerwood Fiction Uncovered Prize and was the *Observer*'s Thriller of the Month. Robinson was hailed as 'among the most impressive voices of Britain's younger generation' by the *Irish Times*. He is a postgraduate of Lancaster University, where he was awarded a PhD in Creative Writing in 2006, and is a Literary Mentor and Reader for the Literary Consultancy. He has appeared at literary festivals around the world, including La Feria Internacional del Libro de Guadalajara, Mexico, and the Edinburgh International Book Festival.

ALSO BY RAY ROBINSON

Electricity

The Man Without

Forgetting Zoë

Jawbone Lake

RAY ROBINSON

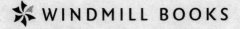

WINDMILL BOOKS

Published by Windmill Books 2014

2 4 6 8 10 9 7 5 3 1

First published in Great Britain in 2014 by William Heinemann

Windmill Books
The Random House Group Limited
20 Vauxhall Bridge Road, London SW1V 2SA

Addresses for companies within The Random House Group Limited
can be found at: www.randomhouse.co.uk/offices.htm

The Random House Group Limited Reg. No. 954009

www.randomhouse.co.uk

A CIP catalogue record for this book
is available from the British Library

ISBN 9780099558798

Typeset in Joanna MT Std by Palimpsest Book Production Ltd,
Falkirk, Stirlingshire
Printed and bound by CPI Group (UK) Ltd, Croydon, CR0 4YY

For

ADRIAN BRISCOE